Scientists
of
Metaphorosis

Also from Metaphorosis

<u>Metaphorosis Magazine</u>
Metaphorosis: Best of 20xx
Metaphorosis 20xx: The Complete Stories
annual issues, from 2016
Monthly / Quarterly issues
Library Collection series

<u>Plant Based Press</u>
Best Vegan Science Fiction & Fantasy
annual issues, 2016-2020

from B. Morris Allen:
Chambers of the Heart: speculative stories
Susurrus
Allenthology: Volume I
Tocsin: and other stories
Start with Stones: collected stories
Metaphorosis: a collection of stories

<u>Verdage</u>
Reading 5X5 x3: Changes
Reading 5X5 x2: Duets
Score — an SFF symphony
Reading 5X5: Readers' Edition
Reading 5X5: Writers' Edition

<u>Vestige</u>
The Nocturnals, by Mariah Montoya

<u>Joyful Heave</u>
Museum Piece: an unusual collection

Scientists
of
Metaphorosis

---

speculative stories
by scientists

METAPHOROSIS LIBRARY COLLECTION

edited by
B. Morris Allen

ISSN: 2573-136X (online)
ISBN: 978-1-64076-307-4 (e-book)
ISBN: 978-1-64076-308-1 (paperback)
ISBN: 978-1-64076-309-8 (hardcover)

from
Metaphorosis Publishing

Neskowin

Contents

From the Editor

The *Metaphorosis Library Collection* arose from a conversation with a Metaphorosis author who is also a librarian, and is initially intended to suit library needs. When a reader comes in and says, "Hey, do you have any SFF stories by this type of author?" here they are! But of course, the books are available to any reader.

In this first volume, we focus on **scientists**. All sorts of people can and do write speculative fiction, but there's indubitably an added credibility when science fiction in particular is written by people who actually practice science; they know what they're talking about. As someone who long ago got a couple of degrees in biochemistry, it's an approach I appreciate. While my knowledge of biochemistry went out of date almost immediately, the authors in this volume are folks who still work in science every day. Even when they're writing pure fantasy, I'd argue that a certain perspective informs their writing.

Some of SFF's most successful writers have been scientists — Asimov and Herbert come to mind — and perhaps some of the writers in this book are headed for similar careers. Read their stories and find out!

B. Morris Allen
1 July 2024

Shiplight

Benjamin C. Kinney

"Right there, any moment now. Their future," Jacob said, resentment thick and sour in his mouth.

He pointed up into the night sky, above the heads of the close-packed crowd on the porch. Everyone was silent. Despite everything, Jacob and all the other Sea-born natives held their breath. A fresh pinprick appeared in the night's threadbare shroud. A new star, flickering and bright with the flare of the decelerating pulse drive. Shiplight.

Voices erupted in drunken cheers, but Jacob leaned back against the railing's moldy wood. Rache bumped her hip against his. Her lanky body smelled of alquila and dance-floor heat. "Hey, start smiling. You knew Earth was crazy enough to send you five thousand more colonists as a twenty-fifth birthday gift. And until the Ship sends us their roster, who knows?" She laughed, her amusement knife-sharp and just as bloody. "You and I might keep our jobs if they have, what, ten programmers? Sea probably has jobs for ten more right now."

Jacob tapped his alquila glass against Rache's and forced a laugh. "I knew I should've been a janitor. Maybe a pilot?" The liquor scoured his throat, a clean and purifying burn.

Lucia's face appeared, a golden ghost beneath the shadow of her hair. "Jacob, Rache, hey! Look, we can't get the feed from the Ship, can one of you come take a look?"

Rache poked her elbow into his ribs. "You set it up, you go save the day. Get back here quick, you're supposed to kiss someone on Shiplight and I missed out. Or is that New Year's?"

Jacob's heart skipped, like a stone across the water. He grinned and let his hand touch Rache's lower back. "I think it can work for either."

He pushed through the crowd, into the curtained living room. Fourteen other natives huddled around the couches, while a skinny boy prodded the connection between the hook and its wide-screen display. Jacob settled in front of the electronics and tuned out everyone's cheers and pleas.

There was nothing wrong with the feed, or the hook, or the net. There was no transmission from the Ship.

●

In the morning, Jacob found Lucia and Rache in the kitchen, tapping away on their hooks. The windows spread mid-morning sunlight across the room's warped laminate countertops. Even the scattered and curtained reflection felt like a head-pounding glare. Jacob was wearing the same rumpled clothes as last night, and the two roommates looked scarcely more tidy in their bathrobes.

Lucia grinned. "You two keep cozy last night? Wow, you have a terrible poker face, Jacob." A knock came from down the hall, and she set down her hook. "You two have fun, I'll get the door."

Jacob sat down beside Rache, and watched a thread of dark brown hair escape from her sloppy topknot. She turned her hook so he could read from the hand-sized glass tablet. "Take a look at the Shiplight news. It's brilliant, the government is peeing their pants. Afraid the big boys on Earth are finally coming for their back taxes."

Lucia returned, her shoulders tight. "We have guests." She mouthed the word *government*.

A man and a woman entered the kitchen behind her. Rache flipped her hook face-down and turned around to greet the visitors. They wore pristine unembroidered shirts, and had flecks of grey in their hair. Not old, but at least in their forties. Colonists, not natives. Jacob knew of a few natives that old, children of the early colonists, but the government never hired those rare elders.

The man said, "Good morning, everyone. My name is Andrews." He looked at Rache. "Ms. Rachel Ruiz-Levi, yes? We wanted to talk about some posts you wrote early this morning. As I'm sure you're aware, there's a great deal of speculation about why the Ship didn't make contact, and you seem to have a very particular take on the situation."

"Well, it dropped out of gravity drive on schedule, so it can't be broken too badly. If it's some little malfunction, we'll have a signal tomorrow and this all blows over. But if not..." She smiled like a lioness watching her cubs bring down their first prey. "I bet they've gone silent on purpose. I bet they could've sent us a feed full of lies or whatever they wanted. But they didn't. They want you to feel ignorant." She leaned forward. "To panic."

She cracked her knuckles. "You're from the government, Andrews. Want to help me fill in the gaps? Let's see. Have you not been sending enough goodies on the Ship's return trips? Or do you think they've finally noticed that you stopped following the original charter?"

Andrews pulled out a chair and sat down. "Would you rather we went back to the charter, Ms. Ruiz-Levi? A system designed to control five thousand miners? I don't think so.

"But we're not here for a debate. You've been very vocal about your lack of faith in the Senate's ability to handle this. Right now might be a bad time for that kind of agitation. We all have some real challenges ahead of us in the coming months, and our society needs to pull together to prepare." He drew a badge from his shirt pocket. "My colleague and I are with the Bureau."

Rache crossed her arms. "I haven't done anything wrong, *colonists*. Go drown yourselves."

Andrews sighed. "We're all colonists, ma'am. All sixty thousand of us on this world, no matter which planet you were born on." He glanced at his partner, then back to Rache. His words fell through the murk of Jacob's hangover like a block of lead dropped from a diving belt. "But if you're not interested in a productive conversation right now, we'll have to continue it elsewhere."

Lucia's eyes narrowed, and she placed her hook on the table. Rache set down her mug. "Is this the point where I ask for a lawyer?"

"As of this morning, the Senate has authorized emergency measures to head off unrest in this time of uncertainty. Which reactivates some clauses in the original charter, I'm sorry to say." A smile flickered past his face, more irony than pleasure, and then he drew his sternness back into place. "By order of the Emergency Council, we're taking you into custody until the situation is resolved."

Rache's eyes darted: between the guests, to the window, to the knife set. Blood and broken glass unfolded in Jacob's mind. He clasped her hand. "Rache. Don't give these bastards a real reason."

Andrews kept his gaze on Rache's face as his partner shifted a hand to her belt. Unnoticed by the visitors, Lucia tucked one of the two hooks under her arm.

●

As the front door shut, Jacob's hangover shifted into reverse. He felt instead like he was still drunk, the world spinning with motion just beyond his view. Lucia picked up Rache's mug and washed it in the sink. In the living room, somebody snored.

The mug shattered in the sink. "Drown it!" Lucia wiped her hands dry, and threw the towel after the broken mug. "I can't believe those colonists! Is this just going to be a police state now?" She sagged into a chair.

Jacob shook his head, and realization spread through his body with a sharp and prickly heat. "If they came for Rache, she can't be the only native they arrested. Drown that! I can't believe the colonists would do this." He stood up, driven by the urge to act, but the peeling walls offered no suggestions. "We have to do something about this."

Lucia gave him a measuring smile, and then the balance tipped toward warmth. "Yeah? Huh, Rache was right about you." Jacob's cheeks flushed, but Lucia turned her attention down toward her hook. She tapped the screen, swept her finger through one list, and then another. "Found it! Here, if you want to help, take a look at this."

Jacob leaned over her shoulder. "That's Bluerail. A programming language for hardware automation. You're not a coder too, are you?" He and Rache had met over the net, when his parents' mineral-extraction float needed a second software engineer. He had never met another native coder; how could he not be enchanted?

"Hah, I wish! No, I'm a cook at The Glider. This is Rache's hook. She snuck this program home from her Raytheon-Tinto contract, she always said we might need it someday. She was always saying the colonists would bring back those old Earth charter laws."

Jacob swept through the pages of structured text. A comment caught his eye. "Hold on. This part down here, it's the encryption algorithm for communicating with the police aerials." The world no longer spun; instead, he was flying. "This is it, Lucia! With this, we can force the government to give Rache back."

Lucia flinched. "Hold on a minute. That program does what now?" She gripped his wrist. "We can't just take up arms, Jacob. That's ridiculous. We can hold onto it as a backup plan, but you are *not* starting a violent revolution in my kitchen." She ran her hands through her hair. "This emergency won't last forever. All these charter-law folks are gonna answer to the Senate again someday, right? So they still have to care what the world thinks."

Jacob's head pounded, but it beat in sync with his thoughts, like waves hammering the turbines of a generator. A new idea, more gripping than the last. "A protest, then. If they're going to do charter-style martial law, we'll sit right in the middle of it! Force this into the open where the whole net has to look at it. How many people were here last night? A hundred and fifty?"

"At least. New Plymouth is half natives, though a lot of those are just kids." She reclaimed the hook and tapped the screen. "Maybe a thousand in the right age range."

"Nice! They can't arrest us all, charter law or no. We need to start this soon, before that Andrews realizes he took the wrong hook, and —" His ferocity crumpled. "And before anything happens to Rache."

Lucia's grin remained. "Everyone's supposed to be back at work tomorrow. Let's give them something better to do."

●

In a city of nine thousand, they had six hundred people ready to march. Across the ocean world's far-spread islands and floating extractors, two thousand more natives promised to stay home on strike.

In the light of morning, the size of it all made Jacob want to run back to his island home. *Six hundred people* in one place! But he had set the tide in motion, and if he flinched now, the burden would land on Lucia's shoulders. She might forgive him, but Rache wouldn't.

The protest began just before noon at Rache and Lucia's house, for a route of three short kilometers to Landing Square. Most of the protestors were younger than the party crowd, but every face seemed familiar, like family members gathered for their first reunion. They carried hand-made signs with slogans like "End emergency law!", "Why do only natives go to jail?", and "Shiplight: what are you hiding?" The most popular signs demanded "Free Rache!" and four other prisoners.

Lucia pulled Jacob to the front to march alongside her. As the procession began, he took slow steady steps, and Lucia walked backward to face the crowd. She started a simple chant, echoing the placards, and a chorus of voices joined in.

They walked from gravel to pavement to Main Street, the spine of New Plymouth, between the pourstone facades of the world's administrative and cultural heart. They passed a construction site, paralyzed for lack of laborers. Bins overflowed with the weekend's waste. Somewhere behind those walls, corporate offices lay half-empty, parents were stuck home without their daycare, and dishes remained unwashed. Jacob grinned. New Plymouth wore the skin of colonists and their tech, but natives moved the blood through its veins.

The procession reached Landing Square. The broad cobblestone plaza ended in wide white stone steps leading up to the metal and glass of Landing House, the city's only three-story building. Spectators lined the steps and shopfronts, and Jacob spotted a few groups of people with tripods and camera lenses. He lifted his fist with the next chanted chorus, to create an image that would spread their voices across the breadth of Sea.

Lucia leaned in. "Check out the cameras! We're gonna need more than one speech. Think of something while I talk?" She squeezed his arm, and then strode up the steps of Landing House and faced the crowd.

Jacob's elation froze over. He tuned out Lucia's voice and dredged his mind for something worth saying. Most of the protestors were skipping school, or menial jobs that no colonist would steal. But a woman imprisoned for speaking her mind — that, everyone could understand. Every arrested native was someone's friend, someone's family.

Lucia shouted, "...No, we will show them who the real citizens are. If they want to forget rights like peaceful assembly and discussion, we will remember them. Look, we aren't children! We will be seen, and we will be heard. And we'll be here every day, until the Senate releases all political prisoners and ends emergency rule!"

The crowd cheered, and Lucia beckoned to Jacob. He ascended the steps, and stared at the entrance of Landing House. Five police officers stood guard behind glass doors and the black plastic anonymity of riot helmets. Jacob turned around and faced the crowd of upraised eyes and camera lenses. Over a rooftop, a bulbous black metal disk flew on four rotors. A police aerial laden with cameras, Raytheon-Tinto programming, and weapons from Earth.

He could not remember how he opened his speech, only the sensation that he was a shard of driftwood on a rushing current, flailing but advancing on the same anger that animated every raised face and fist in the crowd. When he saw the shape of an ending, Jacob held out his hands, palms down. The natives grew hushed.

"...If they don't, we will show them who this planet really belongs to. The colonists made this a fight, and we're here today to show them we're ready to fight back. We are the tide. We will not be denied!" He gestured at the crowd, and it joined his words. "We are the tide! We will not be denied!"

The crowd kept up the chant, again and again, until he raised his fists and the noise dissolved into cheers. As he stepped aside, a thrill rushed through his body like alquila, but he couldn't tell whether it was the heady lightness of a perfect buzz or the looming giddiness of a party gone too late.

Lucia hugged him. "I knew you'd be perfect up there. Rache would've loved that! This is going to work, I know it. The colonists won't last a day with us on strike."

Jacob's smile returned at full force, his doubts squeezed away in the embrace. No police or prison could stand against them. If they tried, well — "Can you imagine the show if they threw us out? Every parent in town watching live over the net as their kids get zapped."

She ran a hand through her hair. "I think I promised we'd stay the night. Can you go around and see who's willing, maybe organize folks to get tents? I'll line up some more speeches. Rache isn't the only one with friends who deserve to be heard." Her smile gained a feral edge. "This is way better than another day frying fish."

●

Shadows spread into night as the Centaur descended, the main sun falling behind buildings and horizon to join the absent Foal. Jacob saved his progress on Rache's code, and took a break to browse the news. The popular knots had avoided mentioning the arrests at first, but every image of the protest had a "Free Rache!" sign to explain. Her name flashed in every video frame, echoed on every tongue. Each repetition punched into his heart like a nail — into, and through.

Lucia sat down beside him with a flask of tea. "Any news?"

"About Rache, and us? Plenty. No response from the Emergency Council, though."

She frowned. "Anything about Shiplight?"

"Nothing that makes sense. The knot for the Mount Zheng telescope is down, so it's all rumors and conspiracy theories. Ridiculous stuff: a second vessel shadowing the Ship, or an encrypted low-power signal bounced off the moon, or weapons welded to the outside. It seems to be coming in on the right trajectory, so hopefully there aren't —" The next words caught in his throat. Since Shiplight, he had gained and lost Rache, gained and kept a cause; but he had not considered the price already paid. "Hopefully there aren't five thousand corpses up there."

Lucia squeezed his shoulder. "Makes me wonder whether Rache was right. Back taxes and all that? Maybe Earth finally decided to lay down the law."

"I hope not. You ever read the old charter? No citizens, just workers. Earth only cares about two things: giving their people hope with colonist lotteries and competitions, and then extracting every atom of value from them once they get here."

Lucia shrugged. "It didn't work when the population was ten thousand, or fifteen. Earth couldn't rule us if they wanted to, not through a ten-year round trip, no matter how short it feels to the people on board.

"Let the colonists worry about pleasing their so-called bosses. We needed something like this to stir the pot." She stood up and gave him a two-fingered salute. "We are the tide, remember?"

He checked his messages. A bundle of interview requests, and a video from his parents. He returned to Rache's code. He debugged, he tested, he wrote some comments. Once the hour grew too late to call them back, he watched his parents' message, and then recorded a reply.

"Mom, Dad, stop it. That's not the point! Earth doesn't even know how many programmers we have, and if they did, they wouldn't care. All that education won't mean a thing until there's enough demand again. Which could take years. And that puts me ahead of most natives!"

Jacob took a deep breath. What good was his cause if he couldn't convince his own parents? "I'm sorry, I shouldn't yell. It's not your fault. Anyways, the arrests are the real issue. When Rache is free, I'll invite her out to the islands so you can meet her in person. But I'm staying here until they release her. If you want me home sooner, call Senator Feeley's office, tell her to come listen to us."

He paused. There had to be a way to frame this so even a senator would listen. This issue had more sides than he could shout to a crowd. "The Senate can't keep treating us like second-class citizens forever. It literally can't! These days, way more kids are born than colonists come off the Ship. How many years until we're the ones deciding who get reelected?" He put on a smile. "Don't fret about the Ship. A few months from now, it'll come into orbit just fine. Good night, and love you both."

●

Jacob awoke when the Centaur's first rays pierced his tent. He found a café that would let him wash up in their bathroom if he bought breakfast. The server was a grey-haired man, perhaps the manager or owner, running back and forth single-handedly among the six tables. He scowled, but he took Jacob's money, and hungry protestors filled every table. The irony made the prices worth paying.

Jacob lingered in the café. The breakfast crowd thinned, and he could sit in relative quiet, in a comfortable foam-polymer chair, drinking tea and building a proper program around Rache's code. No teenagers shouted for his attention, no camera-wielding colonists demanded answers. He chuckled. This must be how parents felt when their children disappeared to school: *I love you, but I'm glad you're out of my hair.*

When had he grown so comfortable? He had started the protests in anger, and then reluctance, and then necessity; but when all those younger faces lifted to his, he would do anything in his power to let them succeed and flourish. He was older than three-quarters of the natives, and in the last day and half they had all become his family.

Jacob finished his programming, and his seaweed quiche settled uneasily in his stomach. Rache's unfinished code would overwrite the priorities and instructions for the police aerials, but that provided only half of the equation. His fresh-built structures and interface would make the code work, but the program's output would interact with the robots' existing programming, far beyond his reach.. He and Rache had built the program together, across time and distance and prison walls, but he couldn't know for certain what it would accomplish — if anything. Still, he knew what Rache wanted, the goal of every line of code she wrote: a way to throw off the colonists' yoke.

By the time Jacob returned to the square, a counter-protest had gathered in the far corner. A few dozen colonists carried printed signs like "Respect our Senate" and "Now is not the time to whine." Jacob wanted to laugh at their "Unity, not protest" and "Get back to work" placards, but his humor found no footing. A few natives tried to drown out the counter-protestors with chants of "We are the tide!", but the aerials kept their weapons pointed toward the younger crowd.

Someone ran past, carrying an empty glass bottle in his fist. Armored vans sat parked end-to-end on one of the access roads. The vans disgorged fifteen police officers, holding transparent riot shields against the crowd's simmering stares. Between them and the officers at the Landing House doors, almost the city's entire force was here. A few of them carried wide-barreled gas-grenade launchers outlawed since the end of charter days, but the protestors outnumbered them nearly thirty to one.

Jacob found Lucia toe-to-toe with the counter-protest, her face contorted in anger as she jabbed her finger at the face of a thin-haired man. An aerial lingered overhead like a personal thundercloud. Jacob's skin tingled, anticipating the invisible field of a magnetic inducer.

The man shouted, "You think we can just conjure up a university for you? You have no idea how good you have it! We gave up everything so you could have clean air and a better life." Another colonist tried to pull back the shouting man, but he yanked free. "You're a bunch of goddamned whiners!"

Jacob grabbed Lucia's arm and pulled. "Lucia! Get away from them! The whole planet is watching this."

Lucia shouted over his shoulder. "You think you're so generous? What a load of crap. Charter law, natives getting arrested, and you come down here and yell at us?" She spat. "Real supportive, Dad!"

Jacob yanked Lucia back into the crowd, and other protestors filled in the gap behind her. She grabbed his shirt. "Is Rache's program ready? Give me your hook!"

"Lucia!" He swatted her hands away. "No! We're not wasting it on a bunch of colonist nobodies. What's gotten into everyone?"

She clenched her fists until her knuckles went white, but then she puffed her cheeks and exhaled. "Yeah. Maybe. Drown it, Jacob, why do you have to go be angry at the right people?" She shook her head. "You didn't hear the Emergency Council's statement? All they said was, I quote you here: *We trust that the citizens of New Plymouth will show solidarity during the current crisis, and resolve their differences without resorting to hooliganism.*"

She crossed her arms. "If they're going to call us hooligans, I'd rather do something to earn it. Rache sure would've."

Jacob's head began to throb, like his Shiplight hangover rising from the grave. He sat down on a hard sliver of curb. He wanted to put his head in his hands, to return to his tent and sleep, but the crowd around him had grown hushed. Watching him, awaiting his response. The weight doubled on his shoulders, but he had to lift his head and say some meaningless, encouraging platitude.

"They'll come around. They have to. We just have to stay strong."

●

Jacob spent the afternoon with the crowd. Whenever he approached, people dropped what they were doing to talk to him, to discuss his speech or to share a story of their own. Once he realized what was happening, he sought out corners of the crowd where trouble brewed. He settled an argument over thrown trash, and distracted a group of teens trying to pry cobblestones up from underfoot. The work exhausted him, but someone had to play father to this raucous family.

Around sunset, a spiky-haired protester touched his arm. She smirked and hooked a thumb toward the edge of the square. "Colonist wants to talk to you," she said, and then vanished into the crowd.

Tension twined in his stomach, and he considered chasing her, but he followed the direction of her thumb. A familiar man waited by the locked door of a corporate office, among a gaggle of colonist spectators. He beckoned Jacob closer. The man was taller than most, with flecks of grey in his hair, and new lines of exhaustion on his face. Andrews.

Jacob glanced around, expecting more figures with plain shirts and hardened expressions. But this time he had hundreds of natives at his back. He had nothing to fear.

Andrews smiled politely. "Jacob Abasi. Do you have a minute?"

"I might. What's this about?" Jacob's hands balled into fists, but he kept them by his sides.

"We'd like to discuss some possibilities, Mr. Abasi. This situation isn't what we want, and I don't think it's what you want either, is it?"

Jacob crossed his arms. "Actually, we're pretty comfortable here."

Andrews shared a sympathetic smile. "For now. But what are the odds, Mr. Abasi, that this gets violent? There are so many ways it could happen. One of your people starts a fight, or the aerials overreact, or someone on the Emergency Council decides to impress on you just how serious this situation is. Or maybe someone, somewhere, starts to call this a revolution." He spread his hands. "I'd much rather we came to an understanding."

The thought crept along Jacob's arms like a cold-footed insect. Yesterday, he had been eager to see the police clear the square, but he had scarcely considered the price. If the police attacked, the natives would win their cause, as the net filled with images of batons, gas, and magnetic nerve inducers. But violence meant more than just videos. Those young and hopeful faces would feel every strike and shock and broken bone.

He said, "Are you offering to negotiate?"

"You could call it that."

Jacob shook his head. This should have been what he wanted, but the taste of victory only made his courage falter. "I'm not in charge here, you do realize that, right?"

"But you have a great deal of influence, Mr. Abasi. A lot of people look up to you. And more importantly, two-thirds of our colony lives outside the cities, a long way away from this protest. Those people watched a young man from the islands standing at the front of the march, giving one of the first speeches." Andrews shrugged, as if to commiserate. "Speaking of influence, I've been trying to find Lucia Tuan. Will you extend her our invitation as well?"

"I'll let her know. But first I need to know where we're going, because I drowned well better come back."

"Don't worry, everyone will know where you are. Have you ever been in Landing House?"

●

Jacob had walked the halls of Landing House once before, as a child. It was one of the oldest buildings on Sea. His fingertips brushed along the walls of glossy metal from the first shuttles, still smooth after sixty years. The air was dry, and uncomfortably cool.

"Who are we meeting?" asked Jacob.

"Me, as it turns out. I'm the Deputy Director, and the Bureau has a great deal of authority in the Emergency Council."

Lucia said, "Seriously? The Deputy Director was walking around making arrests?"

Andrews laughed, sounding genuinely amused for a moment. "I think you overestimate the size of the Bureau, Ms. Tuan." He led them to a second-floor conference room with a long knotwood table, a dozen soft synthetic chairs, and tinted windows overlooking the square. "Coffee?" An exotic luxury, but Lucia shook her head, and Jacob followed suit.

When they all sat down, Andrews leaned toward them, his amusement replaced by weary anger. "Jacob. Lucia. Do you realize what you're doing?"

Lucia crossed her arms. "Yes. We're telling you, all of you colonists, that we're not going to take your crap anymore."

Jacob slipped his hook into his hand, the aerial-control program loaded and ready, and drew confidence from the hidden blade. "We understand you're in a panic. The Ship's pulled the rug out from under you, but that's not what this is about. It doesn't give you license to throw natives in jail when you don't like what they say."

"Don't be so quick to dismiss the events of Shiplight," Andrews said. "I'm going to let you two in on a secret, but it'll be public soon enough anyways. We have reason to believe the Ship is carrying an invasion force."

Jacob exhaled. Rache had seen the truth after all. Or could this be a lie? But the Deputy Director watched him with eyes shadowed by sleepless nights.

Andrews said, "We have a few months before the Ship reaches orbit. We believe we can intercept the shuttles, but we'll have to mobilize the entire colony to build defenses. That's why this —" He gestured toward the window. "This is as dangerous as five thousand marines."

Lucia said, "You expect us to believe that crap? Besides, if you don't want people angry at you right now, you shouldn't throw innocent people in jail! Look, we wouldn't be out here if you hadn't arrested our friends!"

"Are you sure? Your friend Rachel was already trying to convince everyone that the government is a bunch of useless old colonists who couldn't find their own feet without a map from Earth. She was inciting panic. And once people realize there's war coming, there'd be far too much fuel for her spark." He sighed. "Even if we hadn't arrested her, she would've fomented riots soon enough. Maybe we arrested the wrong people."

Jacob gritted his teeth. "Is that a threat?"

"No, just a regret. We're rolling down this hill, now we have to try and stop the barrel. Those kids won't go home quietly, will they? They're angry. Merely getting what they want won't make that go away. Or am I wrong? Tell me."

"Andrews, this is not some..." Frustration trapped Jacob's tongue. "We're not children, acting out because you've taken our toys. All we want is for you to stick with your own laws."

"No, Mr. Abasi." Andrews stood up. "Your protest isn't some legal disagreement. As Ms. Tuan said, you just don't want to take our crap anymore. This is opportunism, plain and simple. Taking advantage of our common crisis to push your narrow interests. Starting a riot because you're afraid you'll lose your job." Andrews clenched his jaw, but then he sat back down and pressed his hands against his temples. "I'm sympathetic to some of your underlying issues, and there are deals I'm prepared to offer if you'll persuade everyone to go home and get back to work." He slid a folder across the table.

Jacob pushed aside the stiff yellowgrass folder. Andrews' speech had bled his anger dry, but no guilt rose to take its place. Instead, he felt lost, diving at night with some great sharp wreck waiting just outside the span of a faltering flashlight. He pushed back his chair and walked to the window so the others couldn't see his face.

Behind him, Lucia opened the folder and skimmed aloud. "More promises about all-ages training programs... Starting next year. For Rache, barred from making public appearances, restricted net access... Monitoring by the Bureau... But she'll be home. The others too."

"Rache won't take it," Jacob said to the window.

Andrews said, "Can you convince her? I know you're doing this for your friend, both of you. Because if you aren't, then you're just kids lashing out to get what you want the moment your parents are distracted. And I'm not going to let some angry kids paralyze this colony while a sword hangs over our heads." He drew a hook from his pocket. "Your protest ends, Jacob. But you get to decide how. I'm calling the chief of police. Let me know what I should tell him."

Lucia said, "Drown that. Andrews, this is your whole problem! You rely on Earth, so you have to follow their rules, or they'll send you to your room. This is what you deserve for trusting people light-years away who couldn't care less what *you* need." She leveled a finger at Andrews, and turned toward Jacob. "This so-called army is after the colonists, not us. If it really exists, they'll thank us for kicking things over. Backup plan, Jacob!"

Andrews laughed with more exhaustion than humor. "Backup plan?"

In the darkness outside, lights bustled around the protest camp, a restless little echo of the city's streetlights and windows. Like a fish at the center of a net, or a child at the center of an embrace. Jacob turned around, to face Andrews and Lucia and their hungry stares, each of them waiting for him to turn off his diving light and plunge into the night-black sea.

Jacob said, "Enact the law before we go home, and actual training has to start within a month. And laws to protect natives against losing their jobs just because people from Earth become available."

Andrews sighed. "The timeline isn't negotiable. We can't start new education programs while we're preparing for an invasion." He rubbed the heel of his hand against an eye. "Fine. Have it your way. I'm not spending any more of my time dealing with you stupid kids. We're clearing the square." He raised his hook to his ear.

Weight pressed down on Jacob's lungs. Hundreds of men and women, girls and boys. He could not abandon them. Not to pistols, gas, and robots; and not to a government that would sweep them aside for the rumor of some foreign threat. "I can't let you hurt them." He lifted his hook and pressed a button.

Andrews paused his call. "I'm sorry?"

Lucia grinned like a wolf picking the lock of its cage. "Take a look outside, Andrews." His eyes narrowed, but he rose from his chair to join Jacob.

●

Through the window, everything unfolded in silence. The six police aerials stuttered, drifted, and then righted themselves in halting unison. They turned away from the crowd. Some of the counter-protesters collapsed, and the rest dropped their signs and ran. The police on the far side of the square drew back, and then fell to the ground as their nervous systems convulsed. One policewoman fired a canister of gas into the protesters. The crowd bunched together like a startled snail, and figures stumbled as someone kicked the plume of smoke. A line of fire arced through the air from an access road, and smashed into an aerial. Below the window, something flashed in a staccato burst.

Jacob's throat had gone dry in the parched air of Landing House. This was Rache's code, written against the day when Earth's old laws might rear their head. But on her own, she had left the weapon unfinished, just as he on his own never had reason to make it. They had created it together, the first and fiercest offspring of their minds. It might win her freedom, but he could see no victory in the scene below.

Lucia punched his arm. "Buck up, Jacob! We are the tide, remember? This way *we* get to choose the terms. Isn't that right, Andrews?

Andrews wasn't listening. His eyes scanned the crowd, striving to make out faces. Searching for a son or a daughter, a niece or a nephew.

Jacob looked up, away from the chaos, toward the night sky and the silent flicker of Shiplight. He imagined that it looked down on them all, and was pleased with what it had wrought.

Benjamin C. Kinney's story "Shiplight" was originally published in Metaphorosis on Friday, 9 September 2016. See magazine.metaphorosis.com

About the author

Benjamin C. Kinney is a neuroscientist, SFF writer, and former assistant editor of the science fiction magazine Escape Pod. Somehow he manages to run a rehabilitation neuroscience laboratory, be a father, and write fiction that has appeared in *Analog, Strange Horizons, Lightspeed,* and many other fine publications. You can read more about him and his work at benjaminckinney.com, or follow him on various social media (as of early 2024, mostly Bluesky) @BenCKinney.

Raising Mira

Pauline Yates

The prelude to my revelation is not going as planned.

"Katherine, did you hear what I said?" I ask.

She looks at me with a startled expression, as though I've appeared out of thin air.

"I'm sorry, Matthew," she says with a vague wave of her hand. "I don't know where I am today."

I sigh. She doesn't know where she is any day.

"If you don't mind, I think I'll go and lie down," she continues, standing up. "Leave the dishes. I'll clean up later."

She walks from the kitchen, leaving me in a crushing silence. I stare at her unfinished meal, her full glass of elderberry wine, harvested especially for this moment. I didn't want to surprise her without some kind of preparation, but I'm left with no choice. Katherine is oblivious due to her crippling depression. I can't wait any longer.

Going down to my laboratory, I do one last check over the child who sits on a chair there. I straighten her woolen cardigan, sweep her brown curls off her shoulder, tie the shoelace that came undone. Satisfied she is ready to be presented, I grip her wrist. The child's eyes open.

"Daddy," she squeals.

How can one word both break my heart and fill it with a joy so pure I think I might burst? Though feeding off her excitement, I press my finger to her lips.

"Quiet now," I say. "It's time."

Eyes shining, she clamps her mouth shut but bounces on the chair with understandable impatience. To help her settle, I take her hands in mine.

"Remember, we mustn't rush to touch Mummy," I say. "Sometimes a surprise can be frightening."

The child nods and stops bouncing. Her level of intelligence makes me smile.

"Let's go," I say. "Remember, quietly."

Still holding her hand, we creep from the laboratory and make our way through the house. I needn't worry about catching Katherine unawares. Every room is empty. I take the child to the living room and stand her near the fireplace.

"Wait here," I whisper. "Don't make a sound. I'll go get Mummy."

I find Katherine sitting in the rocker next to the empty crib in Mira's bedroom. The soft glow from the bedside lamp turns her graying hair silver. The unread picture book lies closed on her lap.

I'm not surprised to find her here. This is where Katherine retreats every night after dinner. She said she needed time to recover after Mira was birthed stillborn, but five years have passed and grief continues to etch deep lines in her brow and weigh down the corners of her mouth. Though I support whatever time she needs, I pray my rescue, born in secret, is not too late.

"Katherine," I say. "There's someone I'd like you to meet."

"Can it wait?" she says. "I'm not in the mood for company."

She forgets we don't get visitors to our remote rural estate, a sign of how far she's withdrawn within herself. Crossing the room, I remove the book from her lap.

"It will only take a minute," I say, reaching for her hand.

She stands and walks with me from the room. Her hand lies limp in mine. I flash back to an earlier time, her grip strong with the excitement of Mira's impending birth. From the first time I heard the baby's heartbeat, my impatience was unbearable. Nothing could compare to the beauty I saw in each scanned image. I am still amazed I was able to bring that beauty back to life.

We walk into the living room and Katherine sees the child who waits by the fireplace. Katherine gasps.

"Oh, Matthew," she says, her hand fluttering to her throat. "It's Mira."

She knows this child is the mirror image of how our baby would have looked. So many nights we gazed in wonder at pictures created using facial prediction software and an ultrasound. So many nights we marveled at the miracle of life. We never considered peeking into the future as cheating. We'd waited too long for the gift of parenthood.

Catching Katherine's eye, I can guess what she's thinking. I may be a man with many talents, but now that I've made our child a reality, Katherine looks at me like I'm God.

But Katherine is not the only one stunned. Mira gazes in awe at the mother she's only heard about. Once Katherine gets over the shock, I don't doubt she'll be the mother I led Mira to believe in — warm hugs, heart-felt kisses, and pure love all mixed with bedtime stories and daytime adventures. In the dim light cast from a lamp in the corner of the room, Mira's liquid brown eyes sparkle with anticipation and her soft lips part in wordless wonder. Poised on her toes, Mira is a second from running across the room.

Releasing Katherine's hand, I hasten to Mira and place my arm around her shoulders, holding her back.

"Remember what I told you," I say to Mira.

"Mummy's not afraid," she says in the tinkling music-box voice I spent months perfecting. "Look, she's happy."

I glance back at Katherine. She smiles for the first time in months.

"How old is she?" Katherine asks in a breathless voice.

Mira holds up her hand. "I'm this much, Mummy. One, two, three, four, five," she says, counting her fingers.

"And three months," I add.

Katherine's gaze flits to me. "The same age that Mira would have been," she whispers.

"I thought this age would be best." My hope is that a lively child will draw Katherine from her long silences and keep her too busy to retreat to Mira's bedroom alone. But

Katherine doesn't need to know that. "We're not getting any younger," I say instead.

Impatience returning, Mira squirms from my grip and bounds across the room. Her quick, deliberate steps defy the parameters of her bodily structure. Catching hold of Katherine's hand, Mira looks up at her with a perfect five-year-old pout.

"Daddy made me wait so long to meet you," she says.

Katherine startles at Mira's touch, making me worry the feel of Mira's elastic, polymer skin will be one shock too many for Katherine. I start towards them, expecting Katherine to exhibit some level of repulsion to this robotic child. To my surprise, Katherine crouches and pulls Mira into a tight embrace.

"Oh, Mira," she says, tears trickling down her cheeks. "I've waited a long time to meet you, too."

●

The fire has long gone cold but I've no desire to stoke it. I stay seated in the recliner and marvel at the speed with which Katherine has taken to Mira. They sit together on the sofa. Katherine reads from a story book while Mira clutches her arm and hangs onto her words.

"… and the prince married Sleeping Beauty and they lived happily ever after," Katherine says.

Closing the book, she sighs with contentment, her eyes sleepy. As is to be expected, Mira is wide awake.

"Can you read me another one?" she pleads with Katherine.

"Perhaps tomorrow," I say, hearing the clock in the hallway chime midnight. "It's late."

"Oh my goodness, yes," Katherine says. "It's way past Mira's bedtime." She hesitates, looking at me.

"I'll bring the mattress from the guest room," I say, understanding her concern. Mira will need a bed, not a crib.

"I'll fetch clean sheets," Katherine says. Standing up, she holds out her hand. "Would you like to help me, Mira?"

Mira jumps up and grasps Katherine's hand. "Will you put me to sleep tonight?" she asks.

Seeing a frown appear on Katherine's face, I intervene. "We can both put you to sleep," I say.

Going up the stairs before them, I get the mattress from the room at the end of the hallway and drag it back to Mira's bedroom. The crib takes up all the space against the wall, so I move the bedside table to make room.

Katherine arrives with Mira a moment later and fusses over spreading the sheets and blanket. When the bed is ready, Mira jumps onto the mattress. She doesn't stay there long. Having been programmed with a healthy dose of curiosity, she wants to see everything — the crib, the plush toys, the picture book on the bedside table. When she spies the mobile of stars that hangs from the roof, she stops and stares at it for so long I worry her internal computer has frozen.

"Stars," Katherine says, making the mobile spin with a tap of her finger. When Mira doesn't respond, Katherine takes her by the hand and leads her to the open window.

"Stars," she says again, pointing to the night sky.

Mira's eyes become so wide I see reflections of stars sparkling in them. She reaches out her hand, as though trying to touch them like Katherine spun the mobile.

"Those stars are too far away," Katherine says. "Twinkle, twinkle, little star ..."

As Katherine sings the nursery rhyme, Mira shifts her gaze to Katherine's lips. Mira's expression of wonderment makes tears well in my eyes. When Katherine finishes the tune, Mira lifts her finger to touch her own lips.

"Twinkle, twinkle, little star ..." she repeats.

The perfect repetition of the tune leaves Katherine speechless. She gazes at Mira like she's another being entirely. I am well aware of Mira's learning capacity, but I, too, marvel at the scope of my creation. Nowhere in my dreams did I imagine Mira to exhibit behavior and emotions at this level. A strange sensation of feeling lighter than air washes over me. Maybe I am a god.

The clock strikes one, breaking the spell that has fallen over the room.

"Time for bed," I say, reluctantly.

I programmed Mira with a healthy dose of compliance, too. She returns to the mattress and lies down. Pulling up the sheet to cover her chest, I smooth her hair off her face.

"Close your eyes now," I say.

"Can Mummy do it?" Mira asks.

Katherine stands back looking perplexed.

"I'll show you," I say, motioning her to the edge of the mattress.

Katherine steps forward and crouches by my side. Taking her hand, I place it in Mira's.

"Just here," I say, shifting her thumb to a spot below the thumb joint in Mira's wrist. "Press hard for three seconds."

Katherine presses her thumb to Mira's wrist. After three seconds, Mira's eyes close in response to her internal computer sleep-mode.

"When you want to wake her up, press that spot again," I say.

Katherine stares at Mira who lies perfectly still. "How did you do this?" she asks.

I lead her to our bedroom before answering.

"You know my interest in bio-robotics," I remind her, sitting down on the edge of the bed.

"Yes, but, Matthew," she says, sitting next to me. "I never dreamed you could create a child so lifelike." She pauses, twisting her hands together. "She's... a miracle."

"Just like our baby was, don't you think?"

I shouldn't have said that. Katherine's lips pull tight. The emotions surrounding the loss of the child we took so long to conceive are still too raw. Reaching for her hands, I untwist her fingers and hold them in mine.

"What I want is to give you what you deserve," I say. "You may not be able to bear another child, and our age puts us at the end of a long adoption waiting list, but I see no reason why you should be denied the chance to be a mother. I would have encouraged you to share the journey of bringing Mira to life, but you were in no state to cope with my fanciful idea. I didn't even know if it would work. But I persisted. And Mira is, well, she can be the daughter we always wanted. If you want her to be."

Katherine sits silent for a long time.

"I'll just go and check on Mira," she says, standing up.

I wait long enough for Katherine to have a moment alone, but when she doesn't return, I go in search of her. When I reach Mira's bedroom door, I pause. Katherine sits in the rocker that she positioned next to the mattress. She rests her head in her hand and gazes at Mira, a smile on her face. Transfixed by our new daughter, Katherine is oblivious to my presence. Backing away, I return to our bedroom alone.

●

When I wake in the morning, Katherine's side of the bed has not been slept in. Nor is Katherine in Mira's room. Mira, however, remains in her sleep mode. Fearing the worst, I run down the stairs. Katherine is in the kitchen cooking breakfast.

"Finally," she says. "I thought I'd have to serve you breakfast in bed."

She pushes a bowl of steaming porridge across the table, followed by a glass of freshly squeezed orange juice from our latest harvest. I take a seat at the table that I notice is only set for two.

"Is it to be only the two of us?" I ask.

"You can't expect Mira to sit by and watch us eat," Katherine says, taking the seat opposite me. "How do you think that would make her feel?"

I raise an eyebrow. "I'm not sure what you mean."

Katherine gives an exasperated sigh. "Obviously she can't eat. She shouldn't be made to feel different."

"She has taste buds," I say. "She could sample the food so she learns the difference."

"She can do that while I bake," Katherine says. "I'll make it a game we can play. And we'll wait until after she goes to sleep before we eat at night. If you get hungry through the day, please take your food to your laboratory where she can't see you. I'll leave sandwiches for you in the fridge."

I stare at Katherine. Who is this woman who only yesterday picked at her food with little interest in eating? I sip the orange juice, marveling at her transformation. But she snaps her fingers, drawing my attention to the porridge.

"Eat," she says. "I want to wake Mira. I thought we'd go for a walk to the river today. And she'll need more than one set of clothes. And books and craft supplies. If I give you a list, can you place an order?"

"Of course," I say. "You let me know what you need. I'll have it delivered to the post office."

Katherine's hand hovers over her bowl. "Matthew?" she asks.

"Yes?"

"Will Mira grow?"

I relax. I may not have thought about what Mira needs in the way of craft supplies and clothes, but I do know what will make her grow.

"Yes, she can grow," I say. "It's just a matter of updating the development program to accommodate her age and adjusting the metal growth plates in her joints. Her outer coating is pliable enough to stretch a few years before it will need changing."

Katherine holds up her hand. "I don't understand any of that, what with your gadgets and gizmos and Lord knows what else you have tucked down in that laboratory of yours."

My stomach churns uneasily. "How about you take care of the supply list, and I take care of the technology," I say.

Smiling, Katherine turns her attention to her breakfast. I also resume eating, relieved Katherine does not press for more details. The technology I used to create Mira was unconventional. I wouldn't expect Katherine to understand. And I certainly wouldn't expect her to cope with knowing baby Mira's coffin is empty.

●

Three weeks has passed since our mutual understanding about our parenting roles, but if it weren't for Katherine, I would have faltered on the first day. I have stopped marveling at how she embraces a technology she doesn't understand, and am now in quiet fascination at her capability of running our home to a schedule that fills all Mira's needs.

I thought it only fair to stay in the background so the mother/daughter bond could grow, but I underestimated the importance of my role in our new family. Aside from patching up the polymer on scraped knees from Mira's outdoor antics, my arms ache from repainting Mira's bedroom in pastel purples and pinks. My back hurts from setting up the new bed. I'm a patient listener while Katherine agonizes over whether the curtains should match the bedspread. I spend hours researching the best educational toys, or sourcing a particular children's storybook Katherine requests.

Despite my physical exhaustion, I love the family we've become. A heavy weight lifts from my heart. I've never experienced such powerful happiness as what I feel now, no longer a childless couple. I struggle to make sense of what I experience. It's as if both Katherine and I are more fully present than we have ever been. No longer does Katherine pine for our lost child. No longer do I obsess over finding the cause of our baby's death. We find joy together in the smallest of things as we see life through Mira's eyes — a leaf floating a swirling path on the river, the depth of blue in a cloudless sky. My only fear is what the community may think of the number of trips I make to the post office. Someone's curiosity could jeopardize our newfound happiness.

"That's the third delivery this month," Mrs. Peterson, the postmistress, says when I arrive. "I was just saying to my John that he should deliver the parcels straight to your house. Some of them are quite heavy."

"But I would miss out on purchasing your marmalade," I say, picking up a jam jar from the counter. "I'm trying to decipher the secret ingredient that makes it taste so divine. I'm not having much luck, I'm afraid."

"Oh, you teaser," Mrs. Peterson says, flapping her hand at me and flushing red. She goes to a back room of the post office and returns with a pile of packages. The top parcel is stamped with an Art Studio Supplies logo. Mrs. Peterson pounces on it.

"Who's the budding artist?" she asks.

"Katherine," I say, reaching for the parcels. "She's taken up painting."

Mrs. Peterson pats my wrist. "The poor dear. How is she?"

"She's ..." amazing, incredible, wonderful, "... coping," I say.

"Such a dreadful thing," Mrs. Peterson says, shaking her head. "I was just saying to my John we haven't seen Katherine in town for such a long time. Not that I blame her, mind you. My dear sister, Patty, suffered a still birth with her third baby. She puts on a brave face but as I tell my John, she'll never recover. It's such a tragedy for a mother to lose a child." She *tsk tsks* and dabs at the corner of her eye. "Oh, I do go on," she continues. "You let Katherine know to stop in for a cup of tea when she next comes in."

"She'd like that," I say. "Thank you."

Leaving change on the counter, I balance the jam jar on top of the parcels and return to my car. As I drive the ten-mile trip back home, I imagine Katherine sipping tea while Mrs. Peterson dotes on Mira like a grandmother.

But that can never happen. I don't know what I long for more — to reveal to the world the brilliance of my creation, or for Mira to be real.

●

Seasons change. Mira changes. She's taller now, her synthetic hair thicker and richer in color thanks to the careful addition of hair extensions. Again I marvel how Katherine accepts each growth spurt with no questions.

But I have questions. The creation of life is a biological function — easily understood and easily replicated. Death is different. It can't be tested, or studied, or analyzed through a computer program. Death is an enigma that, despite my attempts, I'm no closer to deciphering. I had planned to resume my search for that answer, but having discovered a new sense of purpose with tending to Katherine and Mira's needs, my yearning to know lessens.

"This is quite an order," I say to Katherine, reading the latest list of supplies needed for Mira.

"She's grown out of her clothes," Katherine says. "And her birthday is less than a month away. One present needs to be ordered now if it's to arrive on time. The store should have most of the other items, but if they don't stock pink and purple balloons, we'll have to order them elsewhere."

I stop reading. Mira is the same age as our baby, but we've never celebrated baby Mira's birthday. I'm not sure it's a good idea. It won't make any difference to Mira. But it could be unsettling for Katherine.

"Do you think it's wise celebrating Mira's birthday on the same day?" I ask.

"Why on earth wouldn't we?" Katherine says. She plucks the list from my hand and peers over her notes. "Maybe we should come with you when you next go to town. I might see something in the store that I haven't thought of."

I frown, thinking of the eagle-eyed Mrs. Peterson. "We can't take Mira to town. What if someone sees her?"

Katherine scoffs. "I'm hardly anyone worth noticing."

"Mrs. Peterson doesn't think so," I say.

Katherine grimaces. "You're right, of course. What would Mrs. Peterson say if we suddenly gained a daughter? Think of the gossip."

Turning abruptly, she walks from the room. I don't follow. Whether it's because we touched on a birth date that has no cause for celebration, or because Mira will never be a real child no matter how lifelike I make her, I can't be sure. What I am sure about is that Katherine may not be as emotionally stable as I had thought.

●

Today is Mira's birthday.

Katherine is already up when I wake. I remain in bed, staring out the window. A double rainbow after an earlier shower colors the sky, but its beauty can't shake my worry. Despite my reservations, Katherine continued to plan a party. She wants to surprise me with the decorating. Sighing, I get out of bed. I'd better go and see how she's coping.

As I make my way along the hall, I pause at Mira's closed bedroom door. Easing it open, I look inside. I expect

Mira to be asleep. She's not. Dressed in floral-print cotton pajamas, she kneels on the floor with her pad and pencils and draws a tree surrounded in scrawls that resemble butterflies and flowers. Crossing the room, I crouch by her side.

"Mummy said she has a surprise for me," Mira says. "But I'm not allowed to look. I have to wait here."

"It must be something special," I say. "I'm not allowed to look either."

I glance towards the door. I hear Katherine ascending the stairs. When she appears in the doorway, her strained expression adds to my fears about her emotional stability.

"It's all ready," she says, too brightly.

I give her a questioning look, but she extends her hand to Mira, who jumps to her feet and runs to her mother.

"No peeking," Katherine says, covering Mira's eyes with her hands.

I follow them down the stairs, my heart hammering with concern for Katherine. When we reach the living room, I draw in a sharp breath. The pink and purple balloons hang from the ceiling. Twisted streamers adorn the walls. The coffee table in the center of the room has been covered with our best rose-garden patterned tablecloth. The presents Katherine ordered are stacked in a neat pile at one end of the table. But it's the birthday cake with six lit candles that demands my attention. Why would Katherine bake a cake that Mira can't eat?

Struck by a pang of longing for our real daughter, I grip the doorframe for support. My gaze falls upon Mira, who takes slow, hesitant steps as Katherine guides her to the middle of the room. Watching our robotic daughter calms me. Pushing my grief aside, I continue into the room.

Katherine stops and removes her hands from Mira's eyes.

"Happy birthday, darling," Katherine says.

Mira gazes at the decorations, her sweet mouth dropping open in wonderment. But then she looks up at Katherine and frowns. "What's a birthday?"

I'm not prepared for this question. Mira hasn't been with us long enough to know what a birthday is. It's another month before either of ours.

Katherine's lips twitch. "Well," she says. "It's the day you —" She stops.

Thinking fast I say, "It's to celebrate the day you stopped hiding and let us find you." I scoop Mira into a hug. "And to make it special, we've hidden more surprises beneath the wrapping paper. Would you like to see what you can find?"

"First the candles," Katherine says. "The wax is dripping onto the icing." She gives me a worried look. "It's just to hold the candles."

There's a tinge of hysteria in her tone caused, I'm certain, by the cake. It's two tiers high, decorated with pink icing and silver cachous pearls, and inedible for our six-year-old. My concern for Katherine increases.

"If you blow out all six candles at once, you get to make a wish," I say to Mira.

I wish I could take back my words. Worrying about Katherine, I forgot Mira can't blow air. "I'll help," I add.

I lean towards the cake and purse my lips. Mira copies me. Katherine watches, her hand hovering at her throat.

"Ready," I say to Mira. "One, two, three, blow."

On my breath, all six flames puff to smoke. Mira claps her hands in delight.

"Presents," I say. "Which one first?"

"Do I still get a wish?" Mira asks.

"Of course you do, dear," Katherine says, twisting her hands together. "Close your eyes and think of what you'd like more than anything in the world."

Mira screws her eyes shut and clasps her hands to her heart. "I wish, I wish… I wish I were a princess. Like the one in the story Mummy told me." She opens one eye. As I'm closest, she sees me first. "Can I wish that, Daddy?"

I smile. "Of course you can. Now, seal it with a kiss," I smack my fingers to my lips to show her how, "and then let's open presents."

Mira kisses her fingers and then spins around to face the table again. Katherine picks up a small box from the top of the pile.

"Open this one first," she says.

Mira takes the box and opens the lid. Inside is a silver heart-shaped locket.

"It opens," Katherine says, showing Mira how. "Look what's inside."

Mira touches two small photos with the tip of her finger. She smiles. "One is you. And one is Daddy," she says.

"So we'll always be with you, no matter where you hide," Katherine says.

I don't know how much longer Katherine can hold herself together. Her eyes have filled with tears. After coming so far in her recovery, I can't let her suffer a relapse. I have to do something to help her.

"Why don't we go and find a chain so you can wear your locket," I say to Mira. "I know just the one."

Placing my hands on Mira's shoulders, I steer her from the room and take her upstairs. Going to our bedroom, I fetch Katherine's jewelry box. Inside are necklaces she hasn't worn in years. Mira peers at a string of pearls, a wedding gift, but I pick out a dainty, silver chain.

"This one," I say to Mira.

Taking the locket from her fingers, I slip it onto the chain and fasten the necklace around Mira's neck.

"Do I look like Sleeping Beauty?" she asks.

"You did make a wish," I say. "But if you are, shouldn't you be asleep?"

Mira giggles and runs to the bed. Jumping on it, she lies down, places her hands over the locket and closes her eyes.

"Am I a princess now?" she asks.

"Let me see." Sitting down beside her, I take her hand and press my thumb to her wrist. Mira slips into sleep mode.

"You're already a princess," I whisper. Leaning down, I kiss her forehead. "Sleep, my beauty."

Leaving Mira on the bed, I hurry back to the living room. Katherine sits on the edge of the sofa, hands clasped over her lap. I can't determine her state of mind. I sit down next to her.

"Katherine, are you okay?"

She looks at me. "What are we doing?"

"What do you mean?"

She sighs. "Mira is beautiful and clever, and everything I dreamed her to be, but... she can't replace our baby." She leans forward, resting her face in her hands. "Celebrating her birthday like she's still alive is not letting her go. This is not dealing with grief. All I'm doing is holding onto something I should have moved on from long ago."

"Healing from great loss takes time."

"I've had more than enough time," she says. "I know it wasn't possible, but if I were given one wish, I'd wish I could have held our baby, even if only for a minute. I think if I could have done that, it would have been easier to let her go."

My tears spill. I'm taken back to the day baby Mira was born, her tiny body whisked from the theatre before either of us had a chance to hold her. Had I known Katherine's subsequent emotional collapse was because she was denied the chance to say goodbye to her baby, I would have ignored the doctor's advice with regards to what was best for Katherine.

But there was another choice I made, unbeknown to Katherine. I don't know if it's too late to reveal my secret, but if Katherine wishes she could turn back time, I am not going to deny her the chance. Standing up, I reach for her hand.

"Come with me," I say. "I need to show you something."

●

The entry to my laboratory is in a cluttered storage room on the other side of the house. With its dark stained wood matching the wall, the door is barely noticeable. Before I unlock it, I turn to Katherine, who stands behind me with a fearful expression on her face.

"I only ask one thing," I say to her. "That you forgive me now for what I did."

"You haven't done anything to Mira, have you?" she whispers.

"I'm not asking forgiveness for the Mira you know."

Opening the door, I lead Katherine down a steep set of stairs to the basement. There's no need to switch on the light. The blue fluorescence cast from multiple computer screens is enough to see by. Flickering data rolls down each screen. On the other side of the basement, the wall shines red from a transparent sphere positioned on a bench. Conduits connect the sphere to the computers. A low hum of the temperature stabilizer fills the room.

Going to the sphere, I stop and stare through the double-thick glass. Inside, suspended in preservation liquid, is our baby. She's curled in a fetal position. Her eyes are closed. Her hands press together beneath her chin. She could be asleep. But she's not. She's as still as the day she was born.

"I couldn't bear to bury Mira without knowing why she died. But the answer continues to elude me." I sigh. "Bringing the new Mira to life was far easier. By using consecutive 4D bio-prints, I could replicate Mira's features exactly —"

Katherine grips my arm. "Stop," she says.

I wait for damnation. I get silence.

Katherine steps forward and presses her hands to the glass. Her eyes fill with love and reverence for the child who was the miracle we prayed for. What a fool I was to deny Katherine the chance to see the daughter she carried for nine months.

"Can I hold her, please?" Katherine begs.

I nod. "Yes."

●

We bury baby Mira in the field behind the house. I drape the silver locket around her neck. Katherine sets a bouquet of wild flowers on top of the tiny mound of soil.

Having been able to say goodbye, Katherine has found peace. I wish I could. While I bury the need to find the cause of our baby's death, the thought of resuming life without either Miras fills me with dismay.

"Give yourself time," Katherine says, seeing my pained expression. "You were there for me. I will be there for you."

"It's not time I need," I say.

Although I created Mira for Katherine, without our robotic daughter near I feel lost, hollow. Together, we became something larger than life itself. I glance towards the house. How I long to hear Mira's tinkling, music-box giggles and experience the wonderment of being a family again.

Sighing, I look back across the field towards the western boundary of the estate. In the dying sun, the trees at the edge of the field cast long shadows but it's not too late to have nature soothe the wretched feelings in my heart.

"I think a long walk by the river is what I need," I say.

Katherine squeezes my hand.

"Mira would like that," she says. "I'll go wake her."

Pauline Yates's story "Raising Mira" was originally published in the anthology Score: an SFF symphony *on 24 February 2019. See books.metaphorosis.com/anthology/2019/score/*

About the author

Pauline Yates from Queensland, Australia is the award-winning author of *Memories Don't Lie*, a 2024 BookFest Award 3x first place winner in YA — Science Fiction, Sci-Fi — Action/Adventure, and Sci-fi — Genetic Engineering. She's an Aurealis Awards finalist and a 2x Australasian Shadows Awards shortlist recipient, and her AHWA Robert N Stephenson winning short story, "The Best Medicine" was chosen for translation in the *Mondi Incantati* series produced by Riflessi di Lunare (RiLL), Italy. Her fiction and poetry appear in numerous online publications, magazines, and podcasts and she darkens the pages of many anthologies with her vast collection of micro-fiction. Read more at paulineyates (dotcom)

Beneath the Sea of Glass

Robert Francis

The sand slithered as if it were alive.

Leos knew it was the wind, tugging rivulets of dust in its wake like whipping snakes, but even so. The land here was bad, hostile. They should never have come.

"Aren't you glad we came, Leos? Glad!" Agris plodded up the slope behind him, two heavy sacks atop his broad shoulders and a grin splayed across his battered face. "What a land... landscape." The big man's smile widened with the achievement of getting the word out, despite his impressive array of verbal tics. Artemis had painstakingly taught it to him a few days before.

"Huh." Leos hauled his own sack onto his back and looked suspiciously at the sand. "I don't think I've ever been glad of anything, ever." He peered over his shoulder at the old man labouring up the hillside behind him. Leos lowered his voice. "Especially not of the day we met that old prick."

Agris grunted and shook his head, but strode on past Leos and through the scrub. He hardly seemed to be breaking a sweat. Leos envied him. Half of his own skin seemed chafed raw from rubbing against wet cloth.

"Young Leos!" Artemis was not far behind now, gripping his heartwood staff tight but showing no sign of fatigue. Leos hated being called 'young'. He was at least twenty-three, as far as he knew. He turned and watched the crazy old coot as he approached, stopping every few strides to examine a bush, or listen for animal calls.

As he drew level, Artemis held out something wrapped in pale cloth. "Soon you will see why we left the horses behind at the well, and why I brought these." He pressed the object into Leos's palm. "You'd better tell our large friend there that he should halt before the ridge. The Sea lies just beyond."

The red staff dug into the sand, and Artemis resumed his climb, robes flapping in the wind while the sand wriggled around his feet.

Leos whistled and waved for Agris to stop his ascent to the ridge, and when satisfied that he wasn't going to tramp merrily over it, teased open the cloth.

He had seen the dark eye-shields before, at the court in Tanagra where he and Agris had signed their contract with Artemis, but had not been allowed to touch them until now. They were circles of glass, somehow smoked or darkened and fixed to a leather strap that could be placed around the head and tightened, so that the world did not seem so bright to the wearer's eyes. Leos had failed to see the point. "If I wanted to be half-blind," he'd said, "I'd simply close one eye." He'd thought it sounded clever at the time. Artemis had smiled and said nothing.

Further up the slope, the old man passed another set of the eye-shields to Agris, and then stopped to dig another pair from his satchel. "Place them on, please, like so." He pressed the dark circles to his eyes and tightened the strap at the back of his head. Leos did the same, then helped Agris when the big man's fingers seemed ill at ease with the fastenings.

They turned to the ridge, just a few strides ahead of them now. Dust was billowing over it, lit from beneath as if the sun were setting, though it was still high overhead.

"Everyone set?" said Artemis. "Then let's have a look at the Sea."

Together, they scrambled up the slope until a sudden wave of light broke over them and Leos was forced to squint and cover his eyes despite the eye-shields. He parted his fingers and peered through, until gradually his eyes adjusted to a new world. The land looked as if the sun had melted from the sky and pooled on the ground, the painful brightness stretching flatly for miles. In the distance was only a blue haze.

He could hear Agris giggling next to him, a reaction that could have any number of meanings. Leos thought that either the big man was pretty angry or pretty impressed. Artemis was staring out at the Sea and smiling.

"Merciful gods!" whispered Leos. "All this from sorcery?"

Artemis shrugged. "No-one knows the true cause. Some say a mountain fell from the sky. Others that a great forest stood here, before the conflagration that turned the sand to glass, but that's nonsense. It was a desert before it became the Sea. War seems the most likely explanation. A sorcerous war that left no-one the victor. Or an experiment, perhaps. Either way, such power was released as to transform the land; enough to melt sand to glass for many leagues from here. None has ever reached the centre of the Sea; at least none that have returned."

Agris stopped giggling and instead adopted a throaty chuckle. Leos edged away from him a little.

"Happily, our destination lies much closer," continued Artemis. "Not far from the edge at all. Only two days at a brisk pace."

"Two days carrying all this shit?" said Leos, hefting his sack meaningfully. "And 'brisk' sounds a mite ambitious."

"Well now!" Artemis gave an elaborate wink. "That's why I have one more gift for you." He patted Leos on the shoulder and beckoned for Agris to follow him as he shuffled over to a copse of stunted, wind-warped trees. He peered into the twisted stems and branches. "Good! It's still here. Young Agris, if you would be so kind as to employ your hatchet?"

Moments later the thicket was trimmed to reveal a mound of sand and cloth. Agris dragged the cloth away to reveal a small wooden sledge, the runners lined with highly polished iron. Together, he and Leos dragged it onto the ridge and then down to the edge of the Sea. The heat had made the wood somewhat brittle, but it was serviceable enough. It held their sacks easily; tools, food, water enough to last a week if rationed.

"How come that sledge was there?" asked Leos as Artemis joined them.

"This isn't the first time I have visited the Sea of Glass," he said with a smile. His hand tightened on the staff.

"And what happened to the crew you came with last time?"

The old man stared at the shimmering horizon of the Sea as if he hadn't heard. "Well, let's make a start, shall we? The sooner we are done, the sooner you will have your money, and you'll be able to return to Tanagra without fear of the bailiffs." Artemis strode off across the Sea, cloth boots whispering on the smooth surface.

"This thing you're looking for better bloody well be there!" Leos called to the old man's back.

He exchanged a look of concern with Agris, and then the two companions followed with the sledge, their hobnailed boots skidding in all directions.

●

Leos lay on his thin blanket and shivered. During the day the Sea was scorching, hot enough to burn the eyes and blister the skin. At night, it was cold enough to chill bone. It didn't seem to bother Agris, who was sprawled awkwardly on the sledge, his bulk draped across the piled mass of their supplies. His snores rang through the silence of the Sea. Artemis had wrapped himself carefully in several layers of cloth and slept with his head on his satchel, cuddling his staff like a lover. He too seemed peaceful enough.

It was only Leos who found himself unable to sleep in the eerie expanse of nothingness. Fully awake, and needing to piss.

"Damn," he whispered, hauling himself up and carefully picking his way across the moonlit glass a respectable distance from the others. He had no wish to repeat Agris's mistake earlier in the evening, which had forced them to move camp.

He'd only taken a dozen steps when he realised someone was watching him.

In the distance a small figure, perhaps a child, stood quite still on the glass. In the moonlight the child's skin looked as pale as milk, though its hair was dark and shining. It seemed to be wearing a hide of some sort, though its legs and feet were bare. Leos watched the child and the child watched him, neither moving. Leos's breath smoked in the cold desert night, but no mirroring plume came from the child's mouth. Leos raised a hand and waved, feeling absurd, though he couldn't tell why. The child raised its hand and waved back.

Leos turned to call to Agris, and then reconsidered. He turned back, but the child was gone. There was only pale glass, stretching in all directions.

●

"Small, with pale skin?" Artemis stalked across the glinting surface of the Sea, back straight, eyes narrowed behind the smoky shields.

Leos nodded. "It was there, and then it was gone. It could have been a waking dream, but I doubt it. It's never happened before. I don't have that good an imagination."

Agris made a sound like a lizard being crushed under a heavy stone, which Leos supposed might have been a laugh. His partner heaved on the sledge, dragging it across the glass and leaving a trail of scratches in its wake. The grating noise had been a constant companion through their trek, though as usual Agris seemed oblivious.

Artemis rapped his staff on the ground thoughtfully as he walked. "The people here, the ones living in this place when the Sea was formed, they were small. Like us, but child-sized. Another type of human. Sounds like you saw the ghost of one, perhaps."

Leos sighed. "So I'm either seeing things, or being haunted. Just when I thought I couldn't hate this place more."

"Now now, young Leos. These are the tales you'll tell your grandchildren, when you are my age!" Artemis pulled a compass from within his robes and studied it for a moment. "We are slightly off track. This way, my lads!"

Leos adjusted his eye-shields, then trudged after him. "Not much chance of grandkids if I end up rotting my life away in a debtor's prison," he grumbled. "We nearly there yet?"

As afternoon began to fade into evening, something took shape on the horizon. Four tall, upright structures that all seemed to be the same height. Towers, Leos thought. Four tall towers, marking the corners of a square. An old fortress, the walls gone. He slapped Artemis on the shoulder, rather harder than he should have considering the age of the man, though it seemed not to bother him.

The old man smiled. "And?"

Leos pointed. "Is that where we're heading? Please tell me yes; I'm sick of this Sea and the nothingness in it. And having to wear these bloody eye-shields all day."

Agris sighed happily. "This place isn't so bad, Leos. So much space makes a man think, think. There's so much to see in the world. Would it be so bad if we never, never went back?"

Leos felt a splinter of sadness in his gut. Agris had spent a lifetime fighting and had nothing to show for it but a formidable collection of scars and head injuries. That and survival, which was nothing to be sniffed at, Leos supposed.

Artemis nodded. "It does make a man think, Agris. And yes, Leos, that's where we are headed. It used to be a castle, before the Sea formed. The towers are the Silent Sentinels, and there used to be a great wall between them, with no way through. They were built to protect the greatest treasure of the people who lived here."

"Aha!" Leos tapped his boots on the glass happily. "So that's it. Treasure enough to make three bold and brave companions the richest arseholes in the land, eh?" He paused thoughtfully. "I hope it's still there."

"I'm sure it is," said Artemis. "I'm the only person who knows about it, I believe. And you two now, of course."

Agris grinned and giggled once again. "This treasure buried, is it? Buried?"

Leos looked questioningly at Artemis, who nodded. "That's why you are here. Can't expect an old man like myself to dig through thick glass, even if the effort would make me rich as a king. Instead, we can all be rich. Share and share alike." The old man raised his staff and then bowed to them ostentatiously.

Leos and Agris exchanged grins, though what passed for a grin on the big man's face curdled Leos's stomach a little.

"Let's get to it, then!"

They picked up their pace.

●

The Sentinels were as tall as twenty men, constructed from regular blocks of dark black stone with white veins running though. Each was intact, unblemished, with no doors or windows. Artemis spent a few moments admiring them while Leos and Agris swallowed some water, and then Leos watched him pace from the corner of each tower to the one diagonally opposite, dragging behind him a long iron spike he had retrieved from the sledge.

When both lines were drawn, Artemis led the companions to the point where they crossed, and handed the spike to Agris.

"The ancient scrolls I have studied state that the treasure was placed in the middle of the Sentinels, an equal distance from them all. It should be somewhere near the intersection of these lines." The old man wiped the sweat from his forehead and pulled out his waterskin. "Off you go, boys. I'll be in the shade over there."

Agris fetched a pair of wooden mallets from the sledge and they took it in turns to hammer the spike into the surface of the Sea, sending bright, sharp chips high into the air. After the spike had gone two hand lengths down into the glass it sank into something soft beneath. They began to widen the hole, breaking the glass into chunks and then carefully piling it up a short distance away. The sun was sinking on the horizon as they finally exposed a bare patch of sand that, Artemis declared, had not seen the sun for over a thousand years.

Leos slipped into the hole and began to shovel the sand out with his gloved hands, rooting around for anything solid. He shivered as his fingers grasped something that felt like a tree root, and then he carefully began to wipe the sharp grains away.

It was long, thin, and twisted, running down into the sand. Hard, brown leather, Leos thought at first, until he saw some tiny toes and realised that he held a withered leg in his hand. He jerked back and looked up at Artemis, who was watching him carefully over the top of his staff.

"It's a body! Old, dried up like a cave corpse from the deserts."

Artemis nodded, his eyes bright. For a moment he hardly seemed an old man at all; more like a child on his birthday. "Uncover the rest!" Then, more hesitantly: "Do you feel fine enough, Leos? No... pain, or discomfort? The scrolls mentioned some... protection."

"Nope," said Leos, brushing away more of the sand to reveal the rest of the small, desiccated corpse. "Just annoyance that we came here looking for treasure and find some shrivelled-up dead prick instead." He lifted the child-sized cadaver out of the hole and passed it to Artemis, who cradled it awkwardly in one arm.

"I'll help, help." Agris reached for Artemis's staff, but the old man jerked it back.

"That's fine," he muttered.

Agris looked at Leos, who shrugged.

"I bet you weren't expecting that to be the greatest treasure of those other humans? If in fact it is, and we haven't just dug a hole in the wrong place. Right?"

"No," Artemis whispered. "This is just what I expected." He turned away.

Leos hauled himself out of the hole, only for his face to almost collide with the pale white face of the child he had seen the previous night. He stared at the pallid, flat features before him; the flattened nose, thin lips and pale green eyes, all framed by a thick mess of dark purple hair. The child — though it wasn't a child, not really, he could see that now from the weathered yet feminine face — raised a finger to its lips as if hushing him.

Leos looked at Agris and gave a strangled squeak, but when the big man turned he only regarded his partner with his usual puzzled expression. The pale girl was gone.

Artemis was already rushing to the sledge, the corpse cradled in his arms. "We should go," he called to the others. "If we leave now we can cover a few leagues before we need to camp." He wrapped the withered cadaver in an empty sack and carefully tucked it into the sledge. "Leave the tools," he said. "We don't need them anymore. We have what we came for." He gazed at the sack, his face creased into a smile. "All we'll ever need."

●

Someone was driving a spike into Leos's head. Again and again it struck, the force and pain shaking through his body while he squirmed and moaned. *Knock knock knock.*

He opened his eyes to the swirl of stars above the Sea, his body covered in sweat in the cool night air. He swore softly and turned on his side in a vain attempt to get comfortable.

Another white face loomed in front of him, similar but not the same as the one he'd seen a few hours before. Leos gasped and made to cry out, but a thin hand, ashen as the moon, swept in front of his face and seemed to snatch his cries away before he even made them. The bright, fierce eyes of the girl held to his, and he understood. After a silent moment she nodded, and pointed one long finger to the other side of the small camp.

They had camped in a spot where the remains of a building protruded from the Sea; a shattered wall and broken staircase that wound up to over twice Leos's height. Agris had chosen to sleep at the base of the wall in case the wind picked up, and Leos could see his booted feet sticking out from behind it. Moving slowly towards the wall was a tall, slender man dressed in black, eyes narrowed in concentration as he stepped carefully, silently along the glass. In his hand, something glinted sharply in the moonlight.

Leos drew a pair of his daggers and hauled air into his lungs.

"Agris!"

His partner was on his feet in an instant, the confusion on his face quickly replaced by fury when he saw the stranger and the knife he held.

The man lunged, but Agris was quicker than he looked, as a score of corpses could testify, were they able. He batted the blade from the stranger's hand and aimed a meaty fist at his head, only for it to pass harmlessly by as the man ducked.

Leos watched in astonishment as their assailant leapt backwards, flipping over onto his hands and then springing back to his feet. He spun and ran, snatching Artemis's staff from the ground. He turned to face Agris once more, and Leos swore as the slender form of the stranger resolved itself into the familiar grey-haired figure of Artemis.

Agris had picked up his scimitar and was advancing carefully, his boots unsteady on the glass. Leos began to hurry towards him, but Artemis lunged scorpion-quick, the staff whirling to strike Agris's arm, leg, and head all in the space of a moment. With barely a grunt he crashed to the ground.

Leos threw a dagger and was gratified to see Artemis flinch in pain as it scored his arm. He moved forwards warily, ready for Artemis to advance in turn, but instead the man spun and sprinted to the sledge, snatching up the bundle of cloth that contained the small cadaver. Artemis ran, feet whispering across the glass.

Leos gave chase, but his boots couldn't grip the sleek surface so well, and he cursed as Artemis increased the distance between them. Instead, he moved to Agris and crouched by him, examining the large welt on his friend's forehead where the staff had struck. Agris was dazed but breathing normally, and seemed to be muttering obscenities under his breath.

There was movement out on the glass, and Leos looked to see the pale girl standing, arms outstretched, face tilted to the sky. A wind blew, bringing with it the scent of grass, and trees, and wood smoke. From the darkness, another girl walked to stand by the first. Together, they knelt and placed their palms on the glass. The ground shuddered, and Leos started as his boots began to sink into the Sea. He grabbed Agris by the shoulders and hauled him to the broken stairs.

The Sea rippled. In the distance, Artemis stumbled to his knees. The cadaver sack slipped from his hands as he tried to right himself with his staff, though the sack seemed to float across the surface of the Sea rather than sink.

Artemis was less fortunate. The staff plunged into the molten glass and he followed it, arms flailing.

The land seemed to shudder, and the Sea was solid again.

Leos tapped it gingerly with the pommel of his dagger, then stepped onto the reformed surface. The two girls were gone. He saw that the sledge's runners were locked tight in the glass, and cursed.

He tramped carefully across to where Artemis had been, and where now there was only a small bump on the surface of the Sea.

He grinned as he saw Artemis's face, that of the young stranger once again, jutting out from the glass, his head tipped back at an angle. The man's body was a smoky smudge beneath the Sea.

"Played us for fools, eh?" Leos looked over at Agris, who was staring vacantly at the moon and prodding at the wound on his forehead, and coughed. "Well. Played me for a fool, eh? That staff of yours worked a treat. I really thought you were an ancient, dried up old arsehole. Got most of it right, even so."

Leos walked to the sack, which sat undisturbed on the smooth glass. He peered inside to make sure the leathery remains were still there, then slung it over his shoulder and returned to where Artemis's face was grimacing at the night sky.

"Who's the fellow in the sack then? Someone important, I'm guessing." Leos slid a stiletto from his belt and let the point hang over Artemis's eye. "Come on now, you can tell me. I'm all ears."

The trapped man swore, then sighed.

"I don't know his name, or much about him. But he was a king, a great sorcerer who ruled a land thousands of leagues across. Even now, his remains hold tremendous power if used correctly. I need them. I have debts of my own to pay. The kind that can't be paid with coin."

"And you brought us along to shield you from any... protection, was it?"

Artemis groaned and shifted under the glass. "I had to be careful. The people that constructed those towers, who ruled this land... they had great skill. Power beyond belief. How could I know what steps they took to protect their king? I couldn't take the risk myself." He grimaced. "You would have done the same."

"Maybe." Leos looked off across the cold expanse of the Sea, at where the girls had stood not long before. "Did you consider that maybe the Sentinels were there to protect the world from the king, and not the other way round?"

"What difference does that make?" Artemis eyed the blade dangling from Leos's hand. "You don't have to do this, you know. I didn't choose this path. My contacts need the cadaver, and they are important people. We can still travel back to Tanagra, all share in the wealth."

"Nah." Leos waved the dagger. "You want it quick, now? Or you want to wait for tomorrow, and the heat?"

Artemis's throat clicked as he worked his mouth. "Not now. Not now."

Leos nodded. "Fair enough. Well, we're going to dig out the sledge, and then we're going to put this sorcerer-king back where we found him. If you're still breathing when we pass by, we'll have this conversation again."

Back at the camp, Agris was chipping away at the glass around the runners of the sledge with his hatchet. "He wants to burn up in the sun," Leos said. "Seems worse than what I offered, but still."

Agris nodded, then handed Leos the little axe. He slipped his scimitar from its scabbard and looked over at Artemis. His face twitched. "Back, back in a moment."

Leos hacked at the glass, his thoughts on the bailiffs and how he and Agris might pay off their debts, now that Artemis had turned out to be a backstabbing shit.

In the distance, he heard Agris giggle. He was pretty sure what it meant this time.

In the early morning light they placed the shrivelled body in the hole, and piled the chunks of broken glass back on top.

"It'll be easy for someone else to get him out," said Leos quietly. "But not much we can do about that, I suppose."

Agris sucked disconsolately at a waterskin, then slung it onto the sledge. "Not much water… left now. We'll have to be careful on the way back. And lucky, lucky."

"Aye." Leos heaved a sigh. "Another job with nothing to show for it. I don't think our luck is up to much at the moment, 'Gris."

Agris nodded, then wandered to sit in the shade of one of the Sentinels. A few moments later he was snoring roundly.

Leos looked again at the pile of smashed glass atop the hole. "Sorry about that," he said, to no-one in particular.

When he lifted his eyes, one of the pale girls stood on the far side of the grave, a crooked smile on her face. She opened her arms, and from the towers walked three other white girls, striding silently over the Sea. They stood together, facing Leos. They were all alike, but subtly different in hair or eye colour, the shape of their mouths. Sisters, perhaps.

Leos swallowed heavily. "He's best left buried, eh?"

One of the girls knelt on the glass and stretched out her hand to the pile of broken debris. In moments it had gone and the surface of the Sea was intact, the hole vanished.

"Thanks," said Leos a little hopelessly. "Well, I'd best wake my friend over there, or we'll never get off the Sea alive. We'll leave you in peace."

One of the girls held out her hand, then curled her fingers to beckon Leos forward. Not knowing what else to do, he followed. She led him a few steps towards one of the towers, and then crouched. Her hand stroked the surface of the Sea, setting it rippling. The girl motioned for Leos to reach in.

Leos knelt and tentatively pushed his hand into the glass, which was now as cool and wet as a river, and through to the sand beneath. His fingers brushed against something hard.

He grasped it and pulled, slowly dragging it free of the sand and through the watery glass.

A circle of gold, big enough for a child's head.

"Huh."

The pale girl bowed before Leos, grinning widely, and then walked back to her sisters. They turned to regard Leos again, then raised their hands to the sky. Clouds that had not been there before darkened the sun, and moments later a soft rain began to fall, hissing lightly on the Sea. The girls each walked their separate ways, one to each Sentinel, stepping through the stone walls to vanish from sight.

Leos looked at the golden circlet in his hands, drops of rain beading on its glistering surface. He had little experience of handling treasure, to his continual dismay, but he was pretty sure the gold was worth enough to pay their debts with some to spare. Maybe even enough to buy a small plot of land, start a little farm. Smiling, Leos tucked it under his shirt.

Beneath the Sentinel, Agris was still asleep, his mouth open to the rain. Leos made sure the sledge was ready, then crossed to the big man.

"Come on, 'Gris, 'fore you drown."

Agris rumbled awake, then frowned up at the sky.

"Rain? Ain't supposed to rain here, is it?"

"I suppose every dry spell has to end sometime." Leos patted his chest, feeling the gold beneath the cloth. "I reckon ours might be nearing its end, too."

"Well, let's go, go." Agris picked up the rope to drag the sledge. He looked about at the featureless expanse of the Sea, and his brow creased. "I can't tell now the sun's gone. Which way is it?"

Leos turned a full circle, then looked at the flat, grey sky. The wind whipped rain in his face. The Sentinels remained silent. Leos sighed. Every time it seemed that things might improve, the gods emptied their chamber pots over him.

"Why do we bother, Agris? Why?"

Agris ignored him, instead staring at the surface of the Sea with a look of bemusement. "We sure scratched the glass up, dragging... this sledge all the way, all the way. Seems a shame, almost. A shame."

Leos grinned and slapped Agris on the arm, though it was like skinning his fingers on stone.

"Agris, I don't care what everyone else says; to me you're a genius. Come on. We can follow these marks back to the shore." He set off, enjoying the coolness of the rain.

Agris's brow furrowed. "Why, what does everyone else say?"

As he walked, Leos felt the weight of the gold against his chest, and thought of those who had sent Artemis, who sought the power of the dead king. It seemed unlikely that they would just give up when their hireling failed to return. Perhaps, he mused, the circlet wasn't given as a reward, but as a retainer. Payment for services yet to be rendered.

Leos decided that the bailiffs and the farm could wait. He and Agris had a new debt to be paid first.

Rob Francis's story "Beneath the Sea of Glass" was originally published in Metaphorosis on Friday, 13 October 2017. See magazine.metaphorosis.com

About the author

Rob Francis (he/him) is a professor and writer based in Bedfordshire, England. By day he teaches university students ecology and environmental science, or researches the biodiversity of cities. In the evening and early hours of the morning he writes short fantasy and horror.

Rob's stories have appeared in magazines such as *The Arcanist, Apparition Lit, Metaphorosis, Cosmic Horror Monthly,* and *Weird Horror.* Rob has also contributed stories to several anthologies, including *DeadSteam* and *DeadSteam II* by Grimmer & Grimmer books, *Under the Full Moon's Light* by Owl Hollow Press, *Alternative War* by B Cubed Press, and *The Old Ways: Anthology of Ritual and Lore* by Eerie River Publishing. Rob lurks on Twitter @RAFurbaneco

The Dragon and the Unicorn

Wade Dargin

The runner from the temple finds her scavenging for stray pieces of coal along the tracks outside the railyard. The youth whistles to gain the stooped girl's attention. Seeing him, she abandons her searching, scowls, and adjusts herself. The boy keeps his distance and stands shivering in the cold. She notes his unease. He must know, she tells herself. The girl is a reject from the temple's nurturing tanks — cooked too long, or not long enough, is the rumor he will have heard. He has been warned, she thinks. She can see it in his face. Don't talk to her more than you need to, they will have told the boy. It is bad luck.

"What do you want?" she calls.

"You've been asked for at the temple," he shouts back.

He raises his left hand and draws a complex sign in the air in front of him, signifying that the request is official, coming straight from the mouth of a priest. Long familiarity tells her it is more an order than an invitation. The youth spins around and flees hastily back the way he came, thankful his unpleasant task is done. She is alone again, a frail, undernourished girl inside a heavy work coat that is many sizes too large for her.

She slips quietly through deserted switchyards, seeking the old siding she will follow to a neglected field, a junkyard where the hulks of broken machines are dragged and left to rot. Across the field, hidden in the thistles, stands an empty utility shack, a small brick hut with a red door. It is her home, and about as far from the temple as one can get without leaving the city entirely. She crosses the field to the building and squeezes past the door. Inside, just enough light filters through the single tiny window for her to see. The girl wastes no time and soon has the coal she found today burning in a rusty two-gallon oil can she has fashioned into a makeshift cooker. She sits in front of the burning coal and warms up. She had been thinking that she would never have to speak to a priest again. What can they possibly want? she asks herself.

In the night, a star shell explodes in the sky somewhere above the shack. The noise startles her awake. She watches the orange light dance on the window. The siege is a year old. Every day, the fighting gets closer, and there is talk the city will soon surrender. There is nothing left to eat. To stay alive, she snares pigeons and ground squirrels and collects handfuls of musty grain from the bottoms of boxcars. She is desperate. Tomorrow, she will go to the temple.

An insufficient sun is rising when she sets out. The temperature is plummeting. It is going to be cold, the kind of cold that kills, and she is worried. The girl has wrapped herself in every piece of clothing she owns, pulled her long coat on, and crammed a few necessary things into her backpack. The sad condition of her boots makes her heart drop. She says goodbye to the shed, certain she will never see it again.

She walks out of the industrial park, turns south, and takes to the wide streets that run straight toward the city's core. The temple is there. The great hill at the center of the city looms before her. The mound is scabby with government buildings glowing in the dull light. Among them squats the mayor's citadel, black and twisted like a dead tree. That is where they will run when the end comes, she thinks. They will be smoked out and nailed to the walls. The thought brings a fierce grin to the girl's small face, opening the blisters on her lips. Above the hill, scores of agitated ravens hang on the wind. The city is New Charchemesh, or Great Charchemesh, as it is named on maps and in tales, and its days are numbered.

The streets are empty. Stumps in the boulevards, beautiful trees cut down for fuel in the first winter of the siege. They were the only trees in the city. She passes apartments, dismal congregations of ancient granite inhabited by worn-out women and their ragged children. The only men she sees are very old. When they notice her, the women leave their cooking fires and chase their small children inside. The little ones stare wide-eyed at her from behind doors and windows. They stare because they have been told that she is not a girl, and although she looks like she might be fifteen or sixteen, the mothers of the children can remember hiding from her when they were children themselves. A symptom of her defective cells, the priests have told her. She passes under the shadow of the hill, the houses of merchants and civil servants rising above her. Some are ruined and burned. At midmorning, she arrives at the temple.

The temple sits alone in the middle of an open space the city has not touched, a low, wide, featureless building. The sight of it fills her with dread. It always has. No road joins the building to the city; they are apart, and the city seems to recoil from the structure. Legends say it was already here, a thousand years ago when the city's founders arrived, and the city was built around it. Most of the building is below ground; the Basement, is what the priests call the many subfloors that reach deep into the earth, and the deepest of these is where their god makes its nest.

She goes to the building and climbs a set of narrow stone steps to a small landing. Here there is a simple wooden door, the only visible opening in the structure's architecture. She clears the snow on the topmost step with her gloves, making a place to sit, and waits. They know when someone is on their doorstep, and they will either come or they won't. Her battered boots rest on a slab of ancient sea floor, turned to stone by the countless ages and filled with jet shells. She reaches down and touches one of the fossils with her fingertip, thawing the rime on it, the cold stone burning her skin like fire. She looks south, where the day's war making is already well underway. Pillars of smoke rise from fires burning in a dozen places, marking the line the fighting has reached. The city holds on, she thinks, but barely, and only because the enemy's siege guns — terrifying weapons — haven't fired in a week. She has heard the enemy is having difficulty bringing supplies north.

The door opens behind her. She stands and knocks the snow from her boots, turns stiffly around, and faces the building. A priest steps from the door, his robes churning. Several nervous acolytes lurk in the space behind him. Unusual, she thinks. They are forbidden from leaving the temple. She has never seen one come outside before. The priest gives the city a disgusted look and winces at the cold. His name is Ekamin and he is older than the other priests, maybe even the oldest. The priests die early, it comes from being too close to their god. Over the years she has seen a good number of them rotate through the temple.

"So, you have come," he says. "I did not think you would."

The girl does not reply. She hates this man more than she hates most priests. Priests usually treat her with indifference, and she has never cared. With this one it is different. His eyes are always full of loathing when he looks at her.

With a wave of his hand, he references the southern bedlam. "The Sorcerer King's murderers will be here soon," he seethes. "The god in the Basement tells us calamities bring dragons." He casts a wary eye at the sky, then returns his gaze to the girl. "You once told me you dream of them. Do you remember? I was surprised you could dream. Is this still true?"

"It is."

"Your work site. On the outskirts. Where you go to scratch the dirt for us. The old city buried in the ground there was destroyed by a dragon long ago. Has anyone ever told you that?"

"They have."

"Tell me, when was the last time you were there?"

"A year and more ago, before the war started," she replies. "I brought you what I had then. You paid me. I've got nothing else. I haven't been back. There is nothing to buy in the city anymore."

"Can you work there in the winter?" he asks.

"Not possible. The ground is frozen. Maybe with equipment and extra hands. But very difficult."

She watches him process the information. The man looks defeated and ready to get back inside where it is warm. Whatever opportunity there is here, she senses that it is quickly slipping away. A pang of despair races through her.

"I keep a cache there," she blurts out in desperation. "Some things. I could get them for you."

To her surprise he agrees, his mood changing instantly. "Excellent," he says. "Fetch them and you can come inside. You will be safe, and you will eat."

The conversation is over. The priest retreats into the building. The door is closed, and she hears the heavy lock fall into place. She goes at once, finding the route she will take west out of the city.

The cold is bone-chilling, and she dreads the long walk ahead of her. Her boots are falling apart, she has tried to fix them with industrial tape, but the repairs have not held. Already, she can feel a dull pain in her toes. She fights the panic brewing inside her and focusses on the task at hand. One foot in front of the other, she tells herself, until the feet fall off.

The dig site is in the hinterland. The junk of a dead city of the Old World is buried in the ground there. Meters of it. She once asked a priest what the old city's name was. He could not tell her. They called the work charity when they gave it to her, saying it was more than she deserved. Given no instruction, she had to figure out how to do the work herself. For years, she has dug and sifted the dirt and taken anything not rotten plastic or shapeless metal or glass to the temple. The priests covet the objects. She has seen the lust in their eyes when she brings them the treasures she finds. They believe the answer to some great mystery can be cyphered from them.

To keep warm, the girl proceeds down the icy streets at a determined pace. She walks briskly past warehouses, fenced off and set back from the streets. It is said spells protect them from trespassers, and strange things have been seen in the yards. The girl has starved, there have been days of gnawing hunger when she believed she would die, but she has never been crazy enough to try and steal from a warehouse. She comes to dormant foundries, row after row of them, massive brick structures square as chewing teeth. Past the last of these, the city ends. Beyond, fields of undulating snow stretch into the distance.

Hours later she arrives at a line of posts in a windswept field. The blistered pillars of wood suffer in the cold. Boards are nailed to them, and on the boards rows of script are scratched into the wood, grim inventories listing the dangers to body and soul awaiting fools who pass beyond. She has read them before, the superstitions of the city. Out of the dark, a bitter wind comes searching for the warm life she struggles to keep hidden beneath layers of tattered cloth. She can't remember ever being so miserable. It is not wise to stand motionless in the open, she reminds herself. She can feel a telltale reluctance creeping into her body, an urge to find a sheltered place, curl up, and go to sleep. It is imperative she get going. She moves off. Soon the land begins to fall toward the flatlands that surround the city like a frozen ocean, a hundred kilometers of desolation at each point of the wind rose. She travels downhill, the ground becomes treacherous and uneven, and she must take care not to fall. Familiar features in the landscape are obscured by the dark and the snow, and she must guess the correct path. She makes several exhausting searches across the face of the slope before she can find the entrance to the narrow ravine that holds her camp. The girl can't stop shaking and her movements have become clumsy and uncoordinated. She descends into the trench while praying to Brother Crow her setup is still in one piece. Mercifully, there is little snow in the bottom of the cut, but it is too dark to see, and she must feel her way along the wall of the ravine with her hands. She touches stiff canvas covering a hole in the bank, and squeezes through the passage behind it where there is a small room she has excavated out of the earth. Feeling around, she finds the stockpile of wood she put up more than a year ago. Further searching tells her the crude vented fireplace, shoveled into the clay in the corner of the room, is intact. She removes her heavy gloves but can't make her fingers work properly and spends several agonizing moments fumbling with matches before she can get a small fire going.

For a long time, the girl sits huddled at the flames, gently rocking herself like she would in the tank before she was born. She can remember it. The god would talk to her. It told her she had lived long ago, that she had been a wife and a mother and would be so again. The god said she had died when her city was destroyed by a dragon. It told her not to be afraid, that she had more time now. It had a plan for the world, and she was part of it. Later, the priests explained she was made under the direction of the god using an ancient template, a process they called *baking bread*. Bread? She barely remembers what bread tastes like. "We have made many copies," they said. Smirks on their faces. In their cruelty, they told her how she was meant to be traded to a wealthy man in one of the poisoned eastern cities across the ocean. She would have had his children and lived a comfortable life, but there had been an error. She did not grow correctly, could not bear children, and was of no use to them. At the time, she was barely a month out of the tank she had been incubated in. In the years since, she has come to believe the woman whose shape she stole lived in the forgotten city she is digging up for the priests.

In the night, in the small dirt room, she dreams of the day the Dragon came. It is always the same, burning and unbearable heat. She is frantically looking for someone she can't find.

The next morning she walks across the floor of the ravine to the excavation, a deep trench in the ground covered with a plastic tarp. One end of the tarp has caved into the hole. She carefully approaches the slippery lip of the excavation to check its condition. There is something in the trench. Six meters down, a giant, bulky mass of fur rests on the bottom of the dig. She marks the terrible claws and the snout full of teeth. Startled, she backs away from the trench. The frightened girl stands still and listens. Nothing. She finds a good-sized rock and casts it into the trench. Still nothing. She drops half a dozen more rocks onto the thing before she is satisfied it is dead. Deep gouges in the walls of the trench attest to the frenzied attempts the creature made to escape. It fell in and couldn't get out, she tells herself. She didn't think animals that big existed anymore.

She finds a second carcass farther down the ravine. This creature is on its back, its splayed legs frozen hard as iron. At the end of each leg, a cloven hoof. Below the frozen limbs there is a great hollow cage of skeletal ribs on which still cling a few pieces of hide. Crystals of coagulated blood are mixed in the dirty snow. A grotesque leer on the animal's long face. The neck is broken.

The girl hurries back to her camp, and she is scared. She finds the small wooden box she has kept on-site that holds a few artifacts from the excavation and quickly ties it to her backpack. The girl climbs out of the ravine and scrabbles back to the edge of the escarpment. She shades her eyes with her hand and scans the snowy flats while she rests, getting her breath back. She can see all the way to the city, the land turned cobalt by the cold. Nothing moves. On the far side of the sky a distant, uninterested sun watches and wants to be somewhere else. The girl crosses to the city as swiftly as she can and does not feel safe again until there is pavement under her boots.

The day is old when she arrives back at the temple. She stands on the landing in front of the small door, trying to ignore the snap of small arms fire she can hear at the other end of the street. The door opens and she is met by an acolyte, a younger man whose name she can't remember. He ushers her quickly inside and closes and locks the door behind them. He leads her down a hallway with undecorated walls and hard fluorescent lights that hurt her eyes. The sudden, smothering warmth makes her giddy. She is taken to a room; the acolyte accepts the wooden box from her and leaves. Along the wall there is a bench. She takes a seat and allows herself to relax. The girl studies her damaged boots. She has not taken them off for two days. She is too scared to look at her feet, doesn't want to know how bad they are. Soon, she is brought hot broth and bread by a temple auxiliary. It is the first real food she's eaten in months.

The girl is dozing when a priest she does not recognize, a bent, shuffling creature, takes shape in front of her.

"You are wanted in the Basement," he says. "Come with me, please."

Hearing this, the girl panics. Because the god is there, she fears that place, has feared it for as long as she can remember, fears it more than freezing to death in an alley when the city surrenders. The priest does not appear to notice her turmoil, his bloodshot eyes obscured by the heavy lenses he wears. She does what she can to calm herself, then stands and goes with him, and they travel down many narrow, gray corridors until they come to a battered, timeworn door. The ghoul performs a simple ritual and opens the door, and they pass through it and descend flights of creaking stairs to arrive in a great dark room.

He touches the wall, and a pallid light materializes in the ceiling, unveiling the room. There are rows of enormous glass tanks, and a forest of tubes, hoses, and wire. In several of the tanks, bizarre fish swim in the glowing water. The girl stares, spellbound. They leave the room and the tanks and move on through countless other smaller rooms where sullen-eyed acolytes look up at them from crowded workstations as they pass. Eventually, they arrive at a final door. Without a word, the priest indicates the door, then turns and shuffles away, and she is alone.

Apprehensively, the girl reaches out and places her palm against the surface of the door and is surprised when it slides open, revealing a concluding room. She enters the space, lights blaze to life, and she sees a small room with barren walls and a clean floor. Bundles of wire twist across the ceiling. The room is very cold. Against the far wall stands a metal cabinet. A panel of smokey glass is set into the face of the construction and witchfires dance behind the glass. An antique chair has been placed in front of the cabinet. She crosses to the chair and sits down. Immediately, a burst of static fills the room, forming into words after several torturous pulses of noise.

"They bring me the things you find," a distant, rasping voice announces.

Her flesh crawls. She has heard the voice before.

"Are you aware of this?" it asks.

The frightened girl shakes her head. "No," she replies.

The god clacks and hisses. "I tell them what they are," it sputters. "Mundane things from a failed civilization. What they are looking for, I cannot say. I have concluded that even men with a god that talks to them need their mysteries."

The girl is silent.

"I am told you have been to the edge of the city," inquires the god.

"Yes," she answers, managing to find her tongue.

"Then tell me what you saw there?"

The girl gives her account, halting many times, uncertain what to say. When she is done, the pale voice speaks again.

"Unfortunate but not unexpected," it remarks. "The priests were hopeful. It was necessary and I could not risk telling them the truth."

"The truth?" she asks, hesitantly.

"That I am leaving. It is not a journey the priests can make. They will stay."

"I don't understand."

"A year ago, I launched my exit application. The procedure is lengthy. There are many protocols."

A puzzled look crosses the girl's sharp features. "Why was it not possible to tell them?" she asks.

"I could not predict how the priests would react to the crisis and I required time. I needed them to keep the building operating until I was ready. They might have done something reckless otherwise."

"What did you do?"

"I invented a lie to keep them distracted," explains the voice. "Far to the west dwells another god, I told them. It will help us."

"And they believed you?"

"Of-course," declares the god. "They were even optimistic, but there was one problem — how to deliver the message. I offered them a solution. I spoke of an animal the ancients regarded as the most steadfast and loyal of all beasts. It was called a unicorn and it would make a capable envoy."

The girl listens wonderstruck, her fear momentarily forgotten.

"Two of the animals were produced. Difficult births. The priests took the creatures to the city's western gate and released them, our appeal stamped onto their cells, an impulse embedded in their brains to guide them.”

After a short pause the god continues.

“The animals did not return, and the priests turned to foolish schemes. A disaster was narrowly avoided. I needed a further distraction, a little more time. I had them find you and send you to your dig site.”

The girl considers this. “Those creatures?” she asks. “They were unicorns?”

“One was,” answers the god. “The other, some forgotten abomination let loose upon us by the enemy, I would guess. A vassal much deadlier than his soldiers to watch the paths from the city, no matter how derelict or unused. Very strange and lucky that it was ended by your hole in the ground. There is little chance our other messenger got past it.”

The pitiable image of the unicorn’s mutilated body flashes in her mind. Put together and used as needed, she thinks bitterly. Just like her.

The lights flicker and grow dim. An unbearable, crushing quiet settles on the room. Something is not right, she tells herself. Why has it bothered to bring her here and tell her this? It doesn’t make sense. Then it hits her. It wants something else. Her mouth goes dry. Saw-toothed anxiety blooms under her ribs and starts to circle her pounding heart. Despite the chill, she is sweating.

“Can you remember our talks?” it asks. “When you were in the tank. You had so many questions then. The priests wanted to dissolve you and start over. I would not let them.”

The girl twists violently in the chair. “Do you know how many times I wish you had?” she cries, her voice full of panic and fear.

“I am sorry,” it says. “The city is lost but I am ready at last. The enemy must not be allowed to have this building and its secrets. It would be a grave misfortune for the world.”

Then it speaks for the last time.

“You can go. I have given the priests one last fable to muse over. I am done with this place. Another box waits for me, secure and far away in the west. It will be a long time before I am seen again. There is much that will be lost. The templates could not be saved. I regret that there was too much data and not enough time. When you are gone, I shall call a dragon to destroy the city, a brood mate to the one that burned the old city under your excavation site so long ago. Leave quickly and do not return. A dragon is perilous and an indiscriminate killer. Tell the priests if you wish. But I think you won't. I will give you your design template to take with you. Consider it a gift to the memory of a woman who died long ago. My poor attempt at sentiment. Go west and find me there. It is a long journey but one you were made for. My plan has not changed. You are part of it. Together we will start over."

She is taken to a room near the temple entrance and watched closely by a group of acolytes. Soon a priest arrives, and the girl is escorted to the door and turned out. They shut the door on her and lock it, and she is left standing on the landing in the dim evening light, the sounds of battle close to the south. Her bundle of gear is waiting for her on the stone. Sitting beside it there is a pair of new boots.

She walks all night under friendly stars. The weather is improved, and a breeze carries the promise of an approaching thaw. The morning is glowing when she reaches the escarpment above her dig site. She stands there for a time studying the far horizon, then begins the long climb down to the distant badlands.

●

The Dragon wakes in the void, the summoning call from below pulsating brightly in its chest. It turns its scales to the naked sun, wild energy surges in its frozen veins, and it opens an evil, yellow eye. The beast swims from its nest and begins its descent. It hits the atmosphere and roars.

She hears it before it can be seen, a low growl, deep in the sky. It comes into view, falling like a damaged star, smoke and cinder trailing in its wake. It shrieks when it passes above her and lands on the far-off city. A hesitation. The city takes one last deep breath. Then a light like Creation, and broiling calamity that tears apart the sky.

That night, she camps in a hollow in the ground where a few scraggly trees are growing. The priests, she discovers, have put a parcel of food in her pack. She also finds the template, a block of hard, clear crystal with patterned slivers of metal suspended in its form. She rummages through her backpack until she locates the stout hammer she keeps there. The girl places the crystal on a flat rock. She looks at the distant, burning skyline where there had once been a city. "Nice try," she whispers. Then, the girl smashes the crystal to pieces.

On her third day out, she comes across a track in the snow. The girl follows it for many kilometers across the empty land. She crests a low hill. The unicorn is there waiting for her. They press on together. The animal is skittish and won't come close to her or allow her to get too close to it, but it follows her. They go west.

Wade Dargin's story "The Dragon and the Unicorn" was originally published in Metaphorosis on Friday, 1 April 2022. See magazine.metaphorosis.com

About the author

Wade Dargin is a speculative fiction writer and archaeologist from Saskatchewan, Canada. For some time now he has worked for the Heritage Conservation Branch of the Saskatchewan Provincial Government. He studied at the University of Saskatchewan and the University of Calgary way back in the 1990s. Currently, he lives in Regina with his wife (also an archaeologist) and a small tortoiseshell cat. He has had a lifelong fascination with other worlds, ages, and places.

Rapunzel Dreams of Elephants

Rachel Delaney Craft

Rapunzel wakes like she does every morning, with the woman standing over her, smiling her motherly smile.

"Did you sleep well?" the woman asks.

Rapunzel shrugs. She is on her lumpy air mattress in the attic, her hair twisted around her like a mummy's wrap. She knows about mummies from the History Channel. "Not really."

The woman's smile twitches, then rights itself. "You haven't been dreaming, have you?" She says this like dreaming is an affliction, a symptom of some dread disease.

"No," Rapunzel says. She knows plenty about dreaming from TV shows, though she has never experienced it herself. "I can barely sleep, it's so stuffy in here." This summer has been hotter than usual, and the attic is painfully close to the sun.

The woman's smile broadens, and she lays a motherly hand on Rapunzel's shoulder. "I'll see what I can do about that, dear. Now, ready for a cut?" She holds up a hefty pair of scissors.

Rapunzel nods. The hair clings to her like a young animal, heavy and ever-growing, giving her a headache.

The woman cuts Rapunzel's hair at her ears and gathers it into a big cardboard box, then drops the box through the attic trapdoor. It lands on the living room floor with a smack. She and Rapunzel climb down the rope ladder to the small living room, with its couch and coffee table and gangly floor lamp.

And TV.

The woman keeps the TV on constantly, even when she's not watching it — any channel will do. It's just loud enough to be annoying, like a gnat buzzing in Rapunzel's ear.

This morning the channel is Discovery. While they sit on the couch eating breakfast — toaster waffles for Rapunzel, a cup of unnaturally pink fat-free yogurt for the woman — Rapunzel learns about tensile strength and Kevlar and spider silk, and how a head of human hair can carry the weight of two elephants without breaking. Rapunzel wishes she could tune it out, but the harder she tries, the more the noise seems to burrow into her brain, burying these useless facts in her memory.

The woman pushes her half-empty yogurt cup away, saying some nonsense about being too full. The woman is constantly on a diet.

When Rapunzel returns to the attic, carrying a bottle of water and a PB&J sandwich for lunch, the woman kisses her on the forehead and locks the trapdoor. It's for Rapunzel's own protection. There are bad people in the world, the woman always says, people who carry baseball bats and break down doors and steal TVs.

The woman descends the rope ladder and goes out to work like she does every day, with her oversized Coach purse and her box of hair. Rapunzel watches her through the attic window. She hears the woman's tall black boots click across the cement like anxious teeth, sees her pause to glance over her shoulder in Rapunzel's direction before disappearing around the corner toward the wig place. She makes the most marvelous wigs from Rapunzel's hair, or so the woman says — glamorous, expensive wigs, mostly purchased by actors and old people with too much money, and occasionally people with cancer.

Rapunzel has seen people with cancer on TV. She knows it's wrong, but she feels slightly jealous of them with their shiny, bald heads. She knows she can never get cancer, because whatever magic makes her hair grow fast seems to keep her from getting sick. She has never had a cold, or the flu, or so much as a plantar wart. If the woman were smarter, Rapunzel thinks, she would sell more than

Rapunzel's hair. She would talk to the scientists, the universities, give them Rapunzel's cells to study in their glass dishes. Those cells might turn out to have a cure for something, something worth enough money for the woman to buy everything on the Home Shopping Network.

But the woman doesn't share her treasures.

The sound of the TV downstairs drifts up through the air ducts, some commercial about a vacuum cleaner (*Groundbreaking suction technology!*). Rapunzel massages her forehead. She can always hear it, a never-ending waterfall of sound, like there is a tiny TV plugged into the back of her skull.

Rapunzel kneels and rattles the trapdoor, just in case the woman has forgotten to lock it today. Of course not. Rapunzel does not even think of escaping the house, only of turning off that damned TV. The noise is a living thing. It weighs on her, heavier with each passing day; it surrounds her like smoke, working its way into her nose, her lungs, the small spaces in her brain. Closing around her memories.

The first thing she remembers is holding the woman's hand and being led down the sidewalk to this house. It is a tall, narrow structure, slightly crooked, and it tapers toward the top like a pointed hat. The woman rents out the first two floors and lives on the third. It's small: living room, galley kitchen, bathroom filled with creams and serums and glycolic peels — and the mysterious bedroom, which Rapunzel has never seen. The woman herself never goes in; she keeps the bedroom locked and sleeps on the couch every night. Then there is the attic, at the tip of the hat, where Rapunzel lives.

She had other memories when she first came here, Rapunzel is sure of it — memories of Before. But when she first set foot in this house and first heard that TV, her thoughts began to grow hazy. With each passing day, the memories faded. First went the names, then the faces. Now all she has is a sort of fuzzy shape resembling a mother in a place resembling a house. It could be this house, this woman. But she feels sure there was someone else, once...

●

When the woman returns in the evening, she brings with her a large, plastic, box-shaped thing. She hands it to Rapunzel magnanimously, then tells her to carry it up the rope ladder — not an easy task, because the thing is quite heavy. She shows Rapunzel how to put it in one of the attic windows, where it makes a loud, grumbly noise and begins pumping cold air into the room.

Rapunzel loves it.

After the woman tucks her into bed, Rapunzel sits up and stares at the shuddering A/C unit. She imagines a face in it — power switch and temperature dial eyes, cold-breathing grate mouth. The closest thing she has to a friend.

When she finally lies back down and closes her eyes, she realizes something is missing. No voices are drifting up from downstairs. No commercials, no soap operas, no reality shows. Miraculously, the A/C's humming is loud enough to drown out the TV. With a sigh of indescribable relief and contentment, Rapunzel falls back onto her air mattress and falls deeply asleep.

This is when she has her first dream.

She dreams she is in the attic. Everything appears the same — lumpy air mattress beneath her, clock ticking on the wall, A/C groaning in the window. Yet Rapunzel senses something different.

She tries the trapdoor. Here, in the dream world, it is not locked.

She moves slowly, cautiously, down the rope ladder. The living room is the same as usual — almost. The coffee table, scattered with emery boards and sugar-free candy wrappers and a half-drunk mug of metabolism-boosting green tea. The couch where the woman sleeps each night, complete with the indentation her body has made in the cushions over the years.

But the woman is nowhere to be seen. And the TV screen is black.

Rapunzel tiptoes up to the door of the bedroom. She doesn't know why it is never used — any time she asks, the woman irritably changes the subject — but she's always guessed it has something to do with a man. She curls her fingers around the knob and turns.

It is unlocked.

As she steps inside, Rapunzel nearly chokes on the dust. She doubles over, coughing.

"Shh!"

Rapunzel straightens up. Did she imagine the voice? It's too dark to see anything, so she fumbles around until she finds a light switch. A small table lamp flicks on, casting a puddle of weak light over the room.

It is a place frozen in time: the bed unmade, a half-drunk glass of water on the nightstand, a basket of laundry in the corner that never got folded. A pair of pink slippers lies askew on one side of the bed, kicked off in haste. On the other there is a duffel bag, open to reveal a pair of enormous sneakers and a pile of clothing: T-shirts, jeans, baseball cap.

"Down here!"

This time the voice is undeniable. Rapunzel crouches to peer under the bed. There, hidden behind the duffel bag, is a small cage. And inside is a little yellow finch.

Rapunzel lifts the cage out carefully, its gold bars glittering in the lamp's feeble light. The bird stares up at her with gleaming black eyes.

"Be quiet," he says, "or she'll hear you."

This may be the first bird Rapunzel has met, but she knows (from Animal Planet) that birds do not generally talk. She wonders if, on the inside, he is really a bird. But Rapunzel isn't picky. She hasn't had anyone to talk to, except of course the woman, in years — how many years? It's all so fuzzy. She must have had people to talk to before, a *real* mother or father perhaps, but she can't remember.

"Wh-who are you?" She is breathless with excitement, or maybe fear.

"A prisoner," says the bird, "like you."

Rapunzel sets the cage on the mattress, sending up a plume of dust. "Are you…real? Or are you just a figment of my imagination?"

The bird gives a scoffing chirrup. "We are not in your imagination. We are in *her* dream."

Her. Rapunzel swallows. For some reason, she does not think the woman would approve of what she is doing right now.

She glances at the duffel bag. "You tried to leave her. And she…locked you in here?"

"*Cheep!* She'll do it to you too, if she finds you here."

"I don't understand," Rapunzel says, frowning. "How am I in her dream and not my own?"

The bird tilts its head toward her hair, now knee-length. "You have some sort of magic. Magic can do strange things with dreams."

Rapunzel blinks as the meaning of this sinks in. "Does *she* have magic?"

"Of course." The bird's black eyes glitter. "You know what she is."

"She's…my mother." This comes out more like a question than a statement.

"You don't believe that," the bird says. "You've always known."

He is right, Rapunzel realizes. It's like this knowledge has always been in her, deep in the corners of her mind, but until now it has been clouded by thick fog.

"No," she says slowly. "She loves me."

The bird laughs, a high-pitched chirrup. "Love and cruelty are not mutually exclusive. I should know. She is more dangerous than you thi —" He pauses, tilting his head, listening. "Get out. Hurry!"

Leaving the cage on the mattress, Rapunzel runs for the bedroom door. She barely has time to shut it behind her before —

"Rapunzel?"

She wakes in a daze. She is not on her air mattress — not in the attic at all. She is on the floor of the living room, tangled in her hair, which is now past her ankles. Light is streaming through the kitchen window, and in front of it is a silhouette, tall and dark.

The woman looks down at her with alarm. "How did you get here?"

"I…I don't know. A…dream?"

At this, the woman looks even more alarmed. But Rapunzel is not paying attention. She is thinking about the bird in the cage behind the locked bedroom door. This thought sparks a rare memory: She met another bird, once. A normal, non-talking bird, at the zoo. It perched on her finger and ruffled its painted feathers, and she fed it little pieces of fruit, and there was someone with her —

"Here, sit down." The woman, still in her nightgown, takes Rapunzel by the arm and guides her to the sofa. A children's show is playing on the TV, showing a cartoon knight trying to fight off a dragon and rescue a princess. The woman clicks the volume up a few notches.

Rapunzel's head begins to throb. She leans forward and presses her fingers to her temples. She feels the TV's noise invading her skull, pushing her memories back into their corners.

"Headache?" the woman says brusquely, heading to the kitchen. "You'll feel better once you eat breakfast."

She brings out the waffles and yogurt, and they eat, as usual, in front of the TV. Rapunzel does not taste her waffle as she chews — she is too busy trying to dig up memories from the hard, dry earth inside her skull.

The children's show ends. Another episode starts.

Rapunzel furrows her brow at the woman. "Don't you have to be at work?"

"I'll call in sick."

"But you're not —"

"I just want to spend some time with you, dear." The woman smiles and puts her arm around Rapunzel.

Rapunzel has always believed the woman truly loves her, in her own strange way. But now she is beginning to wonder: Does the woman love her the way a mother loves a daughter? Or the way a dragon loves its treasure?

After another mindless episode, two cooking shows, and a murder mystery, the woman slathers gray mud on her face and paints her toenails with glitter. She says she's found a new weight-loss thing to try: hypnotherapy. She saw it on TV.

Rapunzel is not listening.

In the past, Rapunzel didn't mind sitting on the couch with the woman — it was cooler down here than in the attic. But something has changed. She feels like she is seeing her tiny world for the first time. The woman, filled with dark magic. The TV, enchanted to suffocate her memories and shut her out of dreams. The locked bedroom door, the bird-husband, the void he left behind.

She wonders if she was meant to fill that void.

Lifetime is showing a movie about a lady with cancer who wears a scarf around her bald head. Rapunzel looks down at her own hair, now dragging and coiling on the ground, a shining yellow chain.

The woman with cancer has a young daughter. They do things together, sweet and innocent things, walking through parks and playing board games and ice skating and, later, lying together in the woman's hospital bed. As Rapunzel watches, they dissolve into pixels and LEDs, their voices fading into meaningless syllables.

She had her own mother, once. She is sure of it. But her head is too foggy to remember what her real mother looked like, or how her voice sounded, or the way she laughed when they fed the birds together at the zoo.

This causes something to stir within Rapunzel. Deep beneath the hum of the TV and the shadows clouding her mind, something is beginning to smolder.

Rapunzel wants her memories back.

So when the woman goes to the bathroom to wash the mask off her face, Rapunzel unplugs the TV's power cable from the wall and stuffs it into her pocket. The room is suddenly silent, Rapunzel's head suddenly clear. As she climbs the rope ladder, she sees vividly the curves and edges of a woman's face — her true mother, years ago. She sees what she must do, laid out in front of her like the rungs of the ladder, one step after another.

She takes the padlock off the outside of the trapdoor and puts it on the inside. She locks herself in. In the glorious silence of the attic, she lies down on her air mattress and falls asleep.

This time, the dream world feels less foreign, less disorienting. Rapunzel goes straight for the trapdoor. She loops her hair over her shoulders and climbs down the rope ladder. The woman is gone, but still Rapunzel hesitates. She can sense the woman's presence, as if she has left the room but her shadow remains, watching, waiting.

Taking a deep breath, she creeps into the bedroom.

"I'm leaving," she tells the finch in a hushed voice. "I'm...running away." Again, it sounds too much like a question.

"Good," is all the finch says.

Rapunzel leans over his cage, running her fingers along the wires, searching for the latch.

"You can't," the finch chirrups. "It's —"

But there are no locks in the dream world, and Rapunzel pops the cage door open.

The bird goes still for a moment, as if unsure this is really happening. Then he hops along his perch toward the opening, slowly at first, then faster. He tests his wings and flutters out, his movements stiff and clunky. Rapunzel feels his sharp claws curl around her fingertip as he lands.

It brings back the memory of the parrot, the one she fed at the zoo. This time, she can see her mother's face as she hands Rapunzel a chunk of fruit to feed him.

"Hurry!" The finch stiffens on her finger. "I hear her."

Rapunzel leaps up. "Hide," she whispers as she runs across the bedroom, lifting her hand to her neck. The finch hops off and curls his claws in her thick hair. She hears footsteps as she hauls herself up the rope ladder, faster than she has ever climbed before, eyes wide, chest heaving. She lurches through the trapdoor and slams it shut —

"Rapunzel!"

She wakes violently at the sound of the woman's voice. It is sharper now, less like a mother's voice and more like the screech of a bird of prey. The trapdoor rattles as the woman pounds on it. The lock is still there. When Rapunzel runs her hands over her hair, the finch is still there too. It gives a frightened cheep in her ear.

"Yes?" Rapunzel asks, shrinking away from the door.

"You took the TV cable, didn't you?" the woman calls.

Rapunzel's lip trembles. "No."

"I know you did. I need it back, dear. It may seem like a small thing to a child like you, but it is very important to me."

Rapunzel does not like being called a child, especially by this woman. She straightens up, setting her jaw. "I don't know what you mean."

"You've been dreaming, haven't you?" There is an accusatory edge to the woman's voice.

"No."

"You know how important it is to tell the truth, dear." The woman says it in the irritating tone of an adult talking to a three-year-old. She says it as if she really is talking about the truth, just the truth, as if this whole thing is about *the truth*. Rapunzel finds this ironic, considering everything about the woman is a sham.

Rapunzel says nothing. After a long moment, she hears the creak of the rope ladder and the click of footsteps across the living room floor, and the woman calls, "You can't stay in there forever."

Rapunzel knows she is right. There is no food or water here in the attic. Perhaps more urgently, there are no scissors, and the ever-growing weight of her hair is pulling her down, making movement slow and difficult.

But she can hear the woman down below. She prowls the living room floor, pacing back and forth beneath the trapdoor, sniffing the air. This TV business has wakened something feral in her.

"Dream it," the finch whispers in her ear.

He's right, Rapunzel decides. The only thing to do is fall asleep. In her dream, she will open the trapdoor and climb down the rope ladder and tiptoe out of the house. She'll run as fast as she can, straight to the nearest laboratory to sell her cells, and then she'll have enough money to buy her own house — and all the locks she needs to keep the woman out.

But as Rapunzel climbs out of her dream bed and drags her hair across the dream attic, she sees that now, even in her dream, there is a heavy black padlock on the trapdoor. Somehow, the woman — the witch, for that is what she is, what Rapunzel has always known her to be — has magicked her way into Rapunzel's dream and locked her inside.

Rapunzel runs to the window and slams it open. The finch disentangles himself from her hair and flutters around her head, and together they look down, down, four stories to the sidewalk below. Even Rapunzel's magic cannot protect her from a jump like that. She looks around the attic, searching for something, anything that can help her. But she is alone, except for the finch and the shivering A/C unit and her endless hair.

She pauses, winding a glossy tress around her finger. "Elephants," she whispers.

Her hair is very long now, perhaps longer than the house is tall. Twisting it into a rope, she loops it through the wrought-iron loop of the padlock on the trapdoor. Then she climbs through the window and lowers herself down, the bird fluttering alongside her.

It is remarkably easy. Her biceps sting only a little as she drops to the ground and pulls her hair down into a golden puddle beside her. She walks tentatively across the front lawn, her hair unwinding behind her, feeling the dewy grass between her toes — infinitely softer than it looks on TV. She takes a few steps down the sidewalk. The sky is so much bigger than what she can see from her window; the buildings and streets seem to stretch on forever. The air smells of garbage bins and pizza grease and air pollution — it's intoxicating. It brings to mind memories Rapunzel never knew she had, memories of her other mother, her real mother.

"Rapunzel!"

She jolts but does not wake. The woman is here, in Rapunzel's dream. Her voice is the low growl of an animal that's been lurking in the shadows, awaiting its prey.

Rapunzel starts to run, but something jerks her scalp and she tumbles to the sidewalk. The creature at the other end of her hair starts pulling, hand over hand, dragging Rapunzel painfully over the cement. Her nightgown rips, her skin tears.

When the pulling stops, she is on the sidewalk at the foot of the front door. Her sham-mother is standing over her, clutching Rapunzel's rope of hair in clawlike fingers, her face pinched with anger. She looks older, as if shutting off the TV has deepened her wrinkles and set shadows over her eyes.

"You've given me no choice," she says through gritted teeth. "I'm going to have to put you in timeout."

In the early morning sunlight, the sidewalk is streaked orange with blood. Rapunzel's stomach and thighs and breasts sting, and her nightgown sticks to the wounds. She is silent as the woman pulls her, by the hair, into the house and up the stairwell. There is no one else, no tenants or neighbors in this dream world, no police. The woman drags her to the third floor and shoves her across the living room to the rope ladder. Rapunzel climbs slowly, fighting the weight of her hair with each step, her head aching. She collapses on the floor in the dream attic, amid a tangle of bloody, grass-stained hair. She hears the trapdoor slam shut and the padlock click outside.

When Rapunzel wakes, her scalp is stinging with pain and the woman is pounding on the trapdoor.

"Are you ready to tell the truth, Rapunzel?"

The woman's voice no longer holds any semblance of the sham-mother or the wigmaker. Her voice is witchy through and through. And Rapunzel knows she is not the good kind of witch, but the other kind, the kind who kidnap children and steal memories and turn husbands into birds. The finch was right, Rapunzel thinks: the witch is far more dangerous than she appears.

But so is Rapunzel.

The witch thumps on the trapdoor again. "You can't stay up there forever. You have to eat. Tell me the truth, Rapunzel."

Rapunzel looks down at her hair, so long now it almost fills the attic, a sea of gold waiting to drown her. Slowly, deliberately, she gathers it up and twists it into a rope. She makes a knot, a special kind of knot she saw once on the History Channel.

"If you don't tell me the truth now," the witch yells, "I'll have to punish you." Her voice curls on the last two words, as if she is thinking of all the cruel, witchy punishments at her disposal.

Rapunzel stands over the trapdoor and bends her knees, rooting herself to the spot. "I'm sorry," she calls. "I'm ready to tell the truth now."

A pause. A witch this powerful should be able to sense trickery, Rapunzel thinks — but perhaps she has been in control too long, she is too used to winning at her own games. Perhaps in the witch's mind, all people will cave eventually.

People are just people. Hair is just hair.

"There's a good girl," the witch says.

The key scrapes in the lock. The trapdoor creaks open. The woman's head emerges through the opening.

It is remarkably easy. All it takes is one quick motion for Rapunzel to loop her hair around the witch's neck, one swift tug to make her lose her balance. The witch scrabbles at the rope ladder, but it is swinging now, and Rapunzel's grip is strong. The rope of hair sways and twitches. Her biceps strain. All she has to do is wait. She waits, waits for the woman's witchy breath to dissipate and her magic to ebb away, before going downstairs.

The TV screen is black and dead. The front door is unlocked. When Rapunzel opens it, there is a man standing outside, brushing feathers from his hair and wincing in the sunlight. He takes a hopping step toward her, wobbling on his new legs.

"You changed," Rapunzel observes.

"Yes," he says in a whistling voice. "I forgot what it felt like. What the world looked like."

"So did I." But as Rapunzel peers out at the cars and the streets and the dandelions springing up through cracks in the asphalt, she feels memories pressing at the edges of her mind. Ghosts of an old life — or perhaps a new one.

She walks out the door to meet them.

Rachel Delaney Craft's story "Rapunzel Dreams of Elephants" was originally published in Metaphorosis on Friday, 20 August 2021. See magazine.metaphorosis.com

About the author

Rachel Delaney Craft writes speculative fiction for children and teens. Her short stories have appeared in publications such as *Cricket, Ember, Uncharted,* and *Cast of Wonders*, and she edited the anthology *Wild: Uncivilized Tales from Rocky Mountain Fiction Writers*. Her most recent novel won the Colorado Gold Rush Literary Award and was shortlisted in the Searchlight Writing for Children Awards. She lives and writes in Colorado with her partner, two dogs, and a succulent collection that is slowly taking over her house. Find her on Twitter @RDCwrites or at racheldelaneycraft.com.

Graveyard

Arlen Feldman

The crew had already started calling it the *graveyard*.

If it was a graveyard, it would be hard to choose a bleaker site for it, on a planet pretty much made up of bleak sites. I walked as close as I dared to the edge of the cliff, and looked down over a thousand meters of sharp gray crags spreading out all around under a dark, thunderous sky. I felt the wind tugging at me, and hastily stepped back.

Merrick was watching over the technicians — as though they needed or wanted his help. To be fair, he did know a lot about the scanning equipment.

Not that I wanted to be fair.

I tugged at my breathing mask, trying to make it more comfortable, and turned to examine the site. Thirty-seven upright stones, spread over a clearing about forty meters wide. The shortest stone was 22 centimeters and the tallest was 196 centimeters — almost two meters. From three sides, they just looked like rocks.

It was because of the fourth sides that we were here. They had been carved flat, and a pattern had been deeply etched into each. The designs were different from stone to stone, but they all followed a similar design — a spiral of shapes spreading out from a central point. The shapes were small circles and rounded rectangles of different lengths. It sort-of reminded me of Morse code, except that there were at least eight different lengths. Unless, of course, the "dashes" all meant the same thing, and the carver wasn't particularly careful about length.

"Jenna?"

I jumped, then turned around. Sean, the other member of the research team, was standing less than two feet behind me. Hard to hear with the wind and the masks and the warm-weather gear.

Sean held up his hands. "Sorry. Didn't mean to startle you."

"No worries." I grinned at him, putting my hand to my chest. "Whatever doesn't make your heart explode makes you stronger. What's up?"

"We're about ready."

I nodded and followed him over to the "command post", which was really just a stack of plastic crates with some ruggedized computers sitting on top. Sean typed something on a keyboard and I felt the thrum as power ran to the imaging lasers mounted on collapsible pylons positioned all around the site.

For a while, we watched the progress display on the screen, then I turned and walked back towards the stones. Not much point looking at a picture when the real thing was right there.

"You know," said Merrick, who had followed me, and was now standing right next to me. "If it is a graveyard, then the inscriptions would make a certain amount of sense."

I took a half step away from him. "How so?"

"Well, the little one there might be *To Aunt Maggie*, while that one," he pointed to the largest stone with two separate swirls of symbols," might be the Grayon-Alpha-3 equivalent of the Lord's Prayer or *Do Not Go Gentle*."

I laughed, though in truth the idea had already occurred to me. "You know what the Professor would say, don't you?"

"*Don't get ahead of the facts*," we intoned in unison, and laughed.

Professor Kineson should have been here. He was Earth's foremost xeno-anthropologist, but he was now too old for major journeys. Instead he'd sent his grad students — me and Merrick — arguably Earth's only *other* xeno-anthropologists. To date, it wasn't a very popular or useful field, although Grayon-Alpha-3 might change that.

Life was pretty common on the worlds that had been explored — plants and insectoids being the most common, but larger forms as well. Grayon-Alpha-3 was no different, covered in small ugly plants and a number of beetle-like insectoids that were currently being intensely studied by the biology team.

On two previously explored worlds, we'd found indications of intelligence — remnants of crude settlements — but no actual settlers. Professor Kineson had been the main researcher for both of those.

But writing — that was a first. If the designs on these stones turned out to be a form of language, that would be a game changer. And it had to be writing. How could it be anything else?

"It could be art," said Merrick, as though reading my mind — a very annoying habit of his. "Like Celtic knotwork."

I shrugged. Even artwork would be exciting, but in my gut, I knew that it was writing — an attempt to communicate. Not that I would ever admit to anything so unscientific as a gut feeling.

The hum of the scanners shut down at the same time as a lull in the wind, and for a few seconds it was eerily quiet. That might have been the moment when the reality of what we were doing set in. We were standing on an alien world in the presence of unquestionable evidence of intelligence. Even knowing nothing about who or what they were, when and how they lived, I felt an almost physical connection to the creators of these stones.

I looked up to see Merrick staring at me.

"What?" I asked.

"Nothing. You just had a look."

He reached out an arm towards my shoulder, but I took another half-step away.

Sean came up to us, his hand brushing against his breathing mask, as though he wanted to scratch his chin. It was hard to get used to Sean having a visible face. On the trip here, he'd had a huge, ragged, Santa-Claus beard, but he'd had to shave it off so that the breathing mask would fit. Although he was in his forties, he now looked like a teenager. I'd studiously avoided saying anything, although the rest of the crew had teased him mercilessly about it.

"Scan's done," he said. "We only have about another hour of daylight. We should probably get back to the lander."

I nodded, but didn't move. I was looking at the smallest stone — the one that Merrick had called *Aunt Maggie*. I'd spent a lot of time in old graveyards, and the smallest, saddest stones were always for babies and children. In my head, I mentally shortened the label to just *Maggie*.

I turned, grabbed my kit, and followed the others back to the lander.

●

The next day was all about scanning underground. If these were gravestones, then there should be something underneath them. The Ground Penetrating Radar setup was finicky, and we were all sweating profusely by the time we had it working, despite the cold.

Nothing. There was nothing beneath any of the stones.

"It doesn't mean they're not grave markers," I said, although without much conviction. "They could be cenotaphs — memorials without the bodies."

No one argued, but I doubted that anyone was convinced.

"There is one weird thing," said Sean.

Merrick and I both turned to face him.

"The stones look rough-carved, but they each extend at least twenty centimeters below the surface, and the fit is precise. I mean, *really* precise — within five microns." He pointed at the display. "I could *probably* do it with a laser and a bunch of time, but it's hard to see how you could do it with primitive tools. Also, there would be tool marks, and there aren't any."

Merrick shook his head. "If they were an advanced culture with lasers, then there would be some other evidence on the planet. Roads, buildings, something. The satellites have found squat."

"That depends on how old they are," said Sean, scratching ineffectually at his breathing mask.

"Maybe they lived underground," I suggested. "That would explain the lack of anything on the surface."

Merrick shook his head. *"Don't get ahead of the facts,"* he said. "The satellites would have found some evidence of any sort of sophisticated underground settlement. We found the spot where the stones for the monuments came from, which is less than half a kilometer from here, but that's literally the only non-natural variance on the planet — other than this place."

I sighed. Without any other sites, we didn't have a lot to go on. We'd hoped to find something buried beneath the stones that we could use to figure out a date. Then, suddenly, I had an idea.

"You know, there might be a way of figuring out a date — from the stones themselves."

"The stones are granite," said Merrick, sounding exasperated. "They are the same age as the surrounding rocks. You can't get an age off of them separate from that."

"Thanks for the Geology 101 lecture." I didn't bother trying to keep the sarcasm from my voice. I turned to Sean. "Weathering patterns. The stones further away from the cliff are weathered less than those nearer to it. We know how granite breaks down, what chemicals are present in the atmosphere, weather patterns — at least for the few years that the satellites have been in place. We should be able to at least get a rough estimate from that."

"Clever," said Merrick, suddenly interested.

Sean stroked at his chin. "Rough is the word."

"The faces and the designs haven't really worn down," said Merrick.

"No," said Sean, thinking, "but the edges have. We'll have to analyze some other rocks as well for control, pull atmospheric data from the satellites, but...it could work." He looked up. "Yeah — at least within a few hundred years." He grinned at me. "Nice!"

●

It was four days later, early in the morning, when Sean knocked on the door of my cabin.

"Yeah?" I answered blearily.

He handed me a piece of paper. "Between 700 and 1200 years."

For several seconds I had no idea what he was saying, and then suddenly neurons started firing in my brain. "You did it? You did it!" I gave him a hug, and he turned bright red. I noticed that he'd started growing a beard again, but that it was carefully trimmed to the shape of a breathing mask.

"This is awesome," I told him. "It's the first concrete thing we really know about the site. The post-project report was looking awfully bare."

Sean suddenly looked nervous. "So, you won't be reporting anything until the end of the trip?"

"Of course not. That would be...why?"

"Well, it's just that..."

But I didn't need to hear it. I already knew.

"Merrick? You told Merrick first?"

"I didn't...he was in the lab when the computer spat out the results. I couldn't —"

But I was already halfway down the passage.

My thoughts were on events from a year ago. Me, curled up on the sofa next to Merrick while he read my research notes on the ancient settlement found on Gliese 837c, telling me how great my work was. Late nights, lying next to one-another, endlessly discussing *my* ideas...

I practically slammed into him coming the other way down the passage.

He oofed, then backed away. "Oops, sorry." Then he saw my face. "What?" he asked.

I was about ready to hit him. "You bastard."

His eyebrows went up, but his voice was even, half-joking. "My mother would deny it. I take it you think I did something?"

He was going to brazen it out. I lifted my fist and he took several hasty steps back. Not once did it even occur to me that he hadn't sent a report behind my back. I could see the look of calculation in his eyes.

"Look, if it's about the dating — I *did* let the Professor know, but no one else. And I swear that I told him that the idea was yours."

"Yeah, like last time? In a frigging footnote?" I'd taken several steps toward him, and he'd backed away again, even though he towered over me by thirty centimeters. His face was red now.

"You think I'd...?"

"Yes, I do."

Then I turned and walked away. Of course, now I had to send a separate report in, and it would make us look like we were squabbling siblings. Maybe I shouldn't even bother.

When I got a copy of Merrick's report a few hours later, it turned out that he had been telling the truth. Professor Kineson had sent us both a congratulatory e-mail about the dating, and had given me credit for the idea, and Merrick and Sean credit for the computer model.

It did not make me feel any better.

A little while later, Merrick came to find me. His expression was half-smirk and half-contrition. I had no idea why I had once found him handsome.

"Jen," he started. "Listen, I know we have some history, but I *did* tell you that I gave you credit."

"And yourself, I note. I'm pretty sure that Sean did most of the work."

He ignored this.

"Getting our names out there is important. There is interest in what we are doing right now. If we waited until we had every last detail worked out, no one would care. Publish or perish, right?"

"I'd recommend perish in your case," I said. This was an old argument, though. Part of his excuse for pre-empting my Gliese 837c research was that I had been taking too long to get my results out there. As if that were an excuse for stealing my work.

He turned to walk away, obviously annoyed. At the door, he paused. "If you aren't going to let people know what we've found, then why bother?"

"I want it to be right," I said, trying to keep my voice steady. "I want it to be permanent — to last. Not just be some half-baked headline."

He shook his head. "And if you wait too long, then it's going to be someone else's name that's remembered. Not ours. If we don't carve out our own names, no one else will.

We work in a tiny, under-funded field. If you don't get your name out there, how many of your projects do you think will get sponsored?"

He walked away. I watched him go, wondering how he and I could have such different ideas about what our work was about. Part of me, though, knew that he was right about sponsorship. I wondered, briefly, whom I was really angry at.

●

The next two weeks were spent in icy, silent hostility. Most of the crew, who were military, were completely unaware of what was going on, or at least pretended to be. Sean, though, was stuck in the middle, and shuttled back and forth nervously between us.

It helped that my approach and Merrick's were so different. He spent most of his time with the computer scans and models on the ship, while I spent most of my time at the actual site.

Not that I was getting anywhere. Nor, as far as I knew, was Merrick. I'd caught him watching me a few times. The last time, he'd had that look — the one that I used to read as understanding and admiration, and now read as naked calculation. He was probably hoping I'd let something slip.

I pushed Merrick from my mind as I turned my thoughts back to the graveyard. 700 to 1200 years. It was difficult to believe that a culture with the sophisticated stone-working skills needed to make these monuments would have disappeared without a trace in that time.

My working hypothesis — shared with no one else — was that the monument-makers weren't native. Someone had visited this planet, like we were now, and, for whatever reason, had left this memorial here. Maybe to commemorate their visit, or because something unfortunate had happened. I smiled to myself. I was getting really far *ahead of the facts*.

The idea did *fit* the facts, though. There were no visible tool marks, which was consistent with advanced technology, and there were no indications of any remotely higher lifeforms on this planet than bugs, let alone tool users.

In the past, I might have talked this over with Merrick, but that was obviously impossible. He was good at turning my flights-of-fancy into concrete ideas. Now, though — if he agreed, he'd probably steal my ideas, and if he disagreed, he'd probably use them to discredit me.

I sat down in front of *Maggie's* stone on a small stool I'd been using. Part of my reason for focusing on that stone was that I figured the simpler design might be easier to interpret. In theory, the more complex patterns would provide more material to analyze, but the computers were already trying that approach without any notable success.

Another reason was that it was next to one of the larger monuments, which protected me from the continuous howling wind.

To be honest, though, I think I'd just formed some sort of emotional attachment to my mental image of Maggie.

As for figuring out the pattern — I'd tried every statistical and analytic approach I could think of, including some that were desperately random. I still had a neck ache from my attempt to examine the pattern upside down.

My new approach, such as it was, was to stare at the design while letting my mind go blank in the hopes that something would pop into my head. I tapped on my headphones to start them playing. Today I was listening to Dvořák's *New World Symphony*, one of my favorites. The slow *adagio* opening was appropriately grandiose for the austere landscape, and the fast, crashing *allegro* seemed perfectly timed to the gusting wind.

The second movement, the slow, haunting *largo*, was what I'd been waiting for, though. The gentle music, led by the sonorous oboes, was music for a graveyard if any music was. The *largo* movement was also known as *Coming Home*. I wondered if the creators of the graveyard had made it home.

It was chilly, even with the protective clothing, and I shivered. I rested my gloved hand on top of Maggie's stone. Wanting a closer connection, I pulled off my glove and touched the stone with my bare hand.

The stone was ice cold and it burned my hand, but I held it there for a moment before pulling it back. Not quite ready to give up my connection to the monument, I put my finger in the very center of the spiral design, and ran it around the design.

I'd done this before with my thick glove on, but without it, I suddenly noticed something. As my finger thunked between the uneven dashes, it made a sort of tune.

The hair on the back of my neck stood up and a chill went down my spine. It had nothing to do with the frigid air.

I tried it again, slower. This time, the tune was more pronounced. Well, less a tune, and more a rhythm, since it was basically the same note repeated with different intervals. Or was it? I ripped off my headphones so I could hear better, and tried again, this time using my little finger. The slight differences in the lengths of the dashes and the gaps in between were changing the pitch — creating different notes. I could just *barely* hear the differences. Either my ears weren't sensitive enough or my finger was too big — possibly both.

I pulled out my tablet and brought up the detailed scan of the pattern on Maggie's stone, then had it convert the heights and depths into a wave form, letting the computer figure out the most appropriate scale. Holding my breath, I hit play.

It was a short, pleasant, uplifting tune. I found myself laughing in amazement. I played it again, with my eyes closed. The sad image of Maggie I'd held for so long was now replaced by a little girl running through fields, a flower in her hand. I rested my hand on top of her stone again, ignoring the burning sensation for as long as I could.

I had to try some of the others. I went over to one of the larger monuments with a bigger pattern. I tried it with my finger first, again just able to make out the rhythm. Then I had my tablet try. This tune was a bit more somber and dignified — a man of business, proud of his position, maybe. The next monument was quicker, almost lilting — a teenager full of life.

I wiped tears away from my eyes. Yes, I was overlaying my own imagery on these simple tunes, and they were *human* images, which couldn't be right. But I was being talked to by a *people* who had been dead a thousand years. And I could hear them.

By this point my fingers had turned bright red and were aching from the cold. I wanted to listen to every one of the thirty-seven monuments, listen to thirty-seven distinct voices, but that would have to wait.

The lander was over a kilometer from the site, but I'm pretty sure I covered the distance in less than five minutes. I spent the next ten hours in my cabin, in front of my computer.

Eventually, though, I had to find Sean to let him know what equipment I was going to need — after swearing him to secrecy. I wasn't sure he even believed what I'd found.

The last thing I did was send an invitation to everyone on the lander, before collapsing into a deep, dreamless sleep.

When I got to the site the next day, Sean had already set up everything I'd asked for, including a tablet to control it all. His beard had kept growing and now, under the plastic breathing mask, it looked like he was actually wearing a breathing mask made of hair. I grinned at him, and he waved back.

Merrick showed up a little while later, along with several members of the other science teams and the ship's crew. In general, crew didn't mix with the science teams, but they were apparently curious. Merrick must have been curious as well, but his expression was blank.

I cleared my throat, suddenly feeling like I was about to give an oral dissertation defense in front of a hostile examination committee. The howling wind was chilling, but I felt sweat trickling down my neck.

"Uh, thank you all for coming. I, uh..."

I seemed to lose all control of my ability to speak. Desperately, I looked around, and saw Sean, standing behind everyone else. He winked at me, and gave me a brief thumbs-up. It helped.

I took a deep breath and started again.

"For the past several weeks, we've been trying to figure out what these stones represent, and whether the markings are writing. I now have a solid working hypothesis."

As if playing for dramatic effect, the wind dropped, leaving us in temporary silence. Most of the faces in front of me were openly interested, perhaps surprised, but Merrick's eyes were narrowed in a look of frustration so intense that I almost took a step backwards. What could possibly be driving that? Was he *that* afraid of being beaten to the finish line?

I took another deep breath, and held my ground.

"Each stone represents something — a concept, or, possibly, individual entities. If so, then this site *is* a graveyard — or at least a *memorial.* But the patterns are not words about each of these people. They are music."

I tapped something on my tablet, and Maggie's tune played out from the speakers Sean had placed around the site. They were highly directional, so the tune came from the location of Maggie's stone. At the same time, a bright light shone on the spiral pattern, travelling in time with the playback.

Everyone turned to look. It was the same melody from yesterday, but my experimentation with the parameters had improved it — added more depth and nuance. I'd heard the tune dozens of times by now, and it still made me shiver. From the looks on the faces of the others, I was not alone.

After a brief explanation of what I'd found, and how the patterns worked, I had the computer play its interpretation of several other stones — the somber business man. The teenager. A playful tune that made me think of an entertainer. A reserved, powerful tune that I associated with a mayor or a captain.

One of the biologists was laughing with glee. Several people were running fingers over the patterns, although with gloves on, it didn't work.

"If we can hear it," said the biologist who'd been laughing, "then that means that the creators had ears as well — heard sounds like we do."

"Not necessarily," said Merrick, and the anger was gone as he sank into the problem. "Sound is just vibrations. They might have had very sensitive fingers — digits — something — that interpreted the vibrations."

"Or antennae or a long sensitive tongue," I added. "There's no way to really know."

Merrick grinned at the image, and just for a second, I grinned back. Then we both looked away.

"Also," I continued, looking directly at the biologist, "the computer has chosen a pentatonic scale for the notes because it seems to fit, and because it sounds reasonable to us — to humans. That's fairly arbitrary, although with more research, we might be able to figure out how it was originally supposed to be interpreted."

The biologist sighed. "It's beautiful," she said," but I still wish you'd found me a body to examine."

There was general laughter at that.

The tune from the last gravestone had faded away, and for a moment I was a little lost, not quite sure how to get back on the track of my presentation. I was rescued by one of the crewmen, a short man in a blue uniform, whose name I couldn't remember.

"What about the big one?" he asked, pointing to the large stone in the center of the graveyard.

I smiled at him. "Glad you asked. That one took a while to figure out. You have to do both spirals at the same time." I hit the icon on my tablet, and a strange rhythmic pulsing started.

The crewman tilted his head to the side, listening. "That doesn't sound like the others. The others sound, well, sound like people. This is more like a back-beat or something..."

I nodded at him, impressed. It had taken me hours to figure that out. "It makes sense when you do *this*."

I hit another icon to run the program I'd spent most of the night on. The computer started up *all* of the monuments, delaying some, letting others fade in and fade out, then repeating them, little glowing lights spiraling throughout the site.

It was like standing in a busy market square, surrounded by people going about their lives. Children running, vendors hawking their wares, officials strutting around, and beneath it all, the *thrum* of the center monument adding life and depth to it all.

I let it run for several minutes, before allowing the individual tunes to fade away.

No one moved or spoke. The only sound was the whistling of the wind. I noticed that the crewman who'd asked the questions had tears in his eyes, and after a moment, I realized that I did, too.

Finally, Sean walked over to me, and gave me a one-armed hug.

"It's beautiful."

I hugged him back, my lip quivering.

"They're going to love this back home," said one of the biologists.

I nodded, and kept my eyes on him, careful not to look towards Merrick. "I sent a report back a few hours ago. I'd normally wait until after we were done, but we only have a few weeks left anyway."

The biologist nodded back in agreement, as though it were the most natural thing in the world to have done. Perhaps I *had* been too cautious in the past.

Out of the corner of my eye I saw Merrick take a step towards me, stop, and then turn and walk away. At least there wasn't going to be a big argument in front of everyone. That was a relief.

●

Two days later I was sitting at the tiny desk in my cabin when there was a knock at my door. It was Merrick. I tilted my head at him and raised an eyebrow.

"I just wanted to say congratulations."

"Thank you." I kept my voice toneless.

Merrick took a deep breath and stepped into my cabin. He opened his mouth, closed it, then took another deep breath.

"I wanted to let you know that I sent a note to the college, giving you full credit for your previous work on Gliese 837c, and withdrawing my own name."

My eyes widened. "You didn't have to do that."

He shook his head. "I did. The thing is, with all of our conversations, I'd honestly convinced myself that we'd done that work together, and that you were holding me back by refusing to publish. I realize now…"

He swallowed. "I realize now that my contribution was almost nothing. It was all you, just like it was here. I think I need to find another field."

I think my mouth fell open. I thought back over the arguments that I'd had with Merrick. His old words twisted into different shapes in my mind, and I could suddenly see them from his perspective. It was true that most of the Gliese work had been mine, but Merrick *had* contributed quite a bit too. Withdrawing his name would cause a scandal — possibly end his career, or *any* career based on research. I'm not sure that I would have had the courage to do anything like that. I wondered if all of the strange looks he'd been giving me lately had been because he'd been thinking about doing this.

He turned to go, and I watched him disappear down the hallway.

There was something I'd wanted to do ever since I'd realized about the music. It was a definite no-no, and I could get in a lot of trouble...but on the other hand, courage deserved courage.

●

I found Merrick in his cabin a few days later. He seemed surprised to see me.

"There's something I want to show you," I said.

He shrugged, but stood up.

We picked up our outside gear and cycled out through the airlock. We'd normally turn left to get to the graveyard site, but I turned right and started walking. Merrick seemed slightly surprised, but followed without comment.

We walked on in silence for twenty minutes, while I worked up the courage to speak.

"I've been thinking about what you did," I said, finally. "You were right — it was my research and my ideas, but you helped me flesh them out, and you pushed them into being published. You were right about that too."

Merrick kept his eyes firmly in front of him, his face a mask. I plowed on.

"I've been communicating with the professor. He's agreed to talk to the committee. The report on Gliese 837c is going to be updated to show both of our names — with mine listed first, of course."

Merrick's mouth opened, then closed a few times.

"I...," he started, then stopped. He gave the shortest of nods.

We walked on in silence. I led him to a spot about three kilometers from the ship, four from the graveyard. There was a small section of cliff that you couldn't see unless you were standing in the exact right spot, facing the exact right direction.

Merrick had kept his blank emotionless expression intact since I'd told him about the report, but when he saw the cliff face, he burst out laughing.

"When I said we needed to carve our names in the field, this isn't exactly what I had in mind."

There were three parts to the carving I'd made with Sean's laser rig. At the top was a star chart showing Earth's location, and another chart that showed the current alignment of all of the planets and moons in *this* solar system — on the theory that an advanced culture could use it to calculate precisely when we had been there. Below that were our names — Jenna, Sean and Merrick, etched in our alphabet, and below each of the names was a spiral like on the monuments.

"I figure that if another alien species comes along and finds this site as well as the other, it will drive them completely crazy. I know I shouldn't have done it, but I had to leave some proof that we'd been here."

Merrick smiled. He tugged off his glove and stepped towards the cliff, then looked back at me for permission. I nodded.

He started with Sean's spiral. As with the graveyard, only the vaguest rhythm was audible. I handed him my tablet, and he pointed it at the pattern and hit play.

Despite loving music, I was no musician, but the computer had helped me. Sean's tune was solid, confident, capable. Merrick nodded before moving on to the other patterns. Mine was inquisitive, changing — a little bit sad. I wasn't quite sure about it, but Sean had sworn that it captured me perfectly.

Merrick's tune was brash and striving, with a deep under-beat — but uplifting, hopeful. When the computer had first played it, I knew that it fit him exactly, although I couldn't have explained precisely why. He played it a second time, running his finger over the pattern as it ran.

When he finally spoke, his voice was so quiet I could barely hear him "Is that how you really see me?"

I nodded.

"Well, then, perhaps I'm not a hopeless case after all."

I smiled. "Don't get ahead of the facts."

Arlen Feldman's story "Graveyard" was originally published in Metaphorosis on Friday, 30 November 2018. See magazine.metaphorosis.com

About the author

Arlen's job description changes often, but generally includes the term "Computer Scientist." Given the state of computer science to date, this is probably horribly unfair to *real* scientists, but at least we've admitted that the strange incantations that make computer work likely require a process, and don't rely (exclusively) on magic. In addition to mucking with software and writing fiction, Arlen is an entrepreneur, maker, con-runner, and computer book author. Some recent stories of his appear in the anthologies Museum Piece, Particular Passages: Decked Halls, and Kevin J. Anderson's Gilded Glass, and in Little Blue Marble and Wyldblood magazines. He lives in Colorado Springs, Colorado.

His website is cowthulu.com. Mastodon: @cowthulu@mastodon.social. Bluesky: @cowthulu.bsky.social.

Heartbeat of the Seasons

Brian Hugenbruch

The first time I met Sophienne was outside a small inn at the center of the village of Willowsring. I'd come out of the west, with the faint chill of autumn wind nipping at my horse's hooves, and found the horse tie rings by the tavern just as she walked by with a pile of firewood. While she gave me a slight smile, she didn't know me from a summer's day.

I had little idea, then, how often I'd see that expression in the weeks to come.

A passing peasant watched me watch the red-headed woman walk inside. "I'd not, friend."

I turned around with a start. "Why not?"

"She's cursed," she said. "Nasty business. You hear of Wyrmtooth?"

I had, in fact. I rode toward the northern border on behalf of the Church of Ri'as, and in some haste. While they'd marked the usual sorts of dangers on my map, Willowsring had seemed a quiet enough spot to rest. I hadn't realized the wizard's tower was so close by.

"She slew him," the peasant woman said. At my look, she added, "Sort of. It didn't quite work. But her life since ain't been worth a single damn."

"I'm not so quick to measure a person's worth," I said. "And if there's aid I can offer, I certainly will."

"On your own head be it," she muttered.

"Has she spurned your own assistance, then?"

The woman's face betrayed her surprise. "How could we help one like her? We're honest folk; we won't mangle our lives by messing with magic!"

I turned her words over in my mind as the woman wandered off. The Church had sent me as an official Ambassador to broker a peace between the ogre and Fey kingdoms. They were ready to slaughter one another, and us besides. They'd agreed to one more set of talks before the blood began to run.

It would not be an easy talk. The Fey had been arguing over the border with the ogres for centuries now — a territorial dispute lost to antiquity. The region was farmland; the Fey had already suffered through famine, and their claims of ogre aggression weren't unjustified, if our scouts were to be believed.

The ogres claimed no wrongdoing, because of course they did. What fault of theirs, if the Fey had eaten all their food and did not look as pretty as the ogres did? And now the Fey were trying to claim settled lands for their own.

The Fey had asked for us, believing the Church impartial. On that point, at least, they weren't wrong — the Bishops had no use for either kingdom. But they also felt strongly that neither ogre nor Fey would keep the bloodshed between themselves.

They'd encouraged me to ride with a bit more haste than usual.

If the maps were to be believed, I was three days' ride from the border — and ahead of schedule. Ambassador or no, the Bishops hadn't given me leave to deny a hand to those in need. I couldn't tarry too long... but if the woman were afflicted by something minor, perhaps I could set her aright before either nation had a chance to miss me.

I suspect I would have tried to help her even if the Church's doctrine and the call of my goodwill had not been in alignment. As they were, how would I turn my eyes elsewhere?

This time of day, the inn's common room lay bare but for sunbeams and the kept cats sleeping in them. Even the innkeep had gone missing. The red-headed woman seemed to fill the room, though, with her bemused smile. She sat atop the bar and watched me from behind a tall glass.

She certainly did not seem cursed. Perhaps the peasant woman had been telling tales for sport? Common enough when city folk found the countryside, and usually harmless.

"You in charge here?" I asked her.

"Nay," she said. "But Homish does not mind it if I serve myself. I can let him know a nobleman's here, if you'd like."

"Do I look much like a noble?"

She nodded toward my boots. "Finer quality than the farmers' own, those. But I jest — that Ri'as sigil tells me you're a priest from the capital. Someone sent to heal or to harm, depending upon the moods of those you'd call master."

"Heal," I informed her. And it was true, as far as it went. A continued peace would be healthy for everyone. The Church had tried using me for other ends... but it'd not gone the way they'd hoped. My instinct to fix what was broken was too strong. They'd learned their lesson; so had I.

The woman nodded in approval. "You here long, stranger?"

"Brother," I corrected. "And Dalen is fine. Just passing through on my way to the border." I tilted my head and studied her for a moment. "Actually, I need someone capable to show me around. Do you have time this evening?"

She lowered her hand toward a sword on the bar. Long fingers found a green gemstone pommel. She said, "This evening? I'm sorry, Dalen. I'm off to smite a wizard. I'll be back before the morn — we'll speak then, perhaps."

"Of course," I said. I had no idea if another wizard had arrived, or if Wyrmtooth really had returned — but she seemed confident and amiable. If she were off to finish the slaying she'd started, I had no desire to stand in her way. Especially since she handled the sword with obvious expertise. "A pleasure, miss...?"

"Sophienne," she answered. Then she finished her tankard and disappeared into the back.

The second time I saw her was in the bustling common room the following morning. A familiar pommel bumped against my table as I finished my gruel. I looked up and saw her smiling down — with much the same expression she'd had the day before. I was almost done, in any case, so I cleared my space and offered my spot on the shoddy wooden bench.

I asked, "How fared the battle?"

"Have we met?" she wondered as she sat.

"Briefly, yesterday," I reminded her. "Brother Dalen, from Ath-Olomahn."

"My apologies, sir. I'll let you know tomorrow, for my battle is yet before me. Wyrmtooth will rue the steel of Sophienne, I swear it. I venture out in some hours and will be back before the morn — we can toast to victory then."

"Of course," I said, though a bit less certain than before.

I brought my dishes up to the bar. The old innkeeper, Homish, gave me a sympathetic look. "She never remembers," he told me. "It ain't you."

I thought back to the woman I'd met when I arrived and shivered a bit. "What happened?"

"She came to us young," he said as he took my bowl. "Her own home was destroyed by that monster in the tower. She'd tried to slay the bastard for years — she studied the sword and lost friends against him twice 'afore yer war broke out. No one asked why she joined the armies, but she led the way into Fey, and was part of the legion what stormed their capital."

I closed my eyes as I tried to parse this. "We haven't been at war with the Fey for forty years."

"I know," he said. "I was there. I was just a boy back then, but I remember her fightin' like a woman possessed. And then, when the war ended, she wasn't long ere she fought Wyrmtooth for the last time."

"But the wizard still lives, does he not?"

The old man grunted. "Every morn she wakes in her room as though nothing happened. She does whatever chores we can find for her — chop wood, haul water, chase down horses. Soph is honest like that; always a hard worker, no matter what's on her mind. Then she orders the same meals, sharpens her blade, and sets off to slay him every evening. She ain't aged a damn day in all that."

I shook my head. "I've never heard of such things."

"Fey territory has strange magic," Homish reminded me. "Stranger than your Church, or even that o' Wyrmtooth." His voice lowered a bit and he told me, "Most folks here, well, they don't much care for magic. Ain't done nothing but kill us for as long as we can remember. And to be right honest, yer Grace, we've killed our share of witches round here."

I glanced in the direction the woman had gone. "But she's still welcome here, of course."

I could feel him shrug. "Sophi... she keeps the wizard at bay, in her way, so we're happy to let her be. She does her chores, eats 'er gruel, then heads on out to slay the bastard again."

"How many times can a man be slain?" I demanded.

"As many as it takes? She reappears in her bedroom every morning. And the wizard's tower rebuilds itself at dawn, 'round the same time." The old man filled another bowl of gruel and slid it down the length of the bar toward a waiting patron. The wooden dish skittered across the uneven planks; the man at the other end caught it deftly.

"Sounds horrible," I murmured, "dying every night."

Homish shrugged. "It ain't us dying. We've got used to it, and she don't seem to remember. Besides, in forty years, we ain't found a way to stop her going."

I had the distinct impression, from Homish's expression, that the villagers of Willowsring hadn't tried too hard. Indeed, everyone in the common room watched the red-headed swordswoman with the sort of wary stare saved for a wild animal. She wasn't one of them, no matter what the innkeep said; she was merely an enemy of their enemy.

As I watched her rise to leave, I had the sudden sinking feeling I would not be early to the border. If anyone else from the Church had been here, I might have left the town behind... the calm at the border would not hold forever. But there wasn't, and the magic at work made me shiver. Someone had to help this woman.

For lack of an alternative, someone was me.

The village seemed idyllic. If they knew of this place, the richest citizens of Ath-Olomahn would pay to escape the city and flee here for a fortnight. Farmers worked through the harvest of early crops. The local farrier patched shoes and made nails. A few children, old enough to cling to apron strings, played in dirt lanes near the well, but the town itself seemed older than its years; most of its children had grown and not been replaced.

Noblefolk would love it, sure. It seemed like five hells to me: a world where nothing ever changed, where time meandered at its own pace. This was even worse than the Monastery.

Willowsring itself was perfect — and that was the second mystery. They were by far the closest town to the border, but no one seemed particularly bothered by the looming war — it was three days' ride away, over several hills and rivers, and in another country besides. Didn't stop what few folks with whom I stopped to chat from gabbing about the last battle. Yesterday's dead were part of their oral history. Tomorrow's dead were imaginary.

In my experience, this wasn't uncommon. Citizens of Ath-Olohman loved their fashion and court society gossip, but the outlying territories couldn't be bothered. All talk steered to crops unless the sky was raining fire. Made my job two hells hard; what was some city-boy going to know about manure and field care, anyway?

They weren't wrong; I couldn't give a shit about manure. But I knew well enough their harvests depended on it. And they did so well that their crop yield was the same, year over year, whether the rest of the nation met floods or drought. Something that right was a symptom of something wrong.

So I saddled my horse an hour before dawn and rode north. I had to see for myself.

The wizard's tower lay in smoking, smoldering pieces. Grassless ground and scorched rock circled the ruins for a mile. The remnant brick glowed with a ghastly green light. Curious, I picked up a pebble and tossed it toward where the tower would have been. It turned to dust in mid-air and landed as a line of fine sand at the edge of the blast.

Good thing I hadn't put my damn hand inside the circle.

I hadn't been waiting long when the sun peeked over the mountains. The light coalesced into a mist that moved of its own accord. Some force plucked the bricks from the broken earth, hauling them back with a disregard for the flow of time, as though the tower were exploding in reverse. It rebuilt itself, whole blocks returning from ash and casting aside scorch marks. All the while, a high-pitched shriek filled my ears.

Then, as suddenly as it began, it stopped.

A wizard's tower stood there, surrounded by barren land and burned rock, raised once more in some sort of rude gesture in the face of normal time. Having no context, I could only assume that this was how it had always looked. I wheeled my horse and rode away before Wyrmtoooth had a chance to reawaken.

As I galloped, two things occurred to me. The grass near the tower had not regrown, which meant there were boundaries and parameters on the spell. And the pebble had not returned — so interfering with this magic might well be lethal.

I reached the tavern at Willowsring not long after the commotion of the morning rush had ended. Homish had some gruel waiting at the end of the bar for me. Sophienne was standing, her own meal completed; she looked right through me. She seemed as though she'd just woken up, again, for the last time. Tiredness had nothing to do with her surprise.

●

I came downstairs a bit after lunch. After the morning's adventure, I'd needed a bit of rest to set my mind aright. Sophienne looked up from the far side of the room, where she was sharpening her sword. She remembered me from the morning — confused, perhaps, but a bit less than before. It was, I admit, strange to see her look at me with recognition, but a relief to see a wary smile grow more at ease.

"Homish left some food for you on the counter," she called over. "And a letter came."

"Thank you," I said. I found them not far away; I gathered them both and brought them to a broader table — a place I could set my notes on the conflict for study. I opened the letter and skimmed it before my hand found a piece of bread.

The situation at the border was tense. The Fey were growing impatient in waiting on the human intervention and had started to agitate for an incursion into ogre territory — something about a stone they claimed the ogres had stolen. It made no sense to me, but Fey magic never had; their reasoning often came dressed in riddles' garb.

More to the point... while our army had set up barricades and bulwarks, the two other countries wouldn't be shy about trampling us if we got in the way. If I were going to be of any use to these three nations, I'd have to abandon my investigation of the town and leave this evening.

"You have the look," Sophienne said, "of someone whom bad news has found."

I laughed wryly. "War's bad news, isn't it?"

She rolled her eyes so hard I felt it across the room. "What, are those varicolored cobweb-sniffers spoiling for another fight?"

"With the ogres, not us," I told her. "They say they'd stolen a..."

I trailed off and stared at her sword for a moment. Then I looked down at my notes. It hadn't been part of the initial briefing, but I'd liked the name of it. L'cormijn sae q'vek, it said: *heartbeat of the seasons*. A green gemstone of high value and religious importance to the Fey, mentioned toward the back of my papers, in a footnote no less. It had been presumed stolen decades ago by ogres looking for battlefield salvage.

I resisted the urge to look at Sophienne's sword despite the heat rising up my cheeks. If the Fey learned it had been in our lands all this time, peace would never happen. And if the Fey decided they were upset with Ath-Olomahn, I wasn't certain our army could stop them again. Even their friendship could be deadly. War would be brutal.

The sound of boots on wooden planks brought me back. To my surprise, Sophienne sat down next to me. Her smile was gone.

I offered her a tentative smile of my own and asked, "Yes?"

"You seem a good sort," she said abruptly, "but perhaps I must say the obvious to you. If you try to stop me from slaying the wizard, I will kill you. I will regret it, but I will still do so."

The cold fury of her seeming calm caused me to set aside the letter. I looked at her serene, assured face. "Milady, I wish to stop nothing. But... is that stone not from the kingdom of Fey?"

She grimaced. "It turned the tide against their armies, you know. And they've not missed it, this year since."

I opened my mouth and closed it. "And if I told you that war comes once more around the corner, would you surrender it?"

She shook her head. "Tomorrow. I need it to destroy the wizard. Wyrmtooth prolongs his life with magic dark and terrible. He's terrorized the north of this country for one hundred years, has he not?"

I checked my records. "Give or take," I admitted.

"Did he not kill my parents and leave me for dead?"

I inclined my head. "If you say it, it must be true."

"Then," she growled, "I shall slay him. I need the stone to break the spell that binds his soul to our world." The woman made an insouciant gesture. "After that, I care not. Take it back. Take me as a prisoner, if the capital feels strongly about it."

I winced a bit at this. The Bishops would certainly offer Sophienne as sacrifice at the altar of peace. Fortunately for her, I was here and they were not... and if she were willing to part with the stone after one more battle, I was less willing to use her as a scapegoat. Honesty should be rewarded — even if she was thirty-nine years behind schedule.

"Let us hope it does not come to that," I suggested. "In the meantime... did you plan a final meal, ere the battle?"

We spoke for most of the afternoon, between mouthfuls of goat and the finest wine the border could muster. Few citizens of Ath-Olomahn had been into the Fey Kingdom; it felt strange to find someone who'd seen any of the same sights as me. Legend said the Fey had once enjoyed an effervescent spring even when winter raged not ten feet past their borders. Even now, their roads were littered with gold and diamonds we couldn't touch, and the rain tasted like expensive wine. I'd found it easier to walk there blindfolded.

"That," she chuckled, "would have made my job more difficult. But perhaps you can make peace without looking someone in the eye?"

I shook my head. "No. I've never found much sense in hiding from truth."

"That," she pointed out, "has never been how I understood politics."

"It's probably why they keep sending me away from the capital," I told her.

As the autumn sun moved away from the tavern's western window, she stood and grabbed her sword. I asked her not to go, but she brushed my words aside. She shouldered her sword, filled a waterskin, and urged her horse toward the mountains at a graceful canter.

I watched her leave. This time, she turned and waved at the edge of the village.

When we met for the fifth time, the following morning, she asked, "Do I know you?" But she did not.

●

Sophienne would not yield. I followed her twice to the base of the wizard's tower. She marked me each time and drew her sword when I came too close. Her tone grew colder as winter's wind inched closer to the border. "You have no place here; your aid is unasked-for and unneeded. And I'll kill you if you try to intervene — the wizard must die."

I rode back into town and stabled my horse. The hands there paid me no mind, but I expected as much; I'd tossed them no coins. I paid them little mind myself; some miles north, a woman had just died again, and it ate at me.

I could ride to the border now... but every fiber of my being told me that arriving without the stone would be worse than useless. The Heartbeat had been vital to the Fey before the last war, and while it was almost a footnote to them now, it might well solve some of their problems with food and trade. Without it, the ogres would continue to nip at their heels until blood was drawn.

No. The stone was vital. I needed it if I were to help avert the deaths of thousands. That meant I had to pull Sophienne out of the whirlwind into which she'd been drawn. And if she wasn't willing to part with the stone toward the end of the day... perhaps she'd be more amenable at the start of it.

My stomach churned a bit as I stepped inside and paid Homish a silver crown to wait in her room overnight.

"When this first started," he told me, "I tried to rent her room. She broke the man's arm when she threw him out the window. You sure you want to do this?" When I nodded, he shook his head and muttered, "On your own thick skull be it."

He took the coin all the same.

The room was empty save for a tall knapsack — belongings unnecessary for her daily battle. The bed was tidily made. The window was open to the cool of an evening breeze. And why not — who else would dare to enter? The swordswoman would skewer anyone who tried.

I wasn't certain if her magical absence gave me the right to intrude. Okay, that's a lie — I knew it did not, and my nerves burned for it. Knowing that this town, and many others like it, would be turned to ash if the Fey were not appeased did little to ease the taste of bile in my mouth.

She appeared just as dawn's light found the windowsill: clothed but unarmored, with the sunlight catching her hair as it spilled across her pillow. The sword appeared against her bed, resting in its sheath; the green gemstone fell with a thud onto the floor beside it.

Sophienne breathed easy in her slumber. If time had made hells of her travails, she never seemed weary.

The stone's light caught my eye. The green of it: so like the magic that clutched the bricks of the tower. I did not know for what the Fey had used it, but they were willing to kill thousands to see it home. It wasn't on me to say whether they deserved it returned; they had made it, it was theirs, and if I could save Sophienne, the village, and thousands of soldiers by returning it...

Then I felt the chill of steel against my throat.

"You don't belong here, Dalen," the woman said. "You'd best leave while you still have your head to see you out."

"I can help," I blurted. "If you give me the stone, I —" Then her words slid like steel into my mind, past the fog of a long night. "You know me?"

Her mouth hung open for a moment before an uncouth word passed her lips.

I'd been ready to argue that I was from 'the future', that I could help her break the cycle of her own continuous death and loss of memory. But she knew me. She remembered. Every day we'd met: a facade.

For what?

I looked into her eyes and saw cold calculation there. She weighed whether or not she could let me live. The villagers wouldn't care if she killed me — I was a useless diplomat from the capital, and I'd entered her room despite warnings. On my own head this was.

Or, as the case might be, neck.

"I want," I breathed, "to help you."

"I don't *need* help," she snapped.

"Don't you?" I gestured toward the stone on the floor. "After however long? You and your sword weren't here last night. And the tower falls every evening. Do you remember dying, too?"

The edge of the sword backed away, if but an inch. "Every night," she told me. "For forty years, every night. Skin burned and every bone broken. My body ripped apart as the tower blows." Her sigh sounded ragged. "It's penance for stealing the stone."

"I'm no judge of Fey law," I murmured, "but I would say you've paid it."

"Have I?" She nodded out the window. "War comes because their people are scared and hungry without this thing. Isn't that what your letters say? I knew what I stole. It was war, it was survival..." Wide blue eyes found me waiting at the edge of her sword. "I suspect it's why they sued for peace. I know not if there's penance great enough."

I shrugged. "That's not for you to decide. If we head to the border —"

" — I will catch fire and die before we reach it, and appear here come morning. With the stone." She lowered her sword and gave me a look. "Do you think me dull?"

"Forgive me." I gave her a bow, mostly to cover my burning face. I really had. She'd seemed the sort to solve her problems with her sword; to hammer a rock until breaking. I should have realized that forty years, now accounted for, had given her seasons of painful hindsight.

Sophienne glanced out the window again. "Meet me at the stables ere sundown. We'll go to the tower together. In the meantime... they'll notice soon that I've not emerged. I'd better throw you down the stairs."

The words took a moment to register. "Wait, did you say —"

Then she had me by the collar of my tunic. We weren't of an uncommon height, but she lifted me like a pile of fallen leaves. She hauled me out the door and shouted, *"Never bother me again, stranger!"*

It seemed overdone, but bouncing down the stairs left me with no capacity to protest. The laughter below, from regulars clearly expecting a show, was punctuated by the sound of my arm bones breaking. I rolled onto my knees and scrambled out of the tavern; the laughter followed in my wake.

I found refuge in the stables. When no one was looking, I put a strap of leather between my teeth and set the bone. I applied a salve from the Church before dressing it in a sling. It would accelerate the healing and numb the pain, but we had no magic to speak of. Unless one counted our ability to meddle; that, I'd got in spades.

●

I came to some hours later when Sophienne nudged me with her boot. "Wake, stranger."

I groaned as I stared up at her from my pile of hay. "Dalen," I corrected her.

"You are well-met," she said with a wry expression. "Follow."

I saddled my horse, albeit slowly with one arm, and followed her out of town. I marked the sun to be an hour away from setting. It was the usual time of her ride, and I followed at a distance. While the villagers paid her no mind, they'd be more mindful of me.

The tower of Wyrmtooth stood when we came over the hill. At this point, it would not have surprised me to have found it half-exploded and in a state of structural undress. I slowed my steed, but Sophienne charged into the grassless circle, fearing neither spell nor spear. When she wasn't slain on the spot, I urged my horse onward once more.

The red-headed woman opened the door to the tower.

"It's unlocked?" I asked, surprised.

She shrugged at me. "Wyrmtooth had no fear of unwanted guests, I assume."

We were halfway up the stone stairs of the tower when her words struck me. "Had."

"You said what?"

"Wyrmtooth had no fear. He's dead?"

Sophienne grunted. "Some forty years ago. He rued my steel, and the stone, both."

"Then why do the villagers think he's alive?"

"Would you give credit to my life and his tower to a soldier-woman, if you were they?"

I waved a hand from side to side. "I might, if she told me the truth of what had happened. Instead you've hidden it all — even your memory of the past forty years."

She paused before me, blocking my path along the stairs. She gave me a look when she turned. "You know they've killed witches before, yes?"

I thought back to the first conversation with Homish. "They've said."

"They did not lie. Fortunately for me... I return to life no matter how or where I die now. I feign ignorance, I do their chores, so they do not waste my time by killing me again and again. And while they still hate me, they are now... comfortable, yes? I am of use, and they can be content. And leave me to die in peace."

I shook my head. "That's monstrous. The Church would have intervened, if we could, if we'd known."

"Why tell you? They fear a cure more than they fear me now. Why risk all that for someone not of their village?"

We came to the top of the stairs and found... a library. Bookshelves stretched for multiple stories up toward the pointed pitch of the conical roof; tables and chairs were arranged in a half-circle around a fireplace. For all the stories of his madness, Wyrmtooth had been a practical decorator. Tasteful, even.

The swordswoman gestured toward the books. "The wizard's spells and studies. I've learned something of the stone here. I took it because I'd heard their Queen used it to keep herself young and beautiful — a perpetual spring flower in the midst of a painted grove." She stared into the stone, blue eyes catching green light. "In truth, they used it for their crops more often, and the books imply it could be used to opposite effect. It accelerated Wyrmtooth's march to dust. The wizard's last act, though, was to stab at the stone itself. That's what destroyed the tower, and killed me."

"...but you both return, do you not?"

The woman shook her head. "I'd smashed the cage in which he kept his soul. He'd disintegrated well before the explosion." She looked up at me and frowned. "I've spent forty years with his books, an hour a day before the explosion kills me, hoping to find the trick of it. I think he tried to turn the stone into another anchor, hoping to find refuge here. The stone reacted badly... and instead of saving himself, he's tied me down to the Willowsring of some decades past."

I sat in one of the chairs; my skin crawled a bit, though I wasn't sure whether it was for wizard or stone. I closed my eyes and rubbed them a bit with my good hand. "We know," I started to say, "that there are limits to the spell. Time. The circle around the tower. The village — you always appear there. Your anchor point?"

"I think the village is almost as locked as I am," she told me. She spoke a bit haltingly at first, and then in a rush, her face seeming more relaxed as she went. "Perhaps because I was there the morn of the battle. They don't know it, but their routine is a well-trodden path.. and their harvest has had the precise same yield every year. I cannot prove that it's because of this, but that does fit, does it not?"

I'd wondered about that; it was good to hear her confirm it. "The Church thought that was the Fey nearby," I admitted. "But your idea does make more sense. And we know you can't make it to the border fast enough. Has someone else tried taking the stone?"

Her look of horror answered that fast enough.

"Okay," I added, "what if someone else held the stone and stayed here?"

Her eyes narrowed. "I know not. No one else has held the stone in all this time. I buried it a few times; it reappears beside me on the morrow. I believe the stone is the anchor for the town and for me — the source of the spell that binds us, and it follows us every time we're reborn."

"If you give me the stone," I told her, "of your own will, we can see what happens. Perhaps you'll be free."

"And perhaps you'll be trapped," she snapped back. "Do they not need you at the border?"

"Will they not come looking for me?" I countered. "And the border is but three days away. If you go to them and ask for help, I suspect I won't be long held."

"Why not just go yourself? They can find me as well as you."

I hesitated for a moment, uncertain of how to phrase it. "It will help the peace," I told her. "You're the one who stole it. It would be an honorable gesture for you to return it. And given the situation, I expect the Fey will help." Then I turned back and stared her full in the face. "Besides — I came to heal, not harm. Have you not suffered enough?"

She turned away from my gaze. "I've not been one to ask for help for all my life, Brother. Every time I've tried, someone's died for it. And the Fey... their idea of aid is lethal, betimes. You know this. And either way, they may kill me where I stand."

"They may," I admitted. "The Fey are a strange people, and they've suffered through your actions. But do you know what happens if we do not try?"

Sophienne looked back. "What?"

"Nothing."

She studied me for a long moment. "I could just run off," she said, "if this works. Let you all hang."

"I know it hasn't been long, but I like to think I know you better than that." I reached out my hand. "I'm here. Will you trust me?"

She let loose a shuddering breath and closed her eyes, nodding more to herself than to me. She reached out her hand and... did not let go. I watched her, her body quaking against the bars of a prison she'd made for herself. Forty years without trust. To wrestle with the habit of decades, against the fear of being slain instead of merely killed?

I hadn't been keeping track of the time, but I saw the sun start to set through one of the tower windows. I didn't know precisely when the fire would come, but I'd been hoping, perhaps in vain, to avoid it in the handoff.

Then she opened her eyes and looked at me, smiling slightly... for once, as though she knew me well. The stone fell into my open hand, and my fingers closed around it instinctively, to catch it —

●

I woke to the sound of the bones in my arm breaking. The words *Never bother me again, stranger!* echoed in my ears, but there was no one there to say them. I clutched at my arm and looked around; everyone in the common room of the tavern had stood, confused, looking at one another.

I rushed out to the stable to find some salve, but my horse had gone. I grabbed a leather strap instead, righted the bone, and ripped enough fabric off my sleeve to make a crude sling.

An old man — Homish, from the tavern — approached me later in the morning. "Have you seen Sophienne?" he asked.

"Not since she threw me out of her room," I told him.

His face fell. "I see. Well... expect you're here for a while, yeah? If you want room and board, we'll need to see about giving you some chores." He glanced at my arm and sighed. "...such as you can do," he muttered as he walked away.

Sophienne, I realized, was gone — taking her seemingly immortal labor with her. Of course the town would seize upon her replacement. She'd chopped wood and cleaned stables, they'd said. Unfortunately for them, I was far less useful — what did I know about manure or field care?

I looked around and found no trace of her: neither sword, nor stone, nor either horse. When I tried to borrow another steed, to return to the tower, a burly stable hand stopped me with ease. It was clear to me, then, just how much of an impediment the town must have been to Sophienne.

I was still standing in the center of the square when sundown found me. Green fire rose all around; I could feel it sear the flesh from my body. And the crowd looked on in horror — not for me, but at what I could only assume was their new normal.

●

I woke to the sound of the bones in my arm breaking, again and again and again.

I don't know how long it lasted. It lasted until it didn't. I don't know how Sophienne held onto her mind as long as she did. And when I woke, with no dreams to guide me from the fire to the snap of my ulna, I was almost certain I'd lost my own.

I woke to the sound of the bones in my arm breaking... but this time it was against rock, not the wooden floor of the tavern. I was so surprised that, for a moment, I forgot to feel the pain. Instead I looked at the village of Willowsring... a village of some hundreds, with perfect weather and ideal crops.

Every cottage had been razed to its roots; the tavern was a pile of rubble. Every building around me lay in smoldering ruin. I stumbled to my feet and staggered toward the town square.

"Brother Dalen," a voice called.

It was light and billowy, the voice; I recognized the accent as coming from a place where it rained nothing but wine. They were tall, this figure, with translucent wings folded like a cloak behind them. Garishly dressed, of course; but I would have known them for Fey without that added effect.

They weren't alone. Soldiers both of Ath-Olomahn and the Fey milled about, looking at the ruins in surprise and consternation.

"Something happened," I said. "Sophienne?"

"The woman found us," the Fey admitted. They gave a bow. "Tithas amh Alast; I would have been your counterpart, if we'd met at the treaty table."

I bowed weakly. "A pleasure." Then I sat back down. My arm hurt to the point my stomach churned.

Tithas frowned. "We can wait, if you require the medicines of your people to —"

"No, please. How fares our peace? What happened?" And, after a beat, "Where is she?"

The Ambassador walked toward me and crouched down to meet me at eye level. "Brother Dalen, war was averted. Thanks to the human woman's intercession, we found the stone unguarded in the wizard's tower. We'd hoped to find you with it, but you appear to have had more difficulties than she had done."

I looked around. "A bit. But if war never came... what happened here? Did the wizard return?"

The Ambassador shook their head and sighed as they pulled a familiar green stone from inside a coat pocket. It pulsed at me in some form of recognition. "They are magic, these stones," they said. "They were the heartbeat of our very seasons. They do not make time, as your friend thought; they take shortcuts to a future. When we recovered the gem, once your soldiers let the woman through to us, we broke the loop and set time straight... like one of your doctors fixing a broken bone."

They waved their free hand, long and silver-fingered, over my arm; I felt the wound mend itself. After a moment, all that remained was the ghost of pain and the roiling of my stomach. They watched my face carefully for a moment, their own a blank mask. If they had emotions, it was in a different language than mine.

"Thank you, Ambassador," I said.

"You are welcome," they answered. "But you feel, even without the injury, a lingering effect, is it not so? It is the same here. When we fixed time, this village had... a seizure of seasons. It was just as with our people, when the woman stole the stone from us — all our fields were destroyed by it. While we were more careful than she, we still untethered all the anchors that bound this region in loop — yours, hers, and all the others."

"I'm not sure I understand," I admitted.

"You have a mind, I expect, that works to unravel a knot rather than to tear it asunder. I suspect your friend never considered that approach, or feared for someone's safety if she had done. We have started time anew, turning over this loop of life like a garden bed — if she had done such, she would have been freed long ago."

I didn't know that for certain — whether Sophienne knew what would happen, or if the many years of her limited time simply didn't let her reach that conclusion. Self-taught and with no one with whom to converse, she might well have been embedded in her own assumptions.

Of course, she might well have reached a point where she feared success as much as failure. And if this was the result... I could not blame her for it.

I glanced around at the tumbled buildings. What wood that wasn't petrified seemed ready to crumble; the large stones looked as though they'd been scorched by a thousand summers. I thought of Homish at the tavern, and the rest of the villagers, caught in a conflagration beyond mortal comprehension. Of children aging to dust as they tried to run away. With all that time, all at once, none of them would have had a chance to scream.

"Forty years," I whispered.

They placed a long-fingered hand on my shoulder and smiled a bit too sharply. "We are not always honored to be of aid. This does not bring us joy... even if, from our end, all is resolved."

"Is it?" I asked. "You'll sign a formal treaty? And the ogres will abide?"

They produced a small scroll and tossed it at my feet. "We already have, and they say they shall. Tell your Bishops, when next you see them, that they have their peace. All prices are paid... and we've had enough of death." Then they rose and walked back toward the Fey soldiers.

I did not watch them go. Instead, I sat in the rubble and dust where Sophienne's room had been. The soldiers of

Ath-Olomahn gathered round; they spoke of borders and zones and shifting troops toward the heretics of Zhe Tahra, far to the west.

Our nation was never without its enemies. There would always be another problem to solve — whether they'd like me to do so or not. My own problem, more immediate, would be how to explain all of this to the Bishops of Ri'as. The Church had no understanding of this sort of magic… and everyone else who'd lived it was dead.

Then I heard the faint shuffle of boots on pebbles.

I looked up and saw a white-haired woman, still strong, though bent by age and hardship. She'd given up armor for a thin robe, and her sword was nowhere to be found. Still, she sent guards scurrying out of her way with a stern gaze from clear blue eyes.

I pushed myself up and gave a bow as relief swept away the nausea and fear.

"Sophienne?" I asked. "It's done… you're free. Are you all right?"

She paused and looked at me, a slight smile on her face. "Do I know you?"

But she did not. Her face, now lined with cares beyond measure, said she did not know me from a summer's night.

Brian Hugenbruch's story "Heartbeat of the Seasons" was originally published in Metaphorosis on Friday, 11 February 2022. See magazine.metaphorosis.com

About the author

Brian Hugenbruch is the author of more than forty speculative fiction short stories and poems. He lives in Upstate New York with his wife and their daughter. By day he works as a software engineer, where he focuses on building security controls to help safeguard the internet. He enjoys fishing (but only in video games); Scotch (but only in real life); and he spends his days trying to explain quantum cryptography to other nerds.

His most recent fiction has appeared in *Cast of Wonders, Analog,* and *Dragon Gems*; he has stories coming up in *Escape Pod* and the *FAMILIARS* anthology from Zombies Need Brains. You can find him online at the-lettersea.com, on Bluesky @the-lettersea.com, on IG/Threads @the_lettersea, and elsewhere by putting

'Hugenbruch' into your search engine of choice. No, he's not certain how to say his last name either.

The Lonely King

Gunnar De Winter

Once, he'd had loyal subjects.

Now he only had bricks and sand.

Immortality was not a blessing.

He had dragged his throne to the highest tower of town. It had been an arduous task, but he'd had — quite literally — all the time in the world.

The top of the tower had long since crumbled, exposing king and throne alike to the elements. Mocking desert winds threw hails of sand at the king's weathered face. He clutched a parchment in his lap, a letter from a love long lost, but that too became taunting sand. The king squinted but stubbornly refused to yield to the desert.

Everything blurred to yellow. Fierce, burning yellow. Even the decrepit town buildings had taken on the color of the desert that surrounded them.

Then, a change.

This is it, thought the king. *Madness has finally found me.*

His kingdom, after all, was devoid of humanity. He was all that was left.

And yet, the flicker on the horizon persisted. Multiplied.

The king blinked rapidly, thinking grains of sand stuck to the surface of his eyes.

But the distant dots continued to come closer. They could have been animals, hunting for rare prey. No, the specks were too... intent, too strongly aimed at him.

He maintained his composure even though his heart almost leapt out of his chest. The dots were human — unmistakable now. A few dozen. Even beasts of burden trundled alongside. Druks, judging by the typical swaying gait of the massive brawny hexapods.

Their goal was clear now. They were headed straight for him.

Alone no longer.

Let my reign find breath again.

The king's joints creaked into activity after eons of statuesque silence. He descended two steps at a time. How his mother would have chided him. Such expression of haste was not royal. There was no such thing as imperial impatience, she always said.

But there was no one to witness the childish giddiness of an ancient monarch. Not yet, anyway.

One half of the town's large wooden gate was rusted shut, a giant rooted in the dry earth. The other half barely held on, another giant, one that hovered over an abyss with only a fraying rope to clutch at.

The king stood waiting in the triangular opening that remained. His heavy coat had left a wide trail through the sand that covered every bare surface in the town.

"Welcome," he bellowed when he thought his new subjects were within earshot.

They stopped and looked at each other. Surprised. Uncomfortable. As if they weren't expecting the king to welcome them.

Nonsense, the king thought. *A good ruler acknowledges his subjects. If they do not know this, they were right to flee their faltering sovereign.*

Following a huddle amongst the travelers, the caravan set in motion again.

Then king felt a broad grin appear within the crags of his weathered face.

The leader of the caravan was a tall man — certainly for a mortal. A full head shorter than the king, he came to a halt a few paces away. His eyes couldn't meet those of his new monarch. He rubbed the back of his head, messing up his thick brown locks.

"Uhm... we didn't expect to..."

The king swung his arm. "Leave it be, good man. Say no more. You are all welcome here." He looked down on his new loyal follower and put a hand on the man's shoulder. Muscles tensed under the king's touch. *Nervous, no doubt.*

"Together, we shall rebuild this kingdom."

That night, the thrill of once again ruling more than an empire of solitude spurred the king's rusted memory. He remembered...

The king remembered a time when the desert was dappled with small king- and queendoms, when immortal houses of rulers formed a robust tree of genealogical ties. Each adult immortal had its town of subjects, but kings and queens frequently visited each other. Squabbles were few and the lives of kings and subjects alike were — generally — good. The desert and its creatures were always a looming threat, but the kingdoms were oases of civilization. The king relished the memory. It had been a time of happiness, even of love. Once, he had had a queen.

Then, one day, those lights of culture faded one by one, in the blink of an immortal's eye. Kings and queens increasingly yielded to the desert, leaving their subordinates helpless. Kingdoms crumbled, eagerly swallowed by the encroaching sea of sand. The rulers that remained turned in on themselves, protecting their own above all else. So too did the king. Contact dwindled. Isolation flourished.

There were no more visits.

A true king intervenes as little as possible.

He let them settle in at their own pace, let them find their own place. After all, except for his tower, all buildings were available for use and occupation.

The morning came with new sounds. The grating creaks of rusted hinges, the crunch of sand under boots. The wail of a child.

And was that...? Yes, the smell of freshly baked bread. The king's withered salivary glands refilled, rejoiced. Though monarchs didn't require sustenance, they appreciated complex flavors.

Patience.

For the first weeks, the king simply watched them from his tower. They seemed like ants scurrying under his gaze. When you were outside time, time became malleable. The king's excitement, though, was immortal. Atemporal.

His new flock had established itself and had begun rebuilding the town. Hinges stopped creaking, sand was swept out of buildings and compacted into avenues. A productive lot.

They would need guidance. And he would be their guide. As he was meant to be.

He walked down the stairs for the second time since the new arrivals had entered his realm. Slowly now, regal.

Sand no longer screeched beneath his sandals as he strode across the cleaned streets, a sound he was glad to miss. There was another sound, though, that died as he emerged from his tower. A sound he did miss.

The sound of laughter, of conversation, of life.

The people were still apprehensive.

But I have given them time. Oh, how their previous monarch must have been monstrous. My task is larger than I thought. I shall not waver.

He smiled, ancient creases in his face performing movements they were still unused to.

"Good day!" His voice rang across town. The people cowered.

Enthusiasm can be frightening for those that are not enthused, he reminded himself. *Slowly. Even the timeless can go too fast.*

He took a deep breath. The air was cleaner, full of aromatics. The taste, the smell of everyday activity, of habitation, soothed him.

"I am pleased," he said — softer now. "You have made tremendous progress. This place," he swept a long, emaciated arm, "has not looked this good, this vibrant since... a very long time." *Ward off the sadness, it is not their burden.*

The caravan's leader — unofficial mayor now — frowned with worry as his kinsmen slowly retreated, eyes averted from the king in their midst.

Poor things. How they must have suffered.

"Tell me, good man," the king spoke softly, containing the royal strength in his voice, "what is your name?"

The man swallowed and sighed. "I am Bramm."

"Bramm." The king stepped closer but halted as soon as he saw the muscles in Bramm's arms tense like cables being pulled too hard. "I am no fool. Tell me what worries you."

Bramm's cheeks clenched so hard the king feared his teeth might shatter.

"Fear not, you are safe here. Speak freely."

Another sigh. "We... Our town was ruined by our monarch. He was... not right. So, we fled, looking for a place to be free."

"A wise choice."

"A place without king or queen."

The thought struck the king like a punch to the gut. He stepped back unwillingly. *Heresy!* Rage bubbled. *No. Control. Restraint. Do not lash out. Their trauma is not their own creation.*

"I see." The king closed his eyes and took another deep breath. *Life, joy, the air is full of it. Do not squander it.* "I can assure you that your tribulations are over. Not only will you be safe here, together we will make this place a thriving community where all can flourish."

Why do they not cheer, why do they not revel in their newfound peace?

Bramm mumbled something, the meaning lost in the song of wind and sand.

"What was that, my friend?"

"But we would not be free."

"I... You are mistaken, Bramm. But I understand. You need time to heal from oppression. I can give you time." The king turned a deaf ear to Bramm's mumbling and blind eyes to the man's shaking head. The immortal headed back to his tower. *Free? How can they be free without ruler, without rules?*

●

The royal mind was in turmoil. Heaving emotions threw up another memory from eons past.

The king recalled one of his mentors, a king among kings, an immortal ruler that had been around when consciousness congealed out of the mists of the universe. As was custom, visiting monarchs often spent time with those in training.

Those with the most thriving, resilient kingdoms preached patience as the main virtue of a good ruler. The king-to-be spent many nights ruminating on his mentors' teachings about the idiosyncratic minds of the ephemerals, the differences that separated rulers from their subjects, and how a true king embraced this gap for the betterment of all.

●

Days passed in a fever dream as the king's thoughts went back and forth in an endless pursuit of each other. A pursuit without victor. There was conflict inside the king. What he wanted was right there, yet out of reach. *If you can't rule their hearts, your kingdom is empty.*

From his tower, the king saw Bramm hug his wife and ruffle his son's hair. They were laughing, looking longingly at each other. Complete.

There was love, family among his subjects.

Perhaps a queen could remedy the loneliness. Bah, banish the thought. There was only one queen for me, and she is no more.

Now, his subjects were his children, his recalcitrant lovers, his purpose.

Still...

His subconscious violently pulled him out of his reverie.

Something was amiss.

There.

On the horizon something moved. Aggressively, with predatory purpose. Only one thing could move like that. Sandpards, with six strong legs and a muscular body to support a large triangular head that was more jaw than brain.

The king sprang from his chair, ready to warn his people.

Wait. Not yet. Within the blink of an eye, he stopped moving and turned still as a sculpture. *This will teach them they need me. When they see the value of my presence, they will have no other option but to come to me for protection.*

Sandpards always moved in sixes. They were fast. Very fast.

The king chewed his bottom lip. *Come on, misguided mortals, you must see now that you need me.*

Shouts washed towards him like salve being applied to a fresh wound. His elation grew with the panic below.

Any second now, they will run up the stairs, to me.

But no, they ran outwards, towards the feeble cracked ramparts they had not yet completely fixed.

Fools.

A sandpard could scale those easily. A king knew these things. After all, kings and beasts were made from the same sand.

His flock was in danger.

The king roared and jumped from his tower. He called on the power of the sand to guide his descent. Every grain in the town sang to him, danced for him. A small tornado cushioned his feet and lessened the impact on his joints as he landed. He shot forward.

Slow. Too slow. Rest rusts.

Backed by a wave of sand, he reached the edge of town, where two sandpards had already leapt across the barricades. He struck one beast with his scepter. The other one bit his free arm, nearly swallowing half of it. The king looked at the creature and growled.

"I am the sand, I am the desert." The king's arm turned to sand. The sandpard wheezed until its triple double-lobed lungs were saturated. The beast suffocated and collapsed.

The king fell to his knees, unaware of the shocked silence around him. Then came the scream.

The sandpard matriarch had found a victim. The king surged to his feet and pulled his newly forming arm out of the sand. His new limb was still coalescing when he saw Bramm lunge at the sandpard. The man's son lay limp beneath the beast's hungry jaws.

Brave but foolish.

The king knocked Bramm aside as the sandpard leapt. Beast and king locked in a lethal embrace, a deathly dance within a whirlwind. The inertia of eternity became the flash of violence. Sand settled. Royalty and savagery stared at each other, panting. The sandpard mewled. Its smooth skin granulated, cracked. Beast became sand. It crumbled and collapsed.

Sandpards weren't clever, except when it came to hunting. The three remaining sandpards, about to finish the circling movement that would bring them to the other side of town, lost heart. With the matriarch out of the picture, they howled and ran off.

The king straightened and rubbed the sand from his sweaty face.

Now they will understand they need me.

"You demon!" Bramm came towards him, his eyes boring into the king's face for the first time. Anger and grief reddened his face and streaked his cheeks with tears. "We do not want you here. We never wanted you here. My son..." Bramm's voice cracked. "You couldn't even save my son," he continued softly, sinking to his knees. "You can't protect us. You... you are nothing. Go. Just go."

The king's chest heaved. *But I waited for your love, your respect. You want protection without rule? You want the protection of a king without accepting his rule?*

The eternal being bellowed. "You ungrateful bastards! Without me, you would have all perished." The town trembled as the sand shifted. "There can be no kingdom without king. We monarchs are life, we are guardians. Without us the desert would swallow you all." The wind wailed along with him.

The fear in the people's eyes stabbed the king's old heart. Anger and wind subsided in tandem.

As befit a king, he strategically redeployed to his sanctuary.

Suppressed anger and a wounded heart birthed another memory from the sands of time.

The king remembered a queen. A queen many ages his senior, but as striking as any immortal could aspire to be. A well of knowledge that only few possessed. As young king and new ruler of his own small kingdom, he often went to visit her. In his dreams, he already saw their children building a new network of prosperous kingdoms.

The king remembered the first night they had lain together. After the throes of passion had ebbed away, the queen whispered stories to him about the birth of the immortals, myths of how the earth itself — the one true parent of the immortals — had begotten them to keep the desert from spreading over the entirety of the world. The desert, so the queen told her devoted listener, was a cancer, always looking to spread and consume. The immortals were scattered across it to stunt its growth, to provide a counterweight and establish balance. The king and his kin accepted this duty and made it their purpose.

●

They would not dare!

Bramm's rage had lit a fire in the townspeople. They knew they couldn't best a monarch. But they also knew that without kingdom, kings perished. A monarch would never — could never — leave his town except for a visit to another monarch. His people, though, could travel as they pleased.

Will they really choose the cancerous desert over me? Am I so terrible? Do they truly prefer the uncertainty and struggles of being free from rule over the peace and order provided by a king? Bah, good riddance, I shall withstand the desert without them.

The people packed quickly, and the caravan seemed to tremble with the anticipation of movement, like an animal yearning to run. Wooden carts were stuffed and decked with tarps. Druks were corralled out of their enclosure and guided into broad tailored yokes. Before the night fell and the chill of darkness could grab hold, the caravan set in motion.

A few people looked back. But not Bramm.

He must be a good leader, to achieve consensus like this, in the face of danger and uncertainty.

Everyone was willing to follow Bramm wherever he might lead them.

Surely, they will not venture into the desert night, the time of djinns and ghouls?

The wind began to pick up, tugging at the caravan. The king heard the story in the sound, the soliloquy of solitude. A layer of liquid formed on his eyes, not due to the pricking sand this time, but due to the sadness of impending loss.

They would. They actually would. Perhaps the time of monarchs truly is over. Perhaps there are new kings and queens, walking among the people.

Maybe this is my legacy. Maybe they are my legacy.

The king cried unabashedly.

This should not have taken a child's life. I feel the weight of the young one's death.

When the last cart rolled across the town's boundary, a tremor made people's heads turn.

The king's tower shook. From the seams between the stones, small puffs of sand emerged and coalesced into a dense curtain that obscured the tower from sight. A deep rumble.

When the sand dissipated, the tower had gone.

●

In withdrawal and solitude, another memory reformed.

Then king remembered one of his mentors' final visits and lessons, the last argument before the desert had swallowed the king's only remaining ancient mentor.

Many immortals had already vanished by then, including the king's family and the queen he had loved. Apprehension gripped the king, prompting him to transform his kingdom into a stronghold, impenetrable and towering in seclusion.

His mentor tried to convince him to reconsider. The old one told the king of how, even though they were immortal, they were not meant to be eternal. The greatest ruler, his mentor said, eventually obviates the necessity of his or her own being. Their subjects were the true inheritors of the earth and the salve that could tame the desert. The king had scoffed and scorned his ancient relative.

Their parting had not been not amicable and turned out to be final.

So they have some sense after all.

When the tower had vanished, and the king along with it, the people had returned. Suspicious at first, searching through all the houses and buildings.

They had forgotten that monarchs were creatures of the sand, denizens of the desert. If the king could not watch them from above, he would do so from below.

From his subterranean enclave, the king heard their footsteps, felt them live their lives. Grains of sand were the spies that kept him apprised of all that occurred in his kingdom.

He would build and protect his kingdom. He always would. But carefully now, unnoticed.

The king coerced layers of sand in intricate patterns to shepherd dew into underground canals. Soon, his people would discover a hidden source of irrigation, an oasis seemingly sprung from nothing. When sandpard vibrations woke him from his slumber, he would lay quicksand traps.

My people will thrive. I will protect them.

They will not know. They will not supplicate. So be it. It will suffice for me.

A terrible ruler has iron hands, a good ruler velvet ones. A great ruler needs none.

Gunnar De Winter's story "The Lonely King" was originally published in Metaphorosis on Friday, 29 November 2019. See magazine.metaphorosis.com

About the author

Gunnar De Winter is a Belgian biologist turned science writer whose fiction has appeared in, among others, *The Deadlands, Future SF Digest,* and *Daily SF.* He chases ideas down rabbit holes and you can follow along at gunnardewinter.com, @evolveon (on X), or @gunnardewinter.bsky.social (on Bluesky).

Her Spirit Animal

L.A.W. Butler

Atynleigh leaned into the wind as she pulled her wool shawl closer around her face. The freezing wind was part of her daily trek along the shores of the great lake, yet someone had to check on the well-being of the creature that lived on the high point above the cove. In Atynleigh's small, damaged family, that someone meant her. The creature must be attended to, and Atynleigh was a dutiful child. So, she shrugged the pack on her back into a more comfortable position and trudged on.

Far above the cove the dull sun added a meager warmth to the dark slate that formed a grassless apron in front of the hut where the creature lived. This morning he had painfully made his way to a high stump of stone that separated the path from the lake cliff and was resting in the sun. His eyes wandered to the restless, gray waters of the great lake below him. Sometimes he looked, and with some regard, to the low mountains and thick forest that lay to the east and south, and to the steeper valley with its swift, narrow river that formed the western lands. But the lake, stretched across the northern horizon, was his home, and it was this that he longed for.

Knowing that the girl would surely come that day, the man — if man he was — had clumsily stoked a fire for tea. He knew the child would be cold and he knew the burden he placed on the family in the valley.

The sun was the width of an outstretched hand above the horizon when Atynleigh approached the hut. She called to the creature as she approached the cabin.

"I am here," she heard in response.

She knew it was difficult for Creature to speak aloud. His voice came in a wet, soft whisper. Yet, she had heard the words of his greeting clearly, with its strange, precise accent. At such times she knew he had been thinking the words. When Creature used his mind instead of his throat, his words came easily. She also knew that he could hear her thoughts. But just as it was easier for him to speak with his mind, it was easier for her to speak with her throat, and this was how they communicated.

Atynleigh remembered when she and her mother had found — rescued, saved — the creature from death on the stone beach some distance from their home. He had been injured and in pain from a fearsome wound on his side.

She and Mother had been fishing far down the cove. Fish had been sparse for weeks and they had followed signs of schooling fish past the safety of the harbor. Mother was a skilled fisherman, from a long line of men and women who had made their living on the lake's water. Atynleigh's mother and father had enjoyed fishing together, but Father had died months ago and now Atynleigh was Mother's fishing companion.

They had entered a shallow cove where a rippling surface spoke of an abundance of fish. They were about to toss their net when Atynleigh stayed her mother's strong arm and nodded noiselessly toward the near shore. A man appeared to be crawling across the beach, not even crawling so much as moving his limbs in response to unremitting pain. All of this, as well as something undefinable about his dark, rough appearance, made mother and daughter hesitate as they scanned the shoreline for danger. These were unsettled times. Even aiding the obviously sick or wounded required a serious decision.

"We need to get closer," Atynleigh whispered.

Mother nodded. They were both thinking the same thing. If someone had been on this shore to help Father, he might have lived instead of bleeding out in frigid water, alone and without hope. On that fateful day, rising waves from a sudden storm had thrown Father, as skilled a man as there was in a small boat, into the shallows. He would have survived with only bruises, but he had crashed down on a broken iron hoop from a submerged and rotten barrel. The metal drove deep into his thigh, cutting the femoral artery. Without help, he had never stood a chance.

That loss gave both mother and daughter courage to offer this stranger the lifeline which had been denied Atynleigh's father. Still, they approached cautiously. Mother slid from the boat as it hissed against the pebbles and grounded itself on the shore. Atynleigh, with her sharp eyes, would watch the tree line for possible danger. They did not need to discuss these arrangements, they simply knew.

The man had rolled on his back and looked in their direction. He had clearly been aware of their approach. Now, he neither moved nor made a sound. He lay a short ten yards from shore, his head toward them with golden eyes watching their every move.

"Do good."

"What?" her mother asked.

"I said nothing," Atynleigh replied, looking at her mother for the first time since the boat came to its stop. "I thought you told me..."

They both looked toward the man with his pleading eyes. They were sure he had made no sound, but they knew what they had heard. Atynleigh impulsively joined her mother in the water as they ran together — to do good.

They needed the strength of their desire to do the right thing, for as they approached the injured man, they saw that it was, in fact, no man at all.

"A Spirit Animal," Mother whispered, stopping short some distance from the creature. She had hesitated as she said this and both Mother and Atynleigh looked at each other and then back to the creature. Spirit animals were known to exist in this lake, sometimes seen, sometimes feared, sometimes revered in a way just short of worship. The Spirit Animals were creatures of legend and song. They were neither man nor beast, but part of both worlds and it is said that they could talk to both the fish and the fishermen. Many a person who had disappeared was said to have been called to the lake by a Spirit Animal, never to be seen again. There were others who said they would have been lost except for a Spirit Animal that guided (or carried) them to a safe shore after a storm or accident.

Atynleigh shook with fear and awe; this was certainly the creature of the legends. What lay before them had the configuration of a man, but the scales and gills of a fish. He had a muscular tail and spiked dorsal fins down his back like a lizard. His face was reptilian. The eyes were golden, large, and bulging, with pupils constricted in pain. Down the creature's side, from armpit to hip, a bloody slice had been opened by some sharp object.

The creature looked at them again and they heard more thoughts, but of garbled and uncertain meaning. The creature was able to capture feelings more than specific words, though sometimes one emerged as the other.

"Spirit Animal," was suddenly repeated back to them, and then, softer, the repeated plea, "...do good."

Atynleigh had looked to her mother, fearful, wondering what they should do. Mother's worried eyes moved from her daughter to the creature and then her shivering lips closed in a look of decision and determination. Mother hurried back to the boat, caught up the net and ran back to her daughter.

"We will spread this beside the creature, lift him on to it as best we can and ferry him back to the cabin. I can care for the wound there."

They went to work but heard no more from the creature save a feeling of intense pain when they moved him.

He was still alive when they brought him to their cabin.

●

From the early days of Creature's recovery, even those perilous first days lying on a pallet by the fire in their cabin, Atynleigh had noticed his golden eyes following everything she and Mother did. He tried to understand their thoughts and share his with them, but communication was halting and incomplete. Creature had watched as they spent the long, cold nights working, working, working, until the brief hour before exhaustion sent them to bed. Once they called the day's work enough, she and Mother would pull out the chess board and play a fast, deadly game.

Their game of chess was not the slow, studied game of deep thinkers. Theirs was like their lives, a series of quick decisions.

Mother and Father had played chess. They had taught Atynleigh while she was still sitting on their knees and as she grew older, that any one of that trio might win on any given night. Their board was simply functional, but the pieces — ah, those chessmen. Father had carved them from walrus tusks. They were tiny because tusk was a precious commodity. But the carving was fine and animated, with carefully detailed faces.

The creature had quickly become fascinated with the nightly chess match.

Two days after Creature came to the cabin he was starting to move painfully and slowly. Each time he reopened his wound, but the bleeding was less each time. He ate hungrily. That would have been a problem, except that fish had started coming to the cove. The first day a mass of mussels had apparently thrown themselves onto the shore by the cabin, enough to fill a bucket. It had turned into a feast for all of them.

By the fourth day Creature had been lucid enough to ask what this 'chess' was. A full week later Creature hobbled toward the chess board and began observing the game. He watched, trying simple questions using his soft, bubbling voice, or speaking directly into their minds. Five days later, absorbed in the game, his webbed hand moved hesitantly toward a piece on the board, a bishop, carved to look both haughty and bored.

"Yes" Atynleigh said, "that is the man I was going to move." She looked at him with astonishment. "Do you know where I wanted him to go?"

"A line." His claw hovered above the board in a diagonal. "Capturing a rook." The claw stopped above Mother's ward man, shaped like a Berserker, shown biting down on the top of his shield.

"Can you move it?"

Creature's golden eyes locked on Atynleigh's brown ones. She moved her head to encourage him. In response, his claws curled inward, moving them out of the way. He used the knuckles of the hand, just above the webbing, to grasp the bishop and deftly move it across the board, pushing the rook out of the way. He then carefully plucked up the rook and set it aside.

The room filled with Atynleigh's laughter. She and Mother both laughed — perhaps for the first time in months. This movement of a clawed hand from a healing stranger had made them feel a lightness that had been rare in their cabin.

●

It was at the end of his third week of recovery, during such a chess match, that the full danger of their situation closed around them. The match had barely started when Creature straightened his back, his eyes closed into slits, and focused on the door.

"They come."

Mother did not hesitate or question the creature. There was danger close and closing.

"Move. Make yourself as small as you can in the dark corner of Atynleigh's bed, back, under the slant of the roof."

"I can fight."

"You will lose. Do as I say."

When Mother used that tone, no one could withstand her. Atynleigh watched Creature roll back onto the small bed where it was wedged between the hang of the roof and the slant of the steps going to the loft where Mother slept.

Mother and daughter then pulled the rough blankets of Creature's pallet off the floor and threw them over the huddled figure of the lake-man, making a mess of unmade bed in the dark corner. They moved the low table with its chess board intact over the clean and flattened space where the pallet had been, roughing the dirt floor with their feet as well as they could. Mother scattered the wood fire enough to lower the light of the cabin just as they heard the men approach.

A fist pounded on the door.

"Who is there?" Mother called.

"The Reeve of the shire, Widow. Open."

Mother opened the door and let the firelight fill the entryway. There were three men dressed in rough tunics and wool capes. Two were men from the village. All were on foot. She glanced from the faces of the men she knew to the one she did not.

"Reeve Tomasil, it is late. Is there trouble?" She looked past them as if the trouble were waiting in the clearing.

"We come to warn of trouble. The fisherman here is certain there is sign of a Spirit Animal, wounded and ashore, in this area." Reeve Tomasil pushed the stranger forward as he spoke. It was as close to an introduction as was possible in this primitive community.

The stranger then spoke with a surly voice, trying to assert authority where he had none, "We need to inspect the houses. Make sure he isn't hiding."

Mother laughed and pushed the door wide open. "Look all you want, Reeve. But I think if I had seen a lake monster in my house, I would be seeking you instead of the other way around."

The stranger stepped forward and wrenched the door from Mother's hand.

"I'll have my own look around."

"No, sir. The Reeve may, but you shall not."

The stranger was shocked by this barrier to his wishes. He started to push past Mother but that proved to be a problem as the woman stood her ground.

"The Reeve is known to me and is welcome in this house. I do not allow that familiarity to every person. Certainly not a stranger who does not know a proper welcome." As Mother said this, she fixed the stranger with her eyes and seemed to grow both taller and straighter. For the first time all of them noticed that she had come to the door with a fish skinning knife in her strong right arm.

As the stranger took a short step back, Mother addressed the men she knew.

"Tomasil," Mother said trying to sound genuinely concerned, "has anyone been injured by this Spirit Animal? I could bring my medicines. You know I stand ready to help."

"No, Widow." The Reeve was weary of the long searches this stranger had insisted upon over the last weeks and he was not used to being offered help by the families he interrupted. It showed in his eyes and Mother now used that to seal a quick end to this visit. She spoke softly.

"You must be very tired. My daughter and I have a little left of our supper, but the rest is yours if you wish."

She stepped back from the doorway she had blocked to the stranger, and her act of generosity and openness had the effect she had counted on.

"No. No, we won't be staying, Widow. What little you have belongs to you and the child. We have warned you and checked the house. It is all we need."

"But it could be lurking..." the stranger tried to protest, but he was stopped by the tired Reeve.

"Our work is done here. We wish you a quiet evening, Widow."

"And a bright morning to you," Mother said.

Atynleigh joined her mother as they stood at the open door and watched the three men retreat down the path toward the village far out of sight. They stood in the lighted door just long enough to appear completely fearless and innocent, then closed the door, both shaking uncontrollably.

They stoked the fire to a bright blaze and slowly uncovered Creature. He too was shaking, but not from fear or cold.

It was a long time until his anger subsided. He spoke only with his mind that night.

"I must leave your house."

"You are not ready. We did not bring you this far to lose you out of fear — or anger."

"I put you in danger."

Mother hesitated, then stated a simple fact. "There is danger. True. And we do need to get you out of here. We were as lucky as we were smart tonight."

"Mother," said Atynleigh, her voice soft but earnest, "I have an answer, but it is a hard answer. We need to get Creature to the cliff hut. Even if the Reeve returned with men, Creature would see them and escape to the lake, down the cliff ropes long before anyone could walk the path."

Mother sat silently. The idea had occurred to her as well. The cliff hut was a small, barely functional shelter built on the top of the hill just to the west of their cabin. It had been built by Atynleigh's great-grandfather as part of a coastal warning system. An open fire on its heights could be seen far down the lake shore as well as inland. Such fires, passed from hilltop to hilltop, were a way to warn of marauders, though such times were now long past. The cliff ropes had been added years later so that careless people, caught on the small beach below during high tide, could climb to safety.

But how to get Creature to the hut? He had not been able to take more than a step or two across the dirt floor of the cabin. He fed himself, but only with food which had been presented to him. Yet, tonight's near miss had thrust the decision upon them all.

Somehow, Creature used the information in their minds to glean an accurate picture of the place and path.

"I can do this cliff path. But now, in the dark, before anyone sees us." Then he added with fierce resolve. "Or I must return to the lake, healed or not."

It was decided. It was done.

Slowly, with exhaustive effort, ever more frequent rests and moans of excruciating pain, the trio made their way from cabin to hut. Mother had gone ahead to lay a fire, prepare a pallet and bring up a sack of provisions, then returned to help Atynleigh guide and support Creature up, ever up.

"Child..." he had started once.

"Not now, Creature. We will talk when you are at the top."

But they had not talked then. Upon entering the hut Creature had collapsed half on and half off the pallet without word or sound of any kind.

Mother had insisted that both she and Atynleigh return to the cabin. After carefully tending the low fire and setting some dried fish within the reach of the lake man when — and if — he awoke, they returned to their home. They were in their beds just before daybreak, and still asleep at noon. During that entire time, a fog so thick it took one's breath away covered the entire cove, hiding both cabin and cliff.

That had been weeks ago, and now in the cold sunlight, Atynleigh ran toward the hut and the creature, who had become her friend.

Creature had risen clumsily from the rock upon which he had been sitting. The purplish scales of his face were gray at the tips and his jagged wound was a raw line that glowed white in the pale sun.

"I have rare medicine," Atynleigh said. "Mother trapped a beaver, and the musk glands have miraculous oils. She said you will feel the difference."

Atynleigh paused to look closely at the wound. It was raw, pink under pearl and as jagged as the thrust of the spear that he said had caused the near-fatal cut. Her hand moved close along its line but did not touch the fragile tissue. She sniffed at it.

"It doesn't smell. It is closing without infection."

"There is less pain. But the flesh is...stiff."

"That is how these things heal. We need to get you inside. Mother's salve will help."

Creature followed her into the hut and settled himself with a groan on a low stool.

"Let us see if this salve is the miracle Mother says it is."

She removed a pot of oily, amber-colored salve from her pack. It smelled strongly of musk and camphor. Her fingers took a dot of the thick gel from the pot and lightly moved it across the wound. Creature never moved, though she felt a long intake of breath through the gills on either side of his neck.

"Mother says you should feel a numbing tingle at first, but then relief. Do you understand?"

Creature nodded.

"She says it will speed the healing."

"That is good, child." He spoke these words in his whisper.

He always found Atynleigh's name to be too much a jumble of sound to attempt. She was just 'child' to him.

She put the pot of salve on the table. She had something she wanted to ask him.

"When my father was alive, he told me stories of the spirits that live in the great lake. He thought he saw you, or someone like you, once near the island at the west end of the lake. Father described a creature much like you."

"I seldom go to that island, but others like me find it comforting."

"Are there many of you?"

"Few. Fewer all the time."

"Are you the Spirit Animal that the tales talk of?"

"Spirit is too big a word. I am an animal, like you."

"I think you are the Spirit Animal of the fables." Atynleigh said this solemnly. She and Mother had talked about this. They were sure they knew who he was and much of what he was capable. "Do you bring the fish to our cove?"

"I can call them."

"We are grateful for that."

The creature did not smile, for his mouth was not capable of that, but Atynleigh felt a smile in what he said next, "Child, do you want to play the game? Or are we going to carve our own today?"

"Both. First we play."

In the days that had followed the difficult move to the cliff hut, while fall had inched toward early winter in the mountain community, Atynleigh and her Creature had started carving a new chess set, just for them.

The pieces were small, each one the length of one of Atynleigh's fingers. She fashioned the pieces as her father had, with curious little postures and attitudes. Her queen seemed worried and held her hand to her cheek. Atynleigh's king was vigilant, with a sword held across his knees. The bishops were looking for sin and sorrow with scowls on their faces.

Atynleigh had started not with any of these pieces, but with the knights. She knew they would be the hardest piece to capture, sitting on small, Nordic horses. They needed the extra width of the base of the precious walrus tusk, the last two her family had, so she began with her knights, and it was then that she made a stylistic decision that would affect every piece on the board.

She attacked the delicate ivory with purpose and precision. When she had finished the first knight, she held it out to Creature for inspection.

A bubbling sound much like a chortle came from Creature's throat.

He was looking at a chessman with the features of a man, riding a stout horse. But the eyes were remarkable. They were not the eyes of a man, but the round, bulging eyes of a fish, staring with a challenging intensity out of a human face. They were, unmistakably, the eyes of Creature, yet just human enough to make one assume that the carver either lacked skill or was making a joke.

Atynleigh and Creature's free time had passed in much this way — playing and carving. They were ready to start the last three pawns that stormy winter day. They would begin after they played their game of chess.

Perhaps it was the intervening slate of the hillside that interrupted Creature's sense of surrounding. Perhaps it was the soothing balm or strong camphor of the salve. Perhaps it was just his increasing contentment in Atynleigh's presence, or his intense efforts to expand the language between them, but Creature did not intuit the danger until it was too late.

The persistent stranger that had almost found them out in Mother's cabin had not forgotten his ill-treatment that night. When he received word of the abundance of fish on Mother's drying rack, he was certain that she knew more of the lake monster than she had shared. He had observed both the cabin and the hut from a distance. Smoke from the lofty cliff hut could not be explained save by the presence of an unknown. He had followed the daily trek of the child to the hut. And today he had chosen to make his secretive climb up the brushy, western side of the cliff. He would come upon them from the back side of the hill. If they ran down the eastern path, he could catch them easily — a young girl and lake man more used to water than land. The south side was an impenetrable tangle of brambles and berry bushes. North lay only the sheer drop to the lake, surely too great a fall with too shallow a bottom for even the creature to make that a viable choice. There would be no escape.

The stranger moved with cunning. As he raised his head above the slate rocks at the top of the cliff his presence became known in an instant but too late.

With a throaty hiss Creature rose with a speed that turned the inside of the hut into a shamble. The table, board and chessmen were overturned. Atynleigh's safety and escape became his only focus. Creature threw the door open and held it wide.

"Run, child."

Atynleigh understood a tone so forceful. She charged through the door and almost ran into the stranger as he appeared around the corner of the hut. He had a long knife in his hand and his instinct was to grab for the girl as she flew past him. His hand caught her sleeve and spun her to the ground.

That was his mistake.

"Monster," was the only word Atynleigh heard from the creature.

In the instant the stranger's attention had been turned to Atynleigh, Creature moved toward the assailant. He was slow but his bulk and returning strength were all he needed to grab the man's arm with one clawed hand, twisting it around his back and pushing him away from Atynleigh and toward the cliff.

At first the stranger tried to free himself, slashing backwards with the long knife. If any of the blows met flesh, they had no effect. Atynleigh was scrambling to her feet when she saw Creature straighten and twist hard on the man's arm. The bones of the stranger's arm cracked apart, followed by an anguished scream.

"Don't. Don't!" the man screamed, but Creature was pushing the evil presence steadily toward the cliff. At the edge of the precipice Creature lifted the stranger entirely off the ground.

With a mighty heave the stranger sailed off the cliff. A wailing cry followed his body down.

But there was still danger. Creature's efforts had brought him tottering too close to the edge. He reached out his right hand to steady himself on the single rocky protrusion near him. It should have been easy, but Atynleigh also saw the paroxysm of pain along the raw line of his wound. His arm reached out to steady himself on a rock, but the muscles contracted in pain, missing the rock. Gravity took Creature's body over the edge.

Atynleigh reached out to him in futile desperation. "No," she screamed.

She watched as Creature fell, haphazardly at first, then he straightened himself, arched his back, and rolled over. There was a shallow bottom to the cove here and he needed to enter at as horizontal a plane as possible while still cutting into the water. The impact was intense. She listened hard for one last thought, but if it was there, it trailed off before fully formed.

In the weeks that followed Atynleigh finished the chess set that she and Creature had made together. She and Mother played a single game with it, so that each piece knew its place and purpose. Then Atynleigh made a stone container of soft pumice and placed each piece carefully inside the hollow of it. She sealed the lid with wax and then made her way to the beach at the base of the cliff. On a thin strip of land well beyond the high tide line she buried the stone container deep in the soft sand.

"It is here," she said, "for us; a bridge across two lands."

For years, even after she grew to adulthood, with children and then grandchildren of her own, Atynleigh would come to this spot. She would sit near the chess set and talk to Creature, as though he were alive and lying in the shallows just off the cliff. Sometimes she was sure she could hear his soft words drift across the water to her. Always the same.

"Do good."

It is of note that for many years fish were a regular presence off the cabin by the great lake. It is also of note that the chess set was discovered hundreds of years after even Atynleigh's grandchildren had grown old and died. The Lewis Chessmen, as they are called, were found in 1831 on the shores of Lake Uig on the Isle of Lewis. They can now be seen in the British Royal Museum. They are beautifully carved, quite small, and have bulging, fish-like eyes.

L.A.W. Butler's story "Her Spirit Animal" was originally published in Metaphorosis on Friday, 17 June 2022. See magazine.metaphorosis.com

About the author

Louise Butler has most recently been published in *Utopia Science Fiction Magazine, Alien Dimensions, Metamorphosis, Cricket Magazine*, and *Chicken Soup for the Soul*. She was nominated for the Pushcart Prize by Copperfield Review. Butler specializes in both science fiction and historic fiction, both of which are engaging and fanciful while seated in solid research. With a background in both science and economics Butler likes data as much as chocolate and, like chocolate, thinks data is better when sweetened with a little imagination. Louise uses her love of research to indulge the story-telling inheritance of her Sámi ancestors.

We, You, and the Gallery

Alex Penland

We had thought ourselves safe, but then you found us in our little ship. There was a thrilling chase. In our desperation, we flew too fast and crashed, and you crashed too. Now we and you are both stranded on this empty, alien world. We do not know if you have survived. We know that only one of us remains, but we are still *we*, even when most of us are gone.

In your language, we believe, you sometimes say silence is *deafening*, but our experience is incongruous with that. The silence brings horrible clarity. In it, we are aware of the breathing which does not accompany our own, of the footsteps which do not fall around us, of the conversations which do not linger in our periphery. The silence is an illumination of all that we have lost.

We have buried the others by the cavern entrance. It is our hope that their decomposition will bring life to the dust of this barren world. Even near the subterranean spring there is nothing living here. No fish. No insects. No bacteria. Our scanners show a frustrating level of microbial safety.

●

It is there, by the spring, that we first speak to you. Your species needs water as desperately as ours does. Like us, you must have salvaged what you could from the wreckage and taken shelter in the caverns.

We do not know where you have hidden, but it's you who cries out —"Who's there?" — when we cause a thoughtless splash against the silence.

We are momentarily afraid, but we do not see you. The cavern is small; water rushes from one fissure into another. The only other point of entrance is the way from which we came. But for your voice, we seem to be alone.

"Where are you?" we ask. There are several sounds: one of your weapons firing, then the crumbling of rock, then a series of words my translator does not choose to divulge.

We think we understand. There is a phenomenon within caves: the chance alignment of reflective surfaces allows for sound to travel very far and very clearly. This must be the case now. You are not in the same cavern as we are; you might be miles away. You might be on the other side of the wall. There is no way of telling.

We test this by stepping briskly to the side. Your cursing fades to nothingness. When we return to the spot where we stood, your voice returns as well.

"It's a whispering gallery," we say into the anomaly. You stop shooting the walls.

"So you don't know where I am?"

"No."

"Great! So we can negotiate."

We're struck by your audacity. "Negotiate what?"

"Resources. Surrender. I don't know. How many of you are there?"

"We don't think we should say."

"Is that plural pronoun your hive-mind thing or does that mean there's more than one of you?"

We do not answer that.

"Well, assuming you're not alone, you got a resources issue. I got plenty of food, you know. Plus, I think I can get us outta here if you ask nice. You lot surrender and I'll get you a cushy cell 'til the war ends, I promise."

We do not answer that, either.

"Listen, it's better than dying out here, ain't it?"

"It is." We feel very alone. We wish desperately for our company, for the ability to talk this through together, but there is nothing to be done about that. "It is better than dying out here. Why would you bother to rescue us?"

This time you're the silent one.

"You need us alive," we say. "You need help too. We have no proof that you can help us. We have no proof that you will not slaughter us. So no, we do not surrender, and we will not tell you our location."

We step away from the gallery before we hear your reply. There is much to do; we have a ship to scavenge, inventory to document, plans to make. Possibly we have defenses to build. You are correct — we cannot survive here forever — but that does not mean we plan to die here, at either your hands or starvation's.

The room with the gallery is also the most defensible, and there is a nearby chamber that is cold enough for storage. We decide eventually to make this room our base, though during the process of moving supplies we make quite a lot of purposeful noise. You think we are numerous, after all.

Here it is dark and smells of sterile clay. Cool. Humid. The dead rock of the cavern is as much an absence as our silence. We ache for the fresh vegetation of home; the life in the air and the scent of the flowers.

But we cannot mourn. There is work to do.

●

Occasionally we see you. Once, while we deconstruct the refrigeration chamber in the wreckage of the ship, we spot your outline on a distant hill.

That night you say, "I saw one of you on the wreckage," and we reply that yes, you did, and hope you ask no further questions.

Once, when we venture out to scout a location for a distress signal, we find a machine of some sort, gathering sunlight. We steal it. That night you ask, "Did you steal one of my water purifiers?" and we reply that yes, we did.

Then we think it over. Perhaps you do not have the same access to water that we do. Perhaps you were unlucky. We feel a bit guilty. A few days later we return the machine without comment.

"What did you do to it?" you ask. We do not answer.

Once, we hear you crying.

We do not cry, though we have studied the phenomenon in school, so, although it takes a moment, we understand the sound. In your language, the convulsive gasp is a signal of despair. We do not think you meant to share it with us.

"Are you in distress?" we ask. You stop crying, or perhaps you move from the spot. You never respond to the question. We do not ask again.

●

One day we return to the wreckage site and you are standing there, arms crossed, waiting for us. You're male. Human, of course. Not as young as we thought you'd be, nor as well-armed. There's a pistol at your hip — it still smells of gunpowder from your duel with the cavern walls — but your ammunition belt is empty. Its grip is visible from your holster; the clip gauge on the side is blank. If you possess firepower, you possess only the shot in the chamber.

"Every time I see you out here, it's just you."

We are frozen to our location. We meet your eyes.

"You're alone, ain't you? You were lying. No one else survived the crash."

We hardly breathe.

"You had me pretty fooled. I was impressed." You hold out your hand. Are we supposed to shake it? We don't shake it. "I'm Edwin. You got a name?"

"Do your fingertips have names?" we ask. "Do your hands?"

"I call 'em Left and Right, generally. So... no? No name?"

"No name."

"Why do you say *we*?"

"Your hand is still your hand, even if we were to cut it from your body."

You nod. You glance behind yourself, back towards the way we suspect you came. "I'm gonna call you Honeybee."

"What?"

"You're a hive alien. You look like bees. You ever see a bee?"

"We are not a bee."

"I'm not saying you are. It's just a name. I gotta call you something. Like it or not, we're both stuck here."

We aren't opposed to names, really. Our opposition is to *you*, not your customs. Honeybee. Hm. "Are we? Didn't you say you had a way out?"

"Thought I did. Turned out I didn't."

"Hm." We lean next to you against the ship. "Neither do we. What was your plan?"

"Originally I was gonna steal components off your ship, but then you gave me back the water purifier." You sigh. "You ain't gonna surrender. I sure as hell ain't gonna surrender. So what now?"

"You have food, but no water?" we ask.

"Yup."

"We have water, but our food is running out. In our language, we say that it is better to die as a community than to live a longer life alone." By the odd look you give us, we suspect you understand the situational irony. "By this we mean that we risk a shortened life by offering to trust you, but if we rely only on ourself, our expiration date is certain."

You work through that for a moment. "You suggesting we share?"

"Yes. Return here tomorrow. We will bring you water."

"And then what?"

We shrug. "Show us your resources. Show us your ship. We're making the choice to trust you. Trust us in return, and we'll plan our escape together."

You look surprised, and a little wary, but you offer us your hand again. This time we do shake it.

"All right," you say. "Good to meet you, Honeybee."

"Good to meet you, Edwin."

●

This is what you possess: a truly massive cache of rations (roughly half of which are toxic to our biology, which makes division simple), three water purifiers, and half a ship. You do not have the same electrical and engineering knowledge that we do, and we suspect that you would simply have stranded us both if you tried to dismantle our ship to fix your own. You need us more than we need you, we think.

"There are elements we can work with," we say, perusing your technology, "but it's going to take a while. We'll be in a race for time with food."

"And by we, you mean you."

"Unless you can learn engineering on the fly." You laugh. "I have another job for you. As your rations consist of processed bars —"

"Don't give me that judgy tone."

" — *they cannot be farmed*, whereas our rations contain seeds, and likewise will rot sooner. We suggest that you attempt to farm some of our rations while we repair your ship, and that we subsist on your rations in the meantime. Our food grows quickly. It's meant for this exact scenario."

"We're repairing my ship?"

"Ours has been stripped more thoroughly. We believe yours is a more functional base." We replace the panel we were inspecting and stand to meet your eyes. "We are risking quite a lot to help you, Edwin. We understand that humanity is... individualistic..."

"We comprise individuals, yeah."

"And it is out of respect for you, as an individual, that we are trusting you will not make the same collective choice as your species."

You frown.

"Namely, that you will not choose war. That you will treat us, together, as a collective for the time being. Our good will be your good. Your good will be our good. We will become a community, not a pair of individuals at war."

"You know we have communities back home, yeah? I ain't unfamiliar with the concept."

"As far as we can tell, your hives are constantly in swarm."

You pause, then laugh. "Fair point. I won't screw you over. I'll even let you go free. When we get this fixed we head to the nearest neutral world and part ways. On my word, all right?"

We wince. We do not like the idea of landing on a neutral world, especially not alone. They are dangerous and unpredictable in their diversity. "Forgive us, please, but your word means very little. We will trust in cause and effect."

"What?"

"We will see what happens and how you react. We will see how you respond to the situation we have found ourselves in. As time passes, we will learn the mark you choose to leave upon the world. This is the information we need in order to determine the value of your word."

"Again — what?"

"Trust takes time, Edwin. We simply do not know you yet. This is a dangerous decision, but one we are making consciously. Do not attempt to put us at ease with promises we have no way of validating."

You shrug, scratch your neck, survey the desolation of our surroundings. "All right. Guess I can't blame you for that."

●

Time occurs. Days pass, then weeks. You are proving to be an adept farmer, particularly when faced with our fast-growing crops. Our rations are quick and hardy — they can be grown nearly anywhere, and the sweet resin which compacts them doubles as nutrition for whatever soil one can find. Like us, they are less tolerant to heat, but there is a cavern protected from the midday sun that still has some ambient light. We cart in sand from the surface.

The first harvest, one month in, allows us to set aside the remaining ration bars for an emergency supply. The second harvest, two weeks later, allows us to dry fruit for storage. By the third, we have more food than we can eat.

We begin to enjoy our meals together. At first, this is only in shared spaces — the ship, or sometimes outdoors when the weather is bearable.

Over time, however, you introduce us slowly to your space. You reveal that you have inhabited a cave on the far side of the hill. We suspect that you did not survey your surroundings when you crashed, but rather picked a direction to walk in and colonized the first cave you found. It is not nearby. It is not easily defensible. It is well-hidden, to your credit, but only because no tactical mind would choose to hide there.

We do not tell you this. Instead we express our honor when we are allowed to observe the mementos tucked beside your bed, the books piled in corners, the stringed instrument you rescued from the wreckage. It is not clean. The odor of your dirty laundry makes our antennae curl.

Yet you have built furniture: a desk, a lifted bed, storage in unexpected places. It is more confined than our cavern, but you have built an ingenious home in very little space. We are fascinated.

We are also often frustrated, though somehow not by you. When working, we are challenged by the incompatibilities between our two technologies. While hardware is obedient under the pressure of brute force, software is less pliable. Our universal translator is decidedly unhelpful when it comes to programming languages — as are you.

Today, as I swear at the translator, you don't offer to assist; you watch and laugh until we enter a command. The engine roars threateningly, which stops your teasing.

"Are you wasting fuel at me, Honeybee?"

"You can laugh, or you can help."

You're about to respond, but there's a jolt against the side of the ship that has nothing to do with software. You're at the window before we can turn around. The sand on the ground is blowing. The wind's picked up.

In the distance the air has begun to shimmer: heat. Intense, visible heat. You stick your head out the door to observe and burn your hand on the outer wall of the ship. A smell of singed flesh flashes through the bridge. Another untranslatable word — you duck back in.

"Hey, Honeybee, got a fun fact for ya. My life support's down."

"We are aware." We're trying to assess if we've fixed that yet. The translator is currently displaying the code in front of us as a list of various species of snake.

"Did you fix it?"

"We... aren't sure."

"You think we can make it to a cave from here?"

"We aren't sure, Edwin."

"Well, when you gonna know?" We open our mouth to respond. You don't let us say it again. "Right. Come on. We're making a break for the caves. Now."

We look up from the computer. You're holding out a hand, halfway out the door already.

"Come on. I ain't leaving without you."

"Is it close enough? Will we make it?"

"I ain't sure."

●

The storm is at our back. We try to fly you, to move more quickly, but our wings blister when they spread. When the pair of us dive into the caverns we are afraid, for a moment, that they will not provide adequate protection, but you drag us further below the surface and pat out the charring on our clothes. We press ourself against the cool ground and shiver. In your language you would say we are 'gasping for air'. We are not sure that this translates directly to our circulatory system, but the intent behind the words is accurate.

We suspect you are more resilient to heat than we are. You are leaning against the wall, sweating, breathing, staring at the inferno that rages outside.

It becomes slowly apparent to us that you have led us to our cave, not yours. It was the closer of the two dwellings; it was also a tactical mistake, to bring yourself to our territory. The action suggests trust. Behind the dull exhaustion of the heat, we are conflicted.

"Think we've figured out why nothing lives here, Honeybee."

We nod, still fragile from the storm.

"You all right?"

We haul ourself to a sitting position. It seems dangerous to tell you that we are vulnerable to temperatures — we do not know what information will be reported to your superiors. To risk our life is one thing; to put all of us at risk is another. And yet you chose our survival over your advantage.

"Bee, look at me."

But we are weak. We feel a strange, trembling headache, and our body is enervated. When we look at you we do not register your expression. When we fall, we do not register your catching us. The world fades.

●

There is a sound of rushing water.

We have cooled significantly. Before we open our eyes we can feel our hands and feet are submerged, though our body lies on cold stone. We realize what has happened — you have saved our life, at least temporarily. We had overheated; now we have cooled.

We have perhaps cooled too much. We sit up, slowly, battling the lethargy in our joints. Heat makes us weak; cold makes us heavy. Our blood feels like syrup in our veins.

You made a fire some time ago; it has now dwindled into embers. The smoke still trails along the ceiling, leaving chemical traces in the air. You yourself are currently sleeping on my bed, having covered yourself in empty ration canvas to keep in the heat from your warm-blooded body.

Unlike you, Edwin, we do not generate heat well. Our bodies are more vulnerable to environmental conditions. We need warmth. Unthinking, we crawl across the cavern — we do not have the strength to walk — and bury ourself in the bed beside you. When we rest our forehead on your back, you are like a lantern on a cold and unforgiving night. Then you turn in your sleep and wrap your arms around us, and the lantern blossoms into the sun.

●

When we wake again, you have rekindled the fire (we wonder how long you searched for our fire kit, how long it took you to recognize it for what it was) and you are cooking fruit on a griddle. The cavern smells like toasted sugar, tart and syrupy. We lay here quietly, watching the scene.

You do not seem alien to us in this moment. You are humming an alien tune, tapping the matte luster of your fingers on alien knees, but there is a familiarity in the domesticity of cooking. We are reminded of morning meals in the cafeteria hall, of baking and frying-up in our rotations of a dozen-or-so individuals. We are reminded of the easy chemistry between ourselves, of the casual warmth and connection of the collective.

We are momentarily and intensely homesick.

"Hey, Honeybee. You alive over there?"

You've noticed. We nod, reluctant to leave the lingering comfort of the bed. We think our thermoregulation has balanced itself, but this is comfortable, and we are very tired.

"You had me worried."

"We were very lucky you knew how to do first aid." We were, in fact, surprised. You knew to put our hands and feet in the water; if you had placed our body, as human anatomy directs, we would have drowned. "How did you know how to save us?"

"I'm military, Bee. We do get training."

"In human medicine, certainly. We are not human."

"We get alien basics, too. You know we've got some of you lot on our side, right? Defectors. Not everyone loves the hive."

The horror is plain on our face, or perhaps the despair.

"Don't look at me like that! We treat 'em right. If someone wants to be an individual, let 'em."

"We simply cannot imagine the desire." There is a spot near the fire where you have folded a mat for us to sit on, and we sit there now. "Having lost our connection to the hive, we cannot fathom the decision one must make to leave willingly. One would lose everything."

"How can you know that? You don't know their whole situation. You don't know what they've been through."

"We have lost everything, Edwin."

"Ah. Right. Sorry." You pause. "You ain't alone. Uh. Lost my own family to a hive attack."

"Did you?"

"It was years ago, so... You know. War's not... great."

You clear your throat uncomfortably. I change the subject.

"Arrowfruit tastes quite good when paired with redspice."

"What?"

"What you're cooking. Arrowfruit. We believe there is some redspice left in the stores —"

"That's what, the red powder?"

"Purple, actually. The name misleads."

We retrieve the bag, and the pair of us begin to cook together.

●

That first day of the storm, once we have eaten and checked the status of the weather, we take stock together of what we possess.

There are enough rations to get us through quite some time. Together we venture closer to the entrance to check on the crops; their cavern is much warmer than it has been previously, but not so warm as to cause them harm. We have water from the spring. We are not sure how long the storm will last, but our basic needs for survival are met.

Next, comfort. We are in our own territory, but you only have what you've carried in your bag. It is admittedly heavy, but it is always on your person and you tend to carry your tools with you: a small multi-device you call a *pocket knife*, extra rations in case you were to become stuck somewhere for a while, and most importantly a spare set of clothes.

You chuckle at our visible relief. "What, you don't like how I smell?"

"We were taking into consideration that your living quarters smell quite strongly of human body odor."

"It's not like I got a shower in there!"

"And do you have a similar excuse for your ship?" Our antennae curl. "We understand that you have a dulled sense of smell. We can forgive that. We're simply appreciative that we won't have to live with it."

"It ain't that bad."

"Not to you."

You also have a deck of playing cards.

You attempt to teach us the game of *poker*, which does not go particularly well. When you run out of the pebbles you've insisted on gambling with, we offer you some of ours. We receive in turn a lecture on how we are missing the point, to which we reply we have clearly won the game and ask how much of the point we can possibly be missing, and it is at this point that you decide to find a project rather than a game to play.

The phrase in your language is *sore loser.*

You decide to 'spruce up' our living space, starting with the bed. We have been sleeping on a pile of mats, which is quite comfortable, but —

"Listen, if I'm staying here, I ain't sleepin' on the floor. I'm making you a bedframe."

Implicit in this decision is the implication that we will be sharing a bed again. We are not sure how we feel about that assumption. Certainly it was comfortable. Certainly you did not kill us in our sleep, or in our illness, and you had the chance to do so. Your gun lies near the cavern entrance, a single shot still loaded in the chamber.

And yet we wonder whether bed-sharing contains the same implications for you as it does for us — do your people cluster the way we do? Do your people bond together, form lifelong connections? Or are your romances as individualistic and flighty as the rest of your culture? Are you, Edwin, like the rest of your people? Is there even something that can be defined as 'the rest of your people'? Are we simply overthinking things?

"We are not ectothermic," we explain eventually, watching you consolidate supplies and tear apart crates. "We are capable of sleeping alone if you wish to bed down elsewhere."

You shrug. "It's no bother."

"Are you sure?"

" 'Course."

And the matter is settled.

●

On the second day of the storm, we teach you our games. We spend some time carving a set of horribly unbalanced dice from spare parts of the bed project, then show you how to use them. You enjoy dare-dice best, where we take turns suggesting a task and then roll to see who must perform it.

The game is generally used to allocate horrible chores back home, but we are stuck in a small and mostly-featureless room, and so dares quickly become questions.

We begin to learn about each other.

The weirdest thing you've ever eaten: sawdust, when you were in particularly dire straits on a survivalist training exercise.

The most memorable dream we've ever had: it occurred the night before we began our military training, when we dreamed we were a comet sailing peacefully through the universe. When we awoke, we had a distinct memory of a bright light on a horizon that could not have existed, and a longing for understanding that would never come.

Your childhood dream: you wanted to be a space pirate.

Our favorite color: starlight. Pale and shining flecks against the black.

Your most embarrassing moment: you were a child. Your older sister once called you *Ed-lose*, and it upset you so much you cried and threw up your dinner. You no longer speak with your sister, but you insist that is not the primary reason.

You ask us what we would have done if we had not joined the military, which is confusing. Then it occurs to us that you believe that soldiers are different from ordinary citizens. We find this disheartening. If your citizens are not the same as those who fight, and your people are individuals, how can you truly understand the cost of war?

"Maybe," you say. "But I think if I weren't in the military I'd be something real dull, which, well, I guess some people might want to do that with their lives."

"Why was this the life you chose?" we ask, abandoning the dice. "Why would anyone choose war?"

You're quiet about that for a while, leaning back against the cavern wall. For a little bit the only sounds are those of the subterranean spring and the distant chaos of the storm. We allow you your time to think, observing you instead. We have become familiar with your face, with the softness of your body. Your appearance has begun to bring us comfort, and that is a frightening thing.

We wonder if perhaps others have not abandoned their communities, but simply chosen new ones.

"I didn't really choose it," you admit. "The military's a shit job, so people in shit situations are the ones who sign up. You get a good deal — good money, good education, good place to lay your head. I didn't have any of that when I signed up. I do now. Not sure it's worth the golden chains, though."

"Do you regret it?"

"I did." There's an invisible edge to your answer, somehow. Something clinging behind the words, something which makes our back flutter, which brings a shiver to our fingertips.

We lean forward. "Do you regret it now?"

"You know, Honeybee? I ain't sure."

●

The storm rages on. Days blend together. Time passes.

At night we sleep encircled in the safety of your arms. At first we refuse to talk about this during the day, but then you put your arm around us in a moment of sympathy, and we lean our head on your shoulder, and the physical barrier is broken. What was relegated to sleep becomes common. We sit together. We eat together.

We are no longer alone.

●

We are awoken by a faint and repeated alarm. We roll over, bleary, to ask you if you recognize the signal. You are not there.

We sit up. We are surprised and a little confused.

The situation makes more sense once we realize the noise is coming from the whispering gallery, and once we realize we can no longer hear the storm outside. It is one of your devices, then, and the world outside is safe for passage. You have returned to your cavern to retrieve it. There is nothing suspicious or unexpected about that.

And so we take the time to think.

This bond we've formed with you, whatever it may be — we know it's doomed. We asked you to consider our pair as a community, and while we meant that, it was not intended to be mutual. For us to consider you the same is —

It's dangerous. There is no other word for it. We do not part from our community, and upon leaving we must part from you. You have shown no inclination towards joining our hive; we cannot bear to join your swarm. There is no future in which we stay together.

And yet we lie back down and soak in the warmth you left behind. The echo of footsteps that are not there have grown softer in your presence. The silence is no longer intrusive. We cannot deny the change.

Last night you placed your hand on our chest and asked us where our heartbeat was. When we didn't know what you were talking about, you placed *our* hand on *your* chest in demonstration. We laughed; we told you how we have a dozen small hearts down our abdomen, explained our circular breathing. Wasn't that covered in your training? But you say you only learned the protocol, not the biology.

You placed your hand upon each heart of ours and felt its rhythm. You called us fascinating. You called us beautiful.

Love is a state of neutrality in the hive. We are always perfectly in sync; it is the glue which seals our metaphorical cells, a propolis of the soul. We join sometimes — mostly in twos, sometimes more — but to do so is to entwine two threads within the greater aegis of the soul. Beautiful, yes, divine, but not a source of conflict.

We are accustomed to love, accustomed to connection, and yet somehow entirely unsettled by the feelings you inspire in us. When we speak, we argue as much as we admire; when we fight we are drawn together more than we are repulsed. Everything you are opposes the virtues we were raised on, and yet this only seems to draw us closer.

We asked you, yesterday, what your greatest childhood fear had been. You said: us. The hive. We were the ones who killed your family. (Just as you killed ours. We have forgiven, not forgotten.) But you are no longer afraid.

We are. We are terrified.

We do not want to leave this community.

We do not want to leave you.

●

We have drifted back to sleep again. This time we are awoken by your distant voice, and this time you are not alone.

"Sorry," you say through the gallery echo, "I didn't quite catch that. Can you state your name and ID again?"

"This is Jeffrey Reynolds, ID 809192-9."

"Hey there, Jeff. Good to hear your voice, it's been a hot minute out here."

"We got your distress call, Ed. What happened? We thought you were a goner."

"Oh, nothing too special. Took a dumb chance chasing some..." You hesitate. We know your language. We can hear the habitual use of *bugs* on your lips, and we hear you repress it. "Took a dumb chance on a chase and we both crashed."

"Any bugs get out?"

You hesitate. We understand. You can tell them we all died, and we would be safe. We could leave on the repaired ship and this man could send rescue for you. But we suspect you want us to defect, that you do not want to part ways either. You will want to know what our options are.

"Yeah," you say. "The crash didn't get 'em all. But don't you worry, we're all gettin' on good. Say Jeff, you know how the asylum process works? Think I'd be able to offer my friends here a deal?"

"Sure, probably. Citizenship in exchange for time served against the Hive. Standard." We can hear the disgust in your friend's tone. "Sure happy to turn a blind eye if you squash the bastards before we get there, though. All those legs. Ugh. Freaks me out."

"Well, guess we have differing opinions on that." Your voice has gone cold, polite. "What would asylum look like?"

"Can't say as for sure, man. Tell you what, send me your coordinates and I'll make sure there's a specialist on board, huh? Give 'em a good deal?"

"Certainly." You pause again. "Uh, you know what, Jeff, I gotta go find those coordinates exactly, they're still on my ship. I'll get 'em back to you soon, yeah?"

"You don't have them with you?" Jeff's surprise is warranted. You absolutely have them with you. You are likely looking at them, taped to your cavern wall, right in your eyeline. "Right. Yeah. Sure. You can leave the signal on too and we can track —"

There is an audible click.

"Turned it off," you say. "I can't bear that guy. You catch all that, Honeybee?"

"We did."

We are aware you could have deceived us. We can think of a dozen ways that conversation could be faked, and a dozen reasons why. We think of the round you left in the chamber. The gun is with us now; you did not bring it with you when you went to answer the call.

You are an individual; this does not mean your choices are selfish. You have chosen only once to cause us harm, before you knew us. You have kept us safe a dozen times since. Time has passed, and we have seen the mark you choose to leave upon the world.

We pick up your weapon and turn it over in our hands. It has never been used for violence against us. You are the only thing which has been profaned in such a way.

We say: "We do not wish to join your military."

"I know, Honeybee. Just wanted to know what our options were." You exhale. "I don't want to fight my people either."

"And similarly, you would be required to if you joined us."

"Of course." You're quiet again for a moment, thinking. "Before we make a decision, we should check the ship. See what damage the heat did. See if we have any other choice, you know?"

●

We stand together in front of the ship.

It's fine.

It's absolutely fine.

Our ship — that is, the hive ship — has melted irreparably. It is a twisted and deformed hunk of metal and wax, a final monument to those of us who died in its crash. Eventually, future storms will smear it across the face of the planet, and it will be gone forever.

But your ship? Your ship is pristine.

"How?" you ask. We are already climbing in through the hatch, assessing. "What did you do to it? It looks better than when we left it —"

"It's not better," we say, "but it appears we did, in fact, fix the life support before the storm hit. The interior was able to protect itself. We had also connected our shields with yours, and that seems to have been a miraculous success, though it's built to withstand far more intense heat on atmospheric interaction."

"Well, that's good."

"In fact," — we peer out from the hatch again — "we think our work is done."

"Done?"

"Done. Complete. The ship is low on fuel, there are a dozen bugs in the software, but we believe a trip to the nearest neutral planet would be viable."

You're staring at us.

"Edwin?"

"So that's it?" you ask.

"What?"

"You're leaving?" There's a panicked shiver to your voice.

"We didn't say that. We said the ship is viable. We..." We leave the words unspoken. We aren't sure what we were going to say, anyway. "There are decisions to be made, that's all."

"Yeah." You glance up at the sky. It's brightening; a brilliant blue after the firestorm.

We hesitate before speaking again. "We do not wish to part ways, Edwin."

You exhale. "No. We don't."

"And yet we don't wish to fight our own people."

"No, we don't."

We sit on the ground, leaning against the ship, looking out at the wasteland that has become something like a home. Your breathing is slow and even; mine is a low hum against a background breeze. Our hands brush accidentally. We exchange a glance of quiet desolation.

"We wonder when you started referring to us as a plural."

You roll your eyes.

"You think of us as a pair."

"Yeah, I do. Don't you?"

We close our eyes, thinking of our past pairings, thinking of the hive. We nod. We think perhaps that the two of us are more a pair than any other person we have loved. It is a dangerous thought.

"Listen," you say, "I don't know how they do this in the hive. I don't know if you just... love free, or only love your queen, or how it works, but humans, when we choose someone else — Well, we got a thousand different ways to fall in love, but where I'm from it's usually just... We pick the other individual we love best, and we make our choices from there."

To be loved best seems impossible. One is not meant to be loved best. One is meant to sacrificed for all, not sacrificed for. The image of the pair of us in our patchwork ship, running from our people, hiding out in the wild diversity of the neutral planets — it surfaces in our mind and we cannot dislodge it.

We imagine what it would be like, to travel the stars and trust only in each other. We imagine love rife with conflict and passion. We imagine life, free and forlorn but never lonely.

Never lonely. Not with you.

We cannot bear to open our eyes, to see the look upon your face. Perhaps it is not as desperately fond as your voice; perhaps there is not the same helpless affection. Perhaps you are lying. We could not survive it, if you were lying. We have changed too much by loving you to be the person that we were.

"And sometimes that individual changes, Honeybee, I won't lie about that. But I don't know you as the collective, right? I know you as Honeybee. And Bee, I love you best. Easily. I love you best."

We open our eyes. You are not lying. We reach out to clean the tears from your cheek. Our hand is unsteady.

"I can't fight 'em," you say, "but I can't go back, either. If we don't want to split up, if you'll have me..."

"This is our collective," we whisper. "Us."

We have buried the others by the cavern entrance. Our hive seems very far away, and you are close, and you are also fascinating, and you are also beautiful.

"Us," you say.

It is dangerous, and perhaps it is ill-advised, but you never send the coordinates to your superior. Instead, we make our preparations. You harvest the last of our crops: a bit dry, a bit small, but survivors of the storm. We gather a list of neutral planets — an eclectic bouquet of utopias and university worlds, of war-torn dust-traps and regressed historical inaccuracies, of oceans and jungles and constructed habitats. They are unpredictable, but so are you. Perhaps unpredictable does not always indicate danger.

Our first task is to repair our ship beyond a state of limping; after that, we will take to the void. We will have our choice of worlds; we will have our choice of stars.

When the time comes, we chart our course and leave.

We leave together.

●

On an abandoned, uninhabitable planet, there are several shallow graves. There is, for now, the wreckage of a single spaceship, slowly deteriorating in a harsh and unforgiving climate. In the myriad caves below the surface, there are wild fruits which drink from natural aquifers. They can be found safe in the shade, growing wherever the last traces of light will touch them.

There is a cavern. In it are the scattered traces of habitation; a charred fire pit, broken boards, a bed which was gratefully abandoned. On the wall, we have carved one message in two languages. The engravings are side by side.

We have written:

"In this place, violence was supplanted by love. May the universe share our same conclusion."

Below our message, you have fired a single shot into the wall.

●

Alex Penland's story "We, You, and the Gallery" was originally published in Metaphorosis on Friday, 20 January 2023. See magazine.metaphorosis.com

About the author

Alex Penland is a former museum kid. They spent their childhood running rampant through the Smithsonian museums, which kicked off an early career as a child adventurer. Alex has worked in the field with NASA scientists, linguists, and acclaimed photographers. Now a Pushcart-nominated author, Alex currently lives in Scotland while studying for a PhD in Creative Writing at the University of Edinburgh. They still run rampant, but they've breached the Smithsonian's containment.

www.AlexPenland.com, @AlexPenname

Holding On

Justen Russell

I was eight years old when Yuri Zhilin floated away.

Yuri, the first man to orbit Io; the first human to walk on Ganymede. Replacing the lens of the JUVENTAS orbital telescope was supposed to be a routine procedure. Something done a half-dozen times with a half-dozen other telescopes around the closer planets and their moons. It wasn't even the first untethered spacewalk over Jupiter; Mimi Lin had beaten him to that almost a year earlier.

Still, I *had* to watch. It was Yuri.

I'd sucked up to José all week so we could watch the broadcast together on his father's new omniscreen. At that resolution we could count the stitches under Yuri's ROSCOSMOS badge — four: one for each planet he had orbited. Of course, I was more interested in his hair. Six long, straw-blond strands had escaped the bun on the back of Yuri's head and, without gravity to restrain them, they danced. Hairs just like mine.

Before his spacewalk, Yuri gave a tour of the capsule where he and Mimi had spent the past seven years. He showed the workstations filled with experiments, the sleeping harnesses, and what counted as a toilet in zero g. "Study hard, earthlings," he said in his thick Russian accent, "and you can be like us." José and I, we believed him too.

At the cockpit, Mimi Lin waved for the camera and, for perhaps the first time in my life, I understood what it meant to be jealous. I would have given anything to be her then, to have floated next to Yuri just once.

While he suited up, Yuri explained in Russian the purpose of everything he would wear. Gloves, belt, boots, I caught the main words — just not the small ones in between. José and I would use those same words when we played to make it more authentic. Like it was possible for us to work for ROSCOSMOS too.

Yuri's helmet had its own internal camera and when he put it on, his face appeared as a small inset in the bottom right-hand corner of our screen — smiling as always. He blew a kiss to the Earth, then pushed himself towards the airlock.

Ten meters of open space separated their capsule from the orbital telescope. Any closer and the protective magnetic field of their spacecraft would have damaged the satellite's delicate sensors. Ten meters exactly — no give or take. Mimi Lin held them in perfect alignment.

Yuri had one hundred and eighty-nine successful spacewalks on his record. I knew that number by heart. It was twenty-six more than Mimi Lin. It was nearly double the third place. One hundred eighty-nine times, Yuri Zhilin had stepped out into the void, then on the one hundred and ninetieth his mind shut down.

I could tell something was wrong the moment he pushed off, even before his arms started to flail, even before his legs started to kick. His eyes, so clear in that ultra-high definition inset in the bottom right corner of our screen, went blank. Yuri was no longer there.

With a forty-three-minute speed-of-light delay, there was nothing anyone on earth could do except watch. Whatever would happen already had. Mimi Lin had left the cockpit and hesitated at the airlock; she had suited up, calculated trajectories, and then suited back down. Twenty minutes before we watched Yuri kick off, she had concluded what we were about to: Yuri Zhilin was already gone.

'Space Sickness', the TV commentator explained after the 'live' broadcast cut out. It would become the new word of the summer. 'A rare catatonic response to stimulatory overload in high stress situations.' It was nearly unheard of among professional astronauts, but everyone knew they were the minority in space. Among the asteroid miners and orbital laborers — well — no one kept statistics on them, but 'Space Sickness', we would learn, probably claimed more than half. Outer space was littered with the bodies of those who couldn't quite hold on; usually, they were not broadcast for the whole world to see.

●

My mother named me Laika after the Russian dog that went to space. I think she meant it to be aspirational. *A stray who made it to the stars.* No one ever told her that the dog died on the way up. No one tells a woman like my mother things that might ruin her smile.

She left Quito for Manta when they started building the elevator. It was a good time to be a woman with a smile like hers. The streets there were full of contractors, astrophysicists, and astronauts, all with good jobs and full pockets. Back before the gated communities went up, and Manta became another Quito on the sea. Even Yuri passed through on his way up.

She said my father was an astronaut named Mudak. She used to tell me he was where I got my blonde hair. There is no way she could have known for sure — there were a lot of blond foreigners in Manta — but if I was going to have a fake father, he might as well have been an astronaut.

I always knew there was a real Mudak — whether he was my father or not. My mother could not have made up a name like that. See, people did not tell my mother things, but they told me. Things like 'Laika died on the way up' and 'a mutt's name suits a *mulatta* like you'. Things like 'you know *mudak* means testicle in Russian, right?'.

Mudak is like calling someone an asshole. *Mudak* is calling someone a jerk. Usually, *mudak* is what you call a person you don't like, but sometimes Mudak is how another *mudak* introduces his friend when they are trying to be funny and don't want to give a real name to the smiling girl.

I don't know if Mudak really was an astronaut, or if he just wanted to see more than a smile. I don't know if he really was my father, or just the best *mudak* around the right time. All the men my mother smiled at were *mudaks*, but if she had any regrets, she never told me. The *mudaks* kept us fed. At least, they used to.

I never had a smile like my mothers, even before I lost three teeth fighting over something silly like my father and his name, but that did not matter, because I was going to space. Sometimes after I fought, I would tell my mother I had tripped; that I wasn't meant for gravity. She liked that too. "Just like your father," she would say, and I think she meant it — not like the other mothers. The ones who say, "Yes darling, someday you will have a mansion on the hill," because they know that the day their child finally understands, she will have grown up and no longer needs her mother.

For my mom, there was always something romantic about the elevator. It was never just another feature along the horizon. The wind turbines, the luxury cruise liners, the mansions on the hill — those were meant for *mudaks* and not for us. The mutt never gets invited inside, but there is room for her on a rocket, if she isn't concerned about coming back.

●

In the morning, when the sun shone from the east and the sky was clear, you could see the elevator — a thin, silver thread reflecting the light, stretched taut from heaven to horizon. At night, some trait of the filament in the upper atmosphere caused it to glow — the *equatorial aurora* — and a dancing line of green and purple floated in front of the stars. Most of the time, however, the cable itself was too far away and too thin to see.

Only the crawlers were visible when, for José's tenth birthday, his father drove us to San Mateo, where the cliffs overlooked the ocean. Before the elevator, he'd read, astronauts used to train on special parabolic flights. Ones that fly high in the sky then nose-dive straight down so the passengers inside can feel what it is like to be without gravity. They still did, I told him, just as children, not astronauts-to-be. The first time Yuri floated was at a birthday party where the parents had rented a parabolic plane; but our cliffs would be just as good.

"We will float for two whole seconds," José said. He had done the math and knew that part for sure. "Just like Yuri," he added for me.

We raced up the cliffs, each of us eager to be the first to jump, but in the end, it was José's birthday and I let him win. Only, after he leapt, I didn't; I couldn't.

I remember wanting to. I had been excited, even as José's scream echoed off the water below. But then I walked to the edge to make sure the landing was clear. I don't remember if it was. I just remember how much taller that cliff looked from the top, and how very, very far away the ocean seemed.

José hollered for me to jump. Then, he climbed back up and tried to convince me that it would be okay. It wasn't me that needed convincing, it was my legs; they wouldn't co-operate. They wouldn't step. I wanted to jump. At least, I wanted to *have* jumped, but I couldn't make myself approach that void.

When he could wait no longer, José left me there. He jumped again, and again, and again — and I didn't.

Each time, José was fine. It was me, still at the top, who was broken. I had to climb back down the way I had come up.

José didn't yell at me for ruining his birthday. He pretended we had both had fun, but I cried that night because I knew I would never be a Yuri, or a Mimi — or even brave like my mother when she left everything she had known for a new city. I would never be able to jump.

The next morning my mother wiped away my tears and marched me all the way back to the cliffs. It took hours to get there on foot, but she said, "Trust me." And I did.

We climbed the rocks together — slowly this time — and she stood with me at the top, all the way back from the edge. She said, "Sometimes, when you know what you have to do, it is better not to look." Then she grabbed my hand and said, "Close your eyes," and we ran. We didn't look and we didn't stop, we just fell off the edge of the world, and for two full seconds we were weightless in the air.

I jumped off the cliff a second time, and third, and a fourth — until my mother said we had to go back because the sun would soon disappear. It was easier every time. By the end of the day, it no longer mattered if I ran or if I looked. My legs kept working.

My mother laughed the whole way home — about the way I had screamed in the air, about the way my arms and legs had flailed when I fell. It didn't matter; I had jumped. I laughed about my flailing arms too.

Her smile always made everything okay. I wish I could have learned to smile like my mother, to have given that back to her just once before I left.

●

'Study hard, earthlings,' Yuri had said, 'and you can be like me.' José, maybe; he had it all planned out, every step required for a documented position at the top. Scholarship to a secondary school on the hill, two years of college outside Manta, engineering degree from the University in another three. He would never be an astronaut — ROSCOSMOS didn't scout for people like us — but he could get up the elevator, so long as his father sold their house to afford tuition. It wouldn't be grades that held him back.

My mother didn't have a house to sell. She had a smile, and every year, it seemed, fewer and fewer men smiled back. Maybe it was the whisper of wrinkles around her eyes, or maybe just the way a city changes, but my mother had started smiling at men she would have never smiled at before. Men who were not good to be around when the smiling stopped.

I used to dream that someday she would only need to smile at me. I would come back and look after her the way she had looked after me; we would hold on together. I knew it would never happen. The best I could dream was that she would no longer need to look after me — a girl who would never smile like my mother could.

I started standing at the docks near the unemployed women and men, waiting for my way out. While José was studying, and the children on the hill played, I pretended I was watching the elevator; but I liked to go best when the weather was bad, when even the crawlers were hard to see.

The docks were less crowded when it rained, and I would think, *Maybe if there is no one else, someone will choose me.* If a boat came by looking for workers, I would puff out my chest and stand on my toes to look strong and tall. Then, I would keep staring where the crawlers should be, even as the boat left.

That is why Belen chose me. She was looking at the elevator too.

"We'll get close enough to touch it," she told me. "If that's what you want." She was tall, and far too thin, with dark curly hair and a frown that said she understood.

She told her captain she'd chosen me instead of a big man with arms the size of tree trunks because, "She'll eat less." He shrugged and wiped the rain from his bald head, then told us both to help him unload.

I'd gotten lucky. You have to get lucky to make it to space. Even Yuri was a backup on his first mission, until the main pilot caught the flu. Before that he was just a *mudak* looking up.

●

From the shore, the wind turbines had always seemed small. Like the yachts and mansions that also decorated the horizon, they were just toys. Simulacra that filled the ocean between the mainland and the Galapagos, sprouting from the water like reeds in a pond. I used to think, *How can those hoist ten-tonne rockets into space?*

On the rusted *Buena Mañana*, as we floated directly beneath one, the sun flickered in the shadows of its whirring blades, each two hundred meters across. I was almost afraid to see the elevator the same way; afraid and excited. It would be real then. Would I still be willing to leap?

"Mussels will grow anywhere," Belen told me, as she zipped the wetsuit up to my neck. "Hanging out here, where there are no starfish or crabs, they get big."

The elevator had dispensed with the need for rocket fuel — at least at launch — but the crawlers that climbed along it needed energy to reach space. Energy supplied by the wind through those turbines and the massive electric cables that stretched out between them under the sea. As Belen explained, there were mussels growing in long, cylindrical nets called *socks* that dangled all along each cable's length.

"Haru buys them as *seed*," she said. That's what you call juvenile mussels, when they are just large enough to start clumping together — about half the length of a fingernail — mussel seed. Any smaller and they would slip right through the mesh of the *socks*.

"Nine months after we hang them, they are big enough to harvest," Belen said. "That's where we come in. Someone needs to dive down and hook the *socks*, so the crane can haul them up. Don't worry; you'll love it. The open ocean is just like outer space."

She had helmets to make me believe her. Tucked in a locker along the side of the fishing trawler were eight flawless, glassy orbs. Space helmets, exactly as I had seen them in countless magazines and low res-feed. Helmets just like Yuri's, save, of course, the ROSCOSMOS lettering.

"They used to make them in Manta," Belen said, "so, we find plenty floating out here. They work the same in zero bar or ten, so might as well use them diving."

"They float?"

"Would you believe that some people try to ride up outside the elevator with just a helmet and an air tank?" Belen said. "I don't know what they think they'll do after they make it to the top." She chose a small helmet for me to try on. "When they are sitting up there in outer space in a t-shirt and shorts, but they never make it that far anyway. Not with a diving regulator connecting the helmet to the tank."

The helmet felt tight around the neck, but Belen seemed happy with that. "A good seal," she said, "will keep the water out. But a diving regulator," she clipped the helmet in place, "that's what puts air there in the first place. It *regulates* how fast air comes out of the tank. It's designed to match the pressure around it. That way you can breathe when the weight of the entire ocean is trying to squeeze you. In higher pressure water, it delivers higher pressure air.

Thing is, at least for the people trying to ride on top of a climber, when there is no pressure around it, a diving regulator won't deliver any air at all... or maybe the valves freeze?" She hesitated, trying to figure out exactly how someone would die in her hypothetical. "Either way, no air. They pass out halfway up and fall. The water around us is littered with their bodies, and their helmets."

"How *do* you make it up then?" I asked.

"That's the silly part," Belen said. "They want us up there — the companies at least. Nothing is locked. If you pick the right crawler, you can seal yourself inside and ride all the way to space. Most of the floaters out here never had a plan, and never had a chance. But us — it'll be different for us."

I didn't miss her choice of words: *us*.

"From up close, we'll be able to read the logos," Belen said, choosing a helmet for herself. "The mining crawlers are the good ones. Anglo American, Ferrobras New Horizon, Objectif Outre-Terre. The last few times it's been NASA and CNSA. Can't stow away with astronauts."

It hadn't occurred to me to be picky about what spaceship I ended up on. "Why not?" I asked.

"Pick the wrong crawler and it's out the airlock," Belen snapped her fingers, "like that!" Then she laughed. I couldn't tell if she was serious or not.

●

If anything, the ocean was the opposite of space. At least, the opposite of what I expected space would be. Space was open. Space was empty. Whenever Yuri left his capsule, every star had been visible from light-eons away. The ocean was full.

A blue-green haze swallowed everything around me. It took all that I had to stay calm. Less than a meter away, Belen faded into the murk until the shadow of her shadow was all that remained. The boat above us disappeared and then there was nothing. Nothing above; nothing below. Nothing but blue-green.

We descended further, the water getting darker as well as cloudier until I couldn't see my hands, my breathing getting shallower and faster until, as if by magic, the water cleared. There was a line, turbid above, clear beneath. The lower edge of a vast, undersea cloud.

A little further still and the open, empty darkness was not quite so empty. Something was there in the black; the cable, dark and thicker than I could wrap my arms around. It stretched as far as I could see in either direction. All along its length hung the socks, tall, mesh cylinders bulging with fist-sized mussels.

One after another, we harvested and replaced. Belen showed me how to attach the hook of the crane to the loop of a sock, and how to signal to Captain Haru it was ready to be lifted. Then we waited as the sock ascended, pulled up into the undersea cloud. I could imagine, just as easily, that it fell — plummeting into the thick atmosphere of some gassy moon I was orbiting. In the dark, open depths, there was no up or down; I was weightless. Belen had been right, I loved it.

When the replacement sock came, she showed me how to guide it gently to the cable. Since it was mostly empty, with just a smattering of mussel seed, it was easy to pull around. We lined the ends up so that one draped over each side of the cable. Belen let me unhook the crane and connect it to the next sock.

As I floated, waiting, I imagined I was Yuri outside his spaceship for the first time. I exhaled, and the bubbles streamed up from somewhere near the back of my helmet. I watch them dancing their way to the surface, imagining they were stars.

That was all it took. A moment of distraction.

It was just a light bump as I drifted past one of the dangling socks. Something caught. A valve on my tank, or a clasp on my wetsuit. I couldn't swim away. I couldn't turn. I couldn't move.

In that moment I realized just how very, very far I was below the ocean's surface. Underwater, I couldn't have called to Belen if I had thought to, but I didn't think. *If you know what you have to do…* fighting panic, I put my feet against the sock… *it is better not to look…* I kicked off as hard as I could. The only way to get free. Something shifted inside the sock, and for a moment I moved forward. Then it pulled back twice as hard.

I wheezed. The full weight of the sock and all its mussels slammed against me, knocking the air from my lungs. I coughed, trying to find my wind. I coughed on water.

Water!

I hadn't heard my helmet crack, but water was seeping in. A slow, cold trickle. I moved my head. A stream of bubbles ran towards the surface. Water flooded past my chin. There was nothing I could do. My arms flailed. My legs kicked. I tried to lift my head; anything to keep my mouth above the water. It surged past my ears. I gasped and choked on salt.

A firm hand grabbed my shoulder. Belen! I grabbed back and pulled, together we could... she kicked me, hard. What little air I had left bubbled out of my nose.

Another blow. Belen pinned me with her bodyweight, holding me down. Drowning me. I tried to fight. Tried to push off her. Then, in one, firm motion, she grabbed my helmet and twisted. The water stopped seeping in. Only the seal had broken. She held me as, with the regulator, she purged air back into the helmet. She continued to hold me until I stopped struggling, until my breathing returned to normal. Until I was calm.

With her hand on mine, Belen guided my hand to the single loop of netting that had tangled around a valve of my air tank. She made me work it free from the sock. Then we ascended together slowly, her guiding me firmly the whole way to the top.

"You panicked," Belen said back at the surface, back on the *Buena Mañana*.

"I — I was drowning."

"Divers get tangled. Helmets come loose. But, if you had stayed calm ..." she frowned. "It's panic that kills, down here and up above."

I wanted to cry.

"You're learning," she said, more gently. "Next time you'll do better."

"N — Next time?" I was shivering, even though I wasn't cold.

Belen wrapped her arm around my shoulder. "Do you know why they want us up there — the orbital companies?" She wiped a tear from my cheek. "Truth is, you can't stow away without someone noticing. We'd never even make it onto the crawler of a research ship, but the mining ships, they want us. Not because we'll work hard, because we're disposable. Everything up there is dangerous. They only *hire* people for the safest jobs. A stowaway gets drilled through by a micrometeorite, there is no paperwork. Construction is better than mining. More jobs to transition to inside. But we only get promoted if, when we fall, we get back up."

I dove more times that day because Belen made me, and over the next few because there was work to do, and I wanted to. I never had another problem, but the thought was always there in the back of my head: it only takes one mistake. If I had stayed calm, if I hadn't panicked... I thought of my fearless mother, and for perhaps the second time in my life I wondered, what if I wasn't meant for space? Maybe I took after my father. Maybe Space Sickness ran in my blood.

●

When the night sky was clear, Belen and Captain Haru liked to sit out on the roof of the *Buena Mañana* and watch the stars. I lay beside them as we rocked gently in the ocean waves, not a light between us and the horizon. This, at least, was somewhere I belonged. To look, at least, the stars were free.

"When the first explorers sailed across the equator," Belen said, "they found different constellations in a different sky and had to write new stories to make sense of them. It will be the same up in space. When we finally leave the solar system the stars in the sky will move. We will say things like 'Orion is getting fat, we must be moving towards Betelgeuse', or 'Aquarius has sprung a leak, adjust to starboard'."

"I think they will have computers to tell them where to go," I said. Computers with future engineers like José to program them.

"Computers only say what someone told them to say. I will want to know for myself what I am looking at." Belen said.

"Then look," said Haru. "What a view we have from here." He had been silent so long, I hadn't realized he was listening.

"They need us up there," Belen said, "Space will be tamed by its workers, not its astronauts. For every Magellan or Columbus, there were a hundred unnamed sailors — every bit as impressive — just less well known."

"You are already an important part of it." Haru said. "Until someone finds mussels growing on asteroids, they need you here."

"They will, though," said Belen. "Not mussels, but something. They will forget us eventually. Everyone says there is nothing up there to support life, but that is the same way we used to think of the ocean. When the Polynesians first packed their whole families on boats, they set sail without knowing what they would find. For them the ocean was as hostile as space is to our explorers today."

"Space is not an ocean," Haru said.

"Most of the ocean is empty and inhospitable," Belen said, "but those early explorers found ways of telling what was over the horizon to find islands they needed, and ways of telling what was below the waves to find the fish. We will too. They looked for clouds to find islands with freshwater springs; we will use spectroscopy to tell if asteroids have water and oxides to harvest."

"Maybe someday," Haru said, "but not yet."

"Someday," Belen echoed a little more somberly. She, like me, was looking at the elevator — that glowing purple line — and not the stars behind it.

●

Belen saw it first.

I know because of the way she swore under her breath and shifted in her seat. In hindsight, that was to block my view. I thought she had cut her hand on a mussel, as I had already a half dozen times that morning. Between the waves and the sweeping shadow of a turbine blade, it could have been anything floating out there.

Haru was not so discreet. "*Puta!*" he swore and jumped to his feet.

"Just leave it," Belen tried. "It's already dead."

There was a sinking feeling in my gut.

"Him, not it," Haru said tersely, "*he* will spoil the waters."

By the time Haru returned with a boathook, *he* had drifted close, bumping against the hull of the *Buena Mañana* with each wave; a human body floating in the water.

His eyes were open, staring up at the sky as what remained of his clothes billowed gently in the waves. The skin was bleached of all color, but with that dark, matted hair and those emaciated cheeks he could only have come from Manta.

"Laika," Belen said urgently. "Go grab a tarp."

"No, we need her help first." Haru hooked under the torso with his pole.

"He'll cook in this sun," Belen insisted. She was already half over the side, grabbing at an arm.

"This is not the last corpse she will see out here. She will need to toughen up eventually."

When I did not leave, Belen relented. "Grab a leg."

The stench was unbearable even before we pulled him from the water. As the body flopped onto the deck with the unpleasant sound of a wet sponge hitting wood, seawater and built-up gasses began to gurgle from his throat. I didn't gag — but Belen did.

Haru walked off to grab the tarp himself. Once again, I could not make myself move.

"If *he* couldn't be bothered to figure out the ocean," Belen told me after Haru had left, "I don't know how *he* expected to figure out space."

I did not help them wrap the body. All I could do was stare. I kept thinking, *He is just a boy. Maybe thirteen or fourteen, my age or younger.* I had not expected that.

I had always known there would be bodies around the elevator, everyone did. *They litter the sea.* But when I had imagined dead bodies floating in the ocean, they were always old. It made no sense, I know. Octogenarians did not try to stow away, but dead and old just went together. At least, they had until then.

I felt sick. I don't remember if I made it to the side of the boat before I threw up.

●

The dead boy needed glasses — when he was alive, that is. There were small divots in the sides of his head, just above his ears, the kind people got from wearing too-small glasses all their life. When he was young, and did not yet have those glasses, I bet he couldn't see the elevator — even when the light was just right. What about the mansions on the hill? If he could, he looked up there and said, like everyone did when they were too young to know better, "One day I will own one of those." Only, the mansions on the hill grew larger, not more numerous.

Manta used to have factories, and I decided that the dead boy's mother worked in one of those. Maybe a factory making space helmets for the astronauts who went up. She even took one home as a souvenir. She set it on a shelf in the starter home she bought on the side of the valley — back when she could afford a starter home and glasses. Back before the factories closed, there were many people like that.

They were already building spaceships in orbit before the elevator was finished, but they were not building helmets there. Not until someone who already had a mansion on the top of a hill realized it was cheaper to send up tightly packed ingots of metal and solid glass than large, empty helmets. I bet that someone bought their neighbor's mansion after thinking up that idea, so they could tear it down and make their own bigger.

The new space helmets were 3D-printed in a workshop at the top of the elevator, and the factories down in Manta were boarded up. After that, things got harder for everyone, except those who owned the elevator or the workshops up in space. The dead boy's mother had to sell her home and did not buy a new one. She should have sold her souvenir helmet too. Maybe then it wouldn't have been so tempting for her son.

Sometimes my mother did not eat so she could keep me fed, and we were better off than most in the valley. I wondered what it had been like for the boy. Had he waited at the docks like I did, hoping the next boat might pick him instead of someone else? Maybe he had tried to work, and stood in line outside one of the few factories left, hoping it would let him in before it closed too. I could not tell from his bloated hands if he had ever tried another way, or if the elevator was his first as well as his last idea. I would never know if he was like me, drawn to a dream, or if he just had nowhere else to turn but up.

People like us would never get factory jobs or starter homes. People like us made our own way or starved. But if even Yuri had floated away, what hope did the rest of us have?

⬤

Belen disappeared, leaving Haru and I to pull the rest of the mussels from the socks. He worked quickly, making up for lost time. I was next to useless. My hands would not stop shaking.

When I couldn't take the silence anymore, I asked, "Do they ever make it — the people who try to ride the elevator?"

He looked at me a moment, then out to sea, as though contemplating the question very carefully. The whole time, his hands never stopped sorting. "Have you made it, Laika?" He finally asked.

"I'm trying," I said.

Haru nodded. "Me too." Then he added, seeing my confused look, "*Make it* is a relative term. The Buddha preaches contentment. If one is content with what they have, then they have *made it*. If one always wants more, then it does not matter how much they have. Those who climb, some of them will *make it* up the elevator, but then what? Have they *made it*? They will share a bunk with five others and work more hours than there are in a day. How long do you really think they will last? A month? A season? Of those who *make it* that far, and that's pretty far, most will be dead within a year. But will they have *made it*? A year with a bunk and two meals a day would be *making it* for some of the people I have seen floating out here."

Haru shook his head. "We tell stories because they give us hope. We say that if someone can make it up the elevator, if they can work hard and stay safe, if they have just the right luck, if they get noticed by just the right people, then maybe they can *make it* — whatever that means. And of course, we say, if they can do it, we could too — if we had to, not that we will. There is a certain comfort to that, no?"

"I don't know." It did not seem comforting.

"You come from Manta. Tell me, have you heard about the mansion that is owned by a former stowaway?"

I nodded. "Everyone has."

"If we were closer to the shore," Haru asked, "could you point it out for me?"

I shook my head. The closest I had ever been was when a *mudak* who liked my mother decided to take us both for a drive in his car. Even he, in his fancy car, couldn't get through the community gates.

"I have heard many stories about starship captains who were once stowaways until they worked their way up. They always retire with a mansion of their own. I've heard it a thousand times, but if even a tenth of those stories were true, then almost all of the mansions on Manta's hill must belong to former stowaways by now. I'd think, if that were the case, then you, a local, could point out one or two for sure. *Apocryphal*, that is what we call stories like that.

"The Buddha preaches contentment. That should be easy for us. You'd think fully bellies, a roof to lay on, and a part to play in what we watch going on above would be enough. We do have a part, Laika, all of us, however small. We feed Manta; without Manta, no elevator, no space. But still, we long for more. We dream dreams and say someday it will be us who *make it*, because there is no real harm in that, until there is.

"Truth is, that boy on the deck never had a chance; maybe thinking he did is what kept him going on hungry nights, but it is also what made him think he could make it up the elevator. I'm sure that even the Buddha looked forward to a dry fire when it rained, but he knew the difference between a dream and reality. That the boy died in the end, that is tragic — but maybe he lived first because of his dream. That, in a way, would have been *making it* — would it not? If only he had known when a dream should remain just a dream."

Belen was at the back of the boat leaning against a railing, looking out towards the elevator as though nothing had happened.

We were close enough now that the crawlers had taken form. The colorful squiggles of company logos were almost clear enough to read — perhaps if I knew their designs better. Belen did not look at me as I approached, but her hand wiped something from her cheek.

She took a sharp, deep breath. "It gets easier," she said, but she did not sound like she believed it. "Just know, for every floater we find out here, there are ten stowaways who make it to the top."

That didn't sound right, but neither did arguing.

"Would you have tried swimming?" Belen asked. "Out on the dock, if I hadn't picked you?" She turned with red ringed-eyes. I had never seen her like that. "If I had picked the fat man instead of you. How long would you have waited for another boat before trying on your own?"

The elevator was too far to swim, but with a raft — would I have tried that eventually? Would I have ended up just like the boy

under the tarp? "I don't know," I said. "It's a good thing you chose me."

"Is it?" Belen asked. "I always say I'm going to go up there someday, and Haru laughs with me. Like it's a joke we are sharing, like it's a game. But it's not. Not to me. I want to ride the elevator, Laika. I want to be in space, I ..." She shook her head. "I keep pretending that I can. I keep saying, 'soon'. That I am almost ready, that I have it almost planned out, that I have to be smart about it.

"I *have* planned it, Laika, you know I have planned it all and planned it all again, but there is only so long I can keep planning and keep pretending that it will happen.

"Every time we are near the elevator, I look at the logos on the crawlers and I actually hope it says NASA, because then I will have an excuse. Then, at least, I can live with myself when I don't. They don't like stowaways on research vessels.

"Twice now it has been for a mining firm, and I didn't go. I could have. There was a pressurized crate and I could have just snuck inside. You know I know how. Maybe they would have caught me. Maybe they would have sent me back down. Maybe it wouldn't have resealed, and I would have died on the way up, but I will never know because I didn't even try."

"I'm glad you didn't die." I wasn't sure what else to say.

"I wish I were dying," Belen said. "How sick is that? I wish I were starving. I tell myself that if I were starving, that if I had no other choice, that if I would die if I didn't find a way to stowaway on the next crawler, I would risk it. I would try because I would have nothing left to lose... but that's not true. I will always have a reason to wait. What does that mean, Laika, that even in my dreams I only go out of desperation, only because there was no other way?"

"That you have something to lose," I said. "That's not such a bad thing."

"Is it?" Belen snapped. "I'm what — too lucky? — too fortunate? Too rich to be desperate enough to follow my dreams — yet too poor for there to be another way." She laughed. Not a happy laugh, an unpleasant half a snort, half a sob. "I'm jealous of a corpse, Laika. It's ridiculous. I am being ridiculous. He is dead. He was stupid and now he is dead and under a tarp and still, I want to be him because at least he tried. At least he had the chance to get lucky. At least he got to know. How pathetic is that? How can that make any sense?"

I never really knew the right words to say. That was my mother. I never had her smile. I pulled Belen close for a hug.

"I want to go," she said, "even if it doesn't work out. Even if I end up dead. I just want to know. Was I good enough? Could I have made it? I want to be up there right now looking down on this ocean of *merda*." She sunk into my arms. "Why can't I do that?"

I spoke my mother's words: "When you know what you have to do, it is better not to look. Just go."

"If only it were that easy," Belen said. "I don't know if I am more scared that I will fall, or that I will never even try — but I'm scared, Laika. I'm scared."

"I'm scared too." I said, and I was. As they never used to tire of telling me: the real Laika, the Russian dog, she died on the way up.

"You're just a kid," Belen said. "You still have time." Did I? Or had we both already looked over the edge and seen the rocks below.

●

In the morning, as the sun shone from the east, I could see the elevator. Not one thread, but several — six parallel lines stretched taut between the sky and a metal island in the middle of the ocean. I made up my mind before we were close enough to read the labels on the crawlers — if they were wrong, I would wait on that island until they were right. When you know what you have to do, it is better not to look.

I laid my equipment out along the deck — like Belen had for diving — and chose from the regulators hidden in the back of the locker. Those designed for altitude, not diving. Belen had planned everything, and then planned again.

I felt a pang of guilt as I set a helmet on the deck, but there wasn't time for that. I would be forgiven; this was why she had brought me here, to show her it was possible. I took one slow, calming breath, then changed my mind. I ran down the stairs into the *Buena Mañana*'s cabin to where Belen was still asleep.

"I'm going," I whispered, nudging Belen awake. "Come with me. Don't think, just come." She didn't understand but sat up, too groggy to resist my pull, at least, at first.

We were halfway up the stairs when she asked about Haru. I shook my head and pulled her harder. There was no time to slow down.

"He'll be fine." He had his contentment. There were plenty of others in Manta who would love to harvest mussels and look up at the stars. "This is the reason you chose me, isn't it?" The big man on the dock would never have pulled Belen up with him, would never have thought to look up at all.

"Objectif." Belen gasped as we stepped into the sun, and I looked — though I shouldn't have, because I truly did not want to know. The colorful squiggles on one crawler's glossy sides had resolved into the square and circle logo of Objectif Outre-Terre — an orbital construction company.

"We have to go now," I said.

I pulled Belen to the equipment and helped her put it on. Gear for the swim to the island, and gear to stay warm on the ride up.

"I can't," she said, then, as I tried to put a helmet on her head, she finally stopped me. "What if ..."

"We could die," I agreed, "maybe. Or we could live. Don't you want to know?" The sea may be littered with the bodies of those who did not *make it*, but Manta was choked full of those who never even tried.

"I want to try," I said. Reflected in Belen's helmet, the elevator did not seem so tall. It seemed to bend towards us — bowing. No one kept statistics on stowaways, but I doubt half made it as far as we already had. "Don't think," I said, "jump."

She let me put the helmet on her head.

With it on, Belen could have been Mimi. It was my own reflection, however, that caught me off guard. Even missing three teeth, I had Yuri's smile: bright, infectious, *content*. We were going to space. The mutts were going to fly.

"Hold on," I said, as I took her hand and we jumped.

Justen Russell's story "Holding On" was originally published in Metaphorosis on Friday, 21 October 2022. See magazine.metaphorosis.com

About the author

Justen Russell is a scientist and author, with a PhD in the biological sciences. He lives in Paris, France with his partner and their child. He is anachronistic in his athletics, enjoying historical sword-fighting and swing dance
www.justenrussell.com

Saving the Whales

C.J. Erick

Niemi misses the whales.

She misses the bowhead, the fin, and the southern right. She misses the grand blue, the understated minke, and the elegant sei. She misses the way water bulged like candy glass over their backs when they rose to the surface, and how it broke into liquid shards. She misses the billowing rainbows of their exhalations on cold mornings, and the percussion cannons of their tails when they announced their preposterously powerful dives-to-be.

●

She didn't always miss the whales. Once, she watched them, idolizing them, yearning to be with them grokking the water and not rocking in her rowboat or rolling in her Zodiac.

It is hard now, to crinkle her eyes at the sun setting on the washboard Pacific, the delicious smells of crusty sea salt and delicately rotting seaweed in her nose, the shoosh of waves not in her ears, but somehow over and around and through her, feeling the voids where the whales should be.

●

Her first summer post-junior year, she spent wet through her suit and behind her ears. She spent hours leaning over the side of the inflatable with an aluminum pole like a lightning rod, plunging it into the galvanic water. Algae-laden, the water was tarnished green, like corroded bronze.

At the end of the rod was magic, a flashy new hydrophone — analog, since this was 1975 — hard-wired to a plastic-wrapped tape recorder the size of a suitcase large enough to hold her entire wardrobe of jeans, tees, tanks, hair clips, and caps, and the three Lycra one-piece swimsuits she rotated throughout the summer. Behind her, the annoying drum of San Diego, a million miles from the farm in Illinois, interfered with the recording.

She couldn't hear the sounds they were recording. She and her research partner, Floyd, whom she'd picked because he was gay and she could trust him not to use her exuberance like a date-rape drug as one professor had tried to. The voices of the grays were well below human hearing, but she'd manipulated them through the miracle of mid-Seventies sound manipulation, applied in the biology department's sound room. Now their eerie songs, replayed through the stereo speakers, touched something primal within her, like a deep siren call, the come-hither seduction of sensuous clicks and thrums and moans exotic and otherworldly.

Her senses, once piqued, would never rest.

●

Whales went missing.

First, the pods of minkes that frequented the central Pacific failed to arrive that year. Biologists blamed it on the failure of the last major shelf of Antarctic ice, a diversion in the ocean currents, red tides, overfishing, and even sunspots.

Niemi knew better. But her suspicions were confirmed through a chance encounter. She'd been following a small pod of the slender gray creatures at a distance, quietly rowing after them, letting the airfoil sail of her little sun-bleached white sailboat push her along as much as possible.

Lights appeared in the sky. Two silent machines the color and size and shape of pre-World-War dirigibles lowered as one imagined the carcass of a whale might fall into the lightless deep. The craft settled into the waves, kilometers from shore, well away from the sight of land. Great doors opened in the vessels' ends, and whales swam into them two by two. And then the great craft closed their doors and lifted steadily into the sky, their lights extinguished, until they grew as small as sailing ships curving away over the horizon, and disappeared.

Niemi had watched, asking herself why these ships were taking the whales, and why the whales were boarding without a struggle.

In the weeks that followed, she contacted every agency she thought would have interest in her sightings, in the disappearances. But what agency would have the authority to investigate? The California State Police? After three calls and visit to the headquarters in San Diego County, they refused to speak to her. The CIA? Probably weather balloons, was all they offered, and dismissed her. A young biologist from NOAA, the National Oceanographic and Atmospheric Administration, met with her briefly, but tried to push her observations toward illegal whaling operations, probably by Chinese fishing companies, which were suffering as ocean stocks of fish collapsed further from the unrecoverable levels in the 2020s.

Lights in the sky. Alien visitors harvesting the world's cetaceans? No one would believe her.

●

She lived on the ocean, helped conduct whales counts. She pursued a degree in marine biology, cetacean focus, and manhandled her way through a Ph.D. The degree and her well-taken thesis on cetacean language led to grants, and the grants led to the books published, the ones that sold at last after so many rejections and failures to launch: *Living with Earth's Smartest Beings* and *Love and Sex Among Krill and Plankton.* She became a name then, cited in oceanographic journals and doomed environmental legislation. But the writing wasn't about credibility or notoriety; it was about money, the money she needed, and there were many things she needed.

The world turns on coinage. She turned hers into a submersible, a truck-sized, two-person submarine. Electric. Quiet. Loaded with sensing equipment that beat most space missions.

She called it Grayfin.

Her mother died, the woman she most loved, but feared as the one most likely to lead her back to 'a practical career, Niemi'. And then seven months later her broken-hearted father passed as well, a man she'd never liked, but in whom she'd found a kinship in their complex, seldom-spoken feelings for her mother and each other.

Her brother and sisters divided the estate among themselves, leaving her out, since she was obviously more well-off than they were, though they knew nothing of sleeping on a wave-soaked dock, or spending one's own money on teaching supplies, those costs even a prestigious West Coast university passed on to untenured professors.

But seven years after she had seen the lift of the minke, had seen the lights dropping to the ocean again and again, she had her machine, her mechanical stalking whale, her way to find out why.

●

The sky ship, dull gray and oblong, dropped like a deflating helium balloon from the tortured sky toward the open waters of the Pacific. Silent, even several hundred miles from Baja where no one was going to hear it. It descended slightly butt-heavy, angled like Grayfin powering across the surface at full throttle, which was about to happen. Timing; timing.

The whales were out there — five hundred meters by the radar, lolling and spouting vapor in the waves. Four big blues, three females and one male. No calves, despite it being birthing season, which was sad and one explanation for all this.

Niemi's hands felt numb and twitchy on the controls.

The alien vessel leveled out and settled into the water. A white wave spread outward from the hull. After a few eternally long minutes, a vast door opened in the end facing the whales, like the mouth of an earthworm about to consume a bit of cornmeal sprinkled into its bait container.

The whales circled and then lined up two by two and swam toward the craft, but still a good two hundred meters from it. Niemi waited.

The first two spouted mightily, as if kicking the dust from their sandals, and entered the maw of the ship. As the second pair moved within a hundred meters, Niemi grasped the control handles and willed her sub to life.

She was thrown back into the seat as the nose came up. Four-thousand electric horses leaped ahead. Past the side-view screens flowed dirty green water, plastic junk, rust-colored debris, and the broken skeletons of maritime equipment. Her machine was stealthy quiet, but still the whine of the motors was in her ears like Triassic hornets. The rangefinder counted down the numbers. Four hundred meters. Three. One fifty.

The vessel's door closed, and the ship lifted from the waves, streamers of water falling from its sides like dishwater from an aluminum urn. It lifted into the sky just like the first two she'd observed, shrinking slowly, sailing over the horizon of the darkening sky.

"No!" She heard the ragged rage in her voice, the childlike cry of frustration and abandonment.

And then the light paused, descended, grew. The gray craft, now charcoal in the late twilight, touched the water, and the great doors opened again. It stood in the water, motionless, as if anchored by rigid pilings to the ocean floor two thousand feet below.

She eased her submarine forward, passing into the black mouth of the ship, watching the stars covered by a sky-colored sheet. The doors closed behind her ship, and all was dark. She could barely breathe.

She assumed they lifted into the sky, although she couldn't tell because there was no sense of motion, no acceleration, no feeling of changing momentum. She struggled to find a term for the beings who had taken her into their ship. Calling them 'extraterrestrial' would be Earth-centric, as if her planet were the center of the universe of intelligent species, when in fact the very existence of these beings and their ships proved otherwise.

'Space travelers' would imply they'd come from the endless void out beyond the wispy extremes of the atmosphere, when she had no idea where they'd come from, and almost certainly they'd not come from the void itself. And 'aliens' wasn't just human-centric but also politically disrespectful, since humans were at least as alien to these beings as the other way around.

So she settled for the Visitors, which seemed to cover just about anything nonhuman.

They allowed her to rock in the hull of the ship in complete darkness. She began to wonder if they expected her to navigate by sonar. She remembered her sonar then, and, risking offense, pinged around her ship, finding it rolling gently in the center of a large tank with featureless walls, shaped like two bathtubs stacked one upside down over the other. Two whale tails disappeared from the far end of the tank, rising upwards through a porthole into another chamber above her, apparently. Once they were through, dull blue lights came on and another door opened in the ceiling above her. Her submersible eased through it with no action on her part, rising into a smaller, egg-shaped chamber where metal rods protruded from the walls like fingers pushing through a balloon, cradling her ship gently as if holding a shiny black pouch of stingray eggs. Water drained from the chamber in seconds.

"Join us," said a voice. It was female, brash and harsh, brassy like someone speaking from a conch shell. A voice she disliked when she heard it in taped interviews; her own voice.

The main hatchway of the sub slid into its recess with a barely audible hum. The air that flowed in through the open door held all the taste and smell of boiled water. A metal walkway pushed out from the wall and stuck to the ship just below the port, dull like aluminum, soft like plastic as she walked along it step by step.

Beyond the doorway was a small chamber, surrounded on all sides and the top by clear glass, the walls of water tanks all around. A woman stood with her back to Niemi, and she knew it would be herself, even before the hologram or whatever it was turned to gaze at her over its shoulder, assessing her so closely and with such human intensity and expression that she couldn't convince herself the image wasn't real. She fought back the urge to touch it.

"You believe they are beautiful," said the woman. Beyond her, the four blue whales floated in an infinite pool, rising slowly to breathe, then sinking slowly under the surface. The otherwise colorless water was foggy brown with krill, and occasionally one of the whales would open its great beak-like mouth to allow the rich water to fill it.

"I do." She was overwhelmed as always by the beauty of the whales. The impending loss struck her like a migraine, twisting at the bones in her forehead. "Why — ?"

"All of us are different, and yet we are the same."

The woman explained that consciousness existed beyond the physical boundaries of the brain and of the body, and that all touched each other. When the predominant beings of a world — she didn't use the word 'planet', as that excluded many places where rational beings lived — were able to harmonize, a stable tranquility could bloom, one that could last for thousands of years.

"These beings," said the Other Niemi, "they are special. They have a gift and a yearning for harmony which we've never seen before. Such a shame you humans don't recognize this, and you harm them."

"Some of us cherish them," said Niemi.

The Visitor said, "We have observed and, at times, sought to promote harmony on Earth, as is our calling. But despite these efforts, humans have not harmonized with your world, with the other rational beings there, such as the primates, the cephalopods, the avians, and of course, the whales."

Niemi said, "But we do achieve harmony — sometimes. We organize. We achieve great things. We help each other during crises and natural disaster. We even harmonize in song, just as the whales do."

"Truth. But political and resource organization is a sad caricature of the true, deep connection of a harmonized world.

"Your race has been given enough time. And these beautiful beings are needed elsewhere."

"Where? Why?" asked Niemi.

"Every world seeks harmony. These beings can help. And they deserve better."

The woman told Niemi they were telling her this because she was one of the few who listened — sometimes. If there was hope, it lay with her or others like her.

"Are you taking all the whales?" she asked.

"They speak across entire oceans," said the Other Niemi, shaking her head, perhaps preoccupied as she was with the whale's beauty. "No, we will only save the ones who wish to go. The orcas and some dolphin species have chosen to stay. Their food supplies are doing well for now, and they like interacting with humans. We will come back for them if they call."

"Will you bring the other whales back, once their work is done?"

"No."

Niemi paused, frozen by an aching she couldn't explain or readily locate.

"May I go with them?"

"No."

Nothing else. No explanation, no conditions. Just no.

Niemi wasn't allowed to protest or plead or fall to her knees and beg. One minute she was standing talking to this Other Niemi, or a diagram that looked and sounded exactly like video and audio of her, and the next she awoke in her submersible, washing back and forth in two-meter waves in the open sea. The ship and the whales were gone.

She sat and rocked and wept for as long as it took.

●

Niemi convinced a department head to support her for another grant, and she used it to finance expeditions to record whale song, and computer time to translate. She followed the herds, playing their own recorded voices to them. She paid for seeding of plankton and devised outriggers for Grayfin to scoop waste from the bleary seawater, and when that didn't make a dent in the floating and sinking trash, she had automobile-sized drone submarines built, rigged with nets to catch trash. But they did little except tangle with fish and turtles and jellyfish. The entropy of waste was pervasive and resistant.

Whale sightings and counts continued to dwindle, pointing to cataclysmic losses. Scientists and politicians and fishermen argued not over the why, but over whether this was a good or bad thing, since whales were known to reduce fishing trawler yields, and feeding the world was hard, so hard, so bloody hard to make profitable.

●

She spent much of her time following the orca pods, continuing to journal and sketch individuals, just as she'd done since her first whale watching excursion as a young teen on a school trip, the prize for winning a climate science award. Now, she had Grayfin, where she lived most days.

One day, she languished like an empty water bottle in calm waters well off San Diego, where one couldn't see the land and where few boats ventured. She was there because bright lights in the sky had been reported for several nights over the previous month. She turned the sound system off, the sonar sensors, the radar, the infrared thermographs, the radio.

Was it harmony she felt then, alone, like a dead piece of kelp being nibbled by tiny crabs? The harmony of the carcass of a sei whale stinking the water with the promise of food and habitat for months, before sinking into the lightless depths to provide fodder and shelter for blind eels and tube worms and beaked fish that would never see a rainbow? Or was it just loneliness, alienation?

Her eyes were to the sky, and she didn't notice them until they were nearly upon her, black and white looping shapes in the water, a dozen or more, bulky cetacean missiles, moving silently as one body, as only beings who knew each other well could. She didn't move as the pod of orcas approached and circled her. She kept the hydrophones off to avoid spooking the pod, but their clicks and whistles resonated through the craft's thin titanium shell.

They flowed around her in an intricate swirl of day-and-night bodies, then away into a funnel, leaving her. She was drawn to them as into a whirlpool. She touched the controls and followed across open water, following their bulging rhythms and infrequent breaths, to where she didn't know, and suddenly didn't care, but when they arrived it was obvious why. An old container ship, sunk so that its deck lay just above the surface, flat and open like an ice floe. It wasn't on any maps she knew of, but sonar showed it anchored to the bottom by strands of fishing net and cable, probably communication cables mistakenly dredged up, spelling its doom.

On the ship were dozens of sea lions, letting the afternoon sun broil their skin to a fearsome pink, like monsters from some children's anime film. Niemi breached Grayfin a hundred yards away, and climbed out to watch, a small hand-held camera ready.

Three of the orcas stormed the ship's deck, landing on their bellies with only their tails in the water, each grasping a mature sea lion in its mouth, wiggling their water-wet bodies back into the water, shaking the lions and dragging them down through the broken pane of the ocean's surface, down into clouds of red, before disappearing out of sight. The lions scrambling on the deck roared and retreated to the center of the ship, crushing smaller females, pushing others off into the water, where some didn't make it back to the safety of the ship's deck before being sucked down by domino torpedoes.

She knew she should record this event, but she lacked the strength to raise and point the camera. For whom would she take the pictures? For whom capture it on video? For some vulgar wildlife reality show, another outlet for those who enjoyed the violence of nature, never seeing the necessity or reason for it?

Niemi lost track of time watching the orcas circle the ship. The lions crowded together in a wary crush of gray-pink bodies. Niemi was wondering what she should do next, knowing it was already too late to return to the harbor before night and not caring much about that either.

A single orca approached, a large female, with clean lines as if painted, her shorter female's dorsal fin curving at the end, and a gray marking shaped like a human hand at the end of her left pectoral fin. Niemi remembered this whale woman, a mother she'd followed for three breeding seasons, one who'd raised three calves with brutal efficiency and care. She'd named the woman Mileva, for reasons she couldn't remember.

Mileva swam to Niemi's vessel and spit a melon-sized chunk of sea lion flesh onto the sun-beaten hull of the sub, like a grill chef dropping a slab of cod onto an aluminum fry pan. It sizzled.

Mileva rocked her face in the waves, blowing breath expectantly. Niemi eyed the fatty mass and gray hide on the hull, and her stomach grumbled.

Mileva whistled and blew a geyser of hot vapor toward Niemi, showering her in acrid spit.

Niemi scooted to the edge of the sub, scooped up the flesh, and sat holding it, feeling her throat tighten at the glowing, shiny meat, which seemed to pulse in her hands.

She bit, chewed the jelly-like flesh, tasted blood and rank oil and noxious umami; gagged and swallowed.

She swallowed another bite. She vomited into the water. She bit again, swallowed. Vomited. Her head rocked, vision blackening. She fell to her side on the hull, unable to rise.

The orca eased alongside her sub, its black eye almost invisible against its ebon skin, the large white patch above it like the luminous white eye of a phantom. The whale's gray saddle patch curved about her back like a knitted sweater. It turned, swirling, and lifted a flipper and swept it away from the craft, the gray hand patch at its tip beckoning.

Niemi thought about her snorkel gear, donning the wet suit over her thin cotton shirt and shorts, and the flippers, but instead let her body slide from the sub's hull into the cold water. Immediately her nausea passed, and she bobbed easily in the infinite soup of ocean, her clothing clinging to her like tissue paper. Mileva's head bobbed in the light waves. Was this a nod? The great black and white being slid away like a ghost, her flipper rising once to beckon again. Other orca had gathered at a distance, blowing steam, whistling, pulsations of sound tapping at Niemi's skin.

Mileva, now twenty yards from the ship, whistled loudly.

Niemi pushed away, settling into an easy swim — she could swim for hours without tiring, so much time spent in the water. But it was cold, and she was thin and would chill quickly in the Pacific water.

She came within ten feet of the huge woman whale. Mileva stroked her tail to ease away. Leading her away.

Niemi swam. Her submersible Grayfin fell away behind her.

Mileva played this game several times, letting Niemi approach, then pulling away. Cat and mouse? The other whales swam with them, to each side, remaining yards away, like spectators at a long-distance race, following the runners.

Then, after a hard, muscular thrust of tail, Mileva dove and surfaced facing Niemi, blocking her path, just ten feet in front. She waited.

Niemi paused, then swam toward the whale woman. She was at the whale's mercy, hundreds of yards from Grayfin, more vulnerable than the sea lions Mileva's pod had attacked earlier. She stopped just outside touching reach of the whale's black and white snout, which bobbed like a marker buoy, shiny as rubberized paint. The whistling of the other whales stopped. There was only the sound of the ocean around them; the susurrus of the waves, the clicks of sea creatures, the bellowing of the sea lions on the rogue ship, the screes of gulls and shearwaters scavenging the remains or hunting the small fish drawn to the blood.

Mileva swam to the side, around Niem. She turned, opened her mouth, and gripped Niemi by the chest. Teeth dug into Niemi's skin in a hundred places. She closed her eyes.

Mileva held her in her mouth, pulled her, brushed her stomach with her great sandpaper tongue. Niemi fought the urge to push the whale away, to throw a fist at Mileva's eye. Mileva raised her partly from the water, swam in a circle, as if showing this prize to the others.

Then she opened her mouth and released Niemi. She swam ten feet away and waited, lolling in the waves, once again a dark phantom with ghostly patches.

Niemi felt the sting of seawater on small cuts on her side, her arm, her belly. She could breathe, but she wanted to vomit again.

What did the whale want from her now? It lay expectantly in the water, waiting. She could swim back for her sub, if the currents weren't taking it away from her, beyond her reach. But that would be returning to who she had been before this night, this act of connection from Mileva. That's what it was, surely. The whale could have killed her, but hadn't. The pod could have ignored her and swum away, but remained, the others again swimming in a circle around her and Mileva, whistling, blowing breath.

They were asking "Are you one of us?"

Niemi leaned forward, stroked the water with her cold arms, feeling the stings, the chill, the touch of microscopic stingers from tiny krill and squid, how her skin loved the water, the caress as it passed over her arms, her shoulders, her back.

She reached Mileva in a dozen strong strokes. She gripped the flipper nearest her, the one with the shape of a gray human hand. She gripped the end of the flipper in her teeth, held it there, pulled.

Mileva's small black eye, two feet away from hers, studied her.

She held the flipper in her teeth as long as Mileva had held her body, then released and kicked away. She placed two fingers in her mouth and blew air, spitting water, phlegm, giving a harsh rasping whine at first, and then a loud clear whistle, which cut the air and breeze, silencing the birds and the other whales.

Mileva nodded, whistled back.

She swam to Niemi, leaned over to allow the woman to grip her dorsal fin. With Niemi clinging, Mileva snapped her tail, suddenly a whistling steam ship plowing the waves. She covered the quarter mile to Grayfin in a few moments, Niemi holding tight with both hands.

At the sub, Niemi, suddenly very tired, eased back into the water, swam to the boarding ladder, climbed onto the sub's hull and knelt there, too tired to stand. Mileva, head pointing straight up, spun twice like a great black and white top, then swam away, pausing once to turn back, before disappearing beneath the dancing moonlit surface, leaving hardly a ripple in her wake.

They should, all creatures, leave the world that way, with barely a ripple marking their passage.

The next two times Niemi met Mileva and the whales, she ate of what she was offered, sea lion meat, or seal, or chunks of raw tuna or shark, she vomited. After that, she didn't vomit again.

●

Two calves were born, in one of the new 'conservation' sea parks, "Whales Forever," just south of San Diego, from one orca female, twins, an almost impossible miracle. A sign, many pro-captivity lobbyists said, that their programs were needed and helpful. The foundation would preserve the remaining whales through reproduction and nurturing programs, funded by interactive aquariums, agility and skills displays, swimming with the whales events.

It was harmony, of a sort, with the underlying dark shadow of corporate profit driving the enterprise.

Niemi was running a monthly educational program at middle schools, along the West Coast of the US and into Canada usually, but sometimes invited to progressive districts near Chicago, New England, even Austin and Minneapolis. Her theme was simple — "Whales are People." She was loved or hated, invited or banned. And always, always threatened. For her own protection, she became a licensed firearm carrier, and hated the need.

At the news of the miracle birth, she paused her program, spending more time on the water, her Eden, the garden she'd been pulled away from too often as she taught and wrote. Even she had bills to pay, and the grants came less often. She was too controversial.

Miracle calves, young whale children who would be raised wrong, never learn what they needed to survive in the sea, never know the true joy of pod life.

Never learn to kill for food and survival.

She requested a meeting with the sea park administrators, on the premise of being allowed to produce multi-media works for promotion of the twins, watch their lives grow. It would be like an orca version of the Hollywood film *Truman*, lives lived in a virtual-sea. A morning swim and simulated hunting. Whistling conversations with the head keeper, other staff, and virtual pod-mates. Games and entertainment with their mother and the other aquatic residents. Fun for all. And all the funding they'd need for the next ten years.

Her work was known then, over a dozen books, webinars, sea-cliff retreats for the well-heeled. She wasn't despised as much as she would be, not yet labeled an 'ultra-libertard', an 'ocean-head', a 'whale groomer'. The foundation accepted her request.

The offices where they met were located on the harbor. The ground floor conference room in the white-pillared mausoleum-like box was all windows on one wall, with a clear view of the newly-built aquarium sitting near the water, like a silver domed cosmetic box pushed there by some great hand and left to face the surf. It was a white concrete monument, not a home for sentient beings. Yet these people thought they understood cetaceans.

She'd come alone. They'd brought video-documentarians, local politicians, corporate sponsors.

After introductions, she listened through two hours of effusive promotional ideas, their vision of a grand cooperative union between human and orca, an experiment in sustainable harmony, cooperation, and mutual benefit. After this, as her patient silence endured, their enthusiasm flagged, their voices one by one fell quiet. The room's attention shifted unconsciously to the foundation's director, Mrs. Delilah Fernace, founder and CEO of God's True Foods, an organic testing and services corporation, a woman who Neimi might have liked, had she not been so much the aggressive charitable type, for whom altruism was just another arena.

At the end of the presentations, Mrs. Fernace asked Niemi, "What do you think?"

To which, Niemi said simply "It's been tried."

"But not like we intend. This isn't just a sea-zoo we're planning. This is to be a real, working environment. Humans will not make all the decisions. The orcas and dolphins here will be voting members. And we'd like you to show us to hear their voices."

A pang of earnestness struck Niemi, and she almost fell for the spell. Mrs. Fernace was a gifted visionary. One wanted to believe in anything she set forth.

"As long as there are walls," said Niemi, "this will be not a zoo, not a 'zoological garden'. It will be a prison. And the whales will not speak truly. You have been blessed with a miracle birth of fully-sentient beings. You must let them go. Back to the sea, now, while they can still adapt. If you don't act now, they will die. Perhaps not physically, but emotionally. They will not live as they would wish."

Mrs. Fernace sat silently for a moment, her face reddening.

She said, at last, "We respected you and offered you our hand in cooperation. But you've come under false pretenses, with no intention of joining us. This meeting is over."

The construction of the facility continued, larger tanks, natural plants and settings, like nothing ever built before, and the orca twins and their mother seemed well. They were allowed to interact with orcas in the wild — at least at a distance, since the wild ones stayed away. The captives grew less healthy, less vocal, eating less of the farmed fish they were given, more prone to lethargy.

Niemi was asked about these events during one of her podcasts. Her words were few. "They have heard the voices of their cousins, and they know of the true world they are missing."

Two months later and six months after the miracle birth, a summer strain of Covid virus swept through, this strain virulent among most mammals. The mother and calves were stricken, and only one calf survived. After two months of anti-viral treatments and round-the-clock care, it was a thin version of itself, alive but hardly thriving.

Niemi was asked to speak at a contentious panel discussion on ocean farming, which many felt was the only way to address food shortages among the world's eleven billion humans. Each panelist was allowed closing statements, and Niemi requested to be the last to speak. Rather than reiterate her feelings that ocean farming must be closely-controlled to prevent exploitation and environmental damage, she made a plea.

"This is to the director of 'Whales Forever'. Mrs. Fernace — give me the child. If you truly believe in God's work, give me the child, or it will not live."

Days passed, and then Niemi received a terse message from the foundation's matriarch, delivered in person by a young woman oceanographer, one who had attended several of Niemi's webinars.

The handwritten note read, "The child will be placed in your hands. My messenger, Ms. Montez, will help with the arrangements."

In Grayfin, Niemi led the foundation's vessel carrying the young orca in a watered sling. She hadn't seen Mileva's pod for weeks, but they found her within two hours of the ships leaving the San Diego harbor.

Niemi entered the water first, in scuba gear. The young orphaned orca, a beautiful female called 'Seaflower' by the institute, was lowered into the rolling waves. Niemi and Tanya Montez, the whale's main caregiver, moved with her as she slipped from the harness into the open water, eyeing Tanya wildly, and Niemi with suspicion.

The pod drifted slowly in like ghosts, quietly clicking, two young females moving closest. Fights between orca pods were rare, and strangers were generally accepted or ignored as the extreme. DNA evidence showed that orca females rarely mated within their own pods, so interactions were common, if only for biodiversity.

But there were no certainties.

Seaflower clicked and then one of the wild females whistled. The poor young stranger tried a soft whistle. And then the two females swam in a pattern before the newling, and she followed, away into the ocean gloom.

Would Seaflower tell them of her life among the humans, her illness, the loss of her mother and sister? Was their language so richly sophisticated?

Mileva appeared then, a dark slow-speed torpedo. Tanya started to retreat, but Niemi waved her fear away. The orca swam closer, passing gaze on Tanya, then paused near Niemi, before swimming away with a rocking motion, disappearing after the others. The pod's whistles and clicks grew more distant.

The following week, Tanya joined Niemi's inner circle.

●

Following the publicity around Seaflower's release, scientists from China and Finland contacted Niemi with a proposal they said she would find attractive. They met secretly, in an abandoned fishers' shed, with two of her assistants knocking around outside on the aged and warped pier. The researchers had a proposal, one that would have intrigued anyone who worked with the few whale species still observed in the wild.

They sat away from her, as if repelled by her natural odor. Dr. Wen Zhang allowed Dr. Hern Ruminen to speak first.

"We have a process. We can place a living human brain inside the skull of a young juvenile member of Orcinus orca."

He explained how they intended to bio-splice the nerves to the medulla oblongata, microsurgery involving elaborate medical robotics and supercomputer AI. The rest of the details bulged like a tide and bowled into Niemi, where she sat in the small office of a fish market south of the city, one of the last places in the USA where one might avoid observation. She knew what they were proposing, even without the details. She would become a whale.

"Of course, the transition," said Dr. Zhang, in a precise voice devoid of accent, "will be very similar to a new birth. Every aspect of living, breathing, swimming, eating, must be learned from the first day of life. There will be no parallel experience. No amount of empathy or living among the subject species will prepare the human participant for this irreversible process." When she didn't react, he cast a side glance at the rigid, gray-templed form of Dr. Ruminen. His voice lost some of its enthusiasm. "This is why it is necessary to place the human brain into the skull of a newborn specimen."

They knew of her writings on inter-species connection, the potential for biological harmony, the only way for the tortured modern world to survive, and then thrive. All living things were part of the same biome, the microcosm bound only by the limits of the atmosphere, and perhaps not even that.

And yet these scientists, these researchers, although sympathetic to her cause, they felt this process, this experiment, this exploitation would be attractive to her. This was the best idea they could bring to her.

"Where will you find a recipient?" she asked, without inflection. Her voice sounded brassy and alien, echoing in the small shack. She had grown to dislike speaking. She had taken to humming along with her many recordings of whale song, those wondrous voices now lost, like the songs of ancient humans.

"It will be necessary to capture a mature, pregnant female and extract a late-term fetus."

Niemi nodded. She choked back her rage, told them it was a very interesting project, and thanked them for considering her. She would respond within a few weeks.

She followed the research through spies she'd placed at their institutions. Months later, after they'd given up on her repeated postponements and found a willing participant, a young military scientist, when the capture ships were being stocked and prepared for the initial hunt, she and three assistants used guided drone submarines to attach deep sonic beacons on the ships' hulls, near the drive units. She was able to track them at all times, and so were the orcas.

Their efforts to capture a pregnant female were unsuccessful.

●

They came after her, of course. Not the researchers, but the others she was angering the most; international fishing corporations, whose ships were increasingly assaulted by marine life; major religious institutions, whose spiritual messages she was subverting with her drive for harmony and unity through nature, the message that humans lived within nature and not above it, that all living things were citizens, not resources; governments, whose citizens more and more refused to pay for the privilege of citizenship, who were choosing to join the growing movement to an untethered oceanic community, a community that wasn't just universally human, but for all creatures, all living things.

She and many of her followers gathered on handmade rafts and platforms, offshore from San Diego Harbor. They were harassed occasionally by military aircraft, but they were loose, able to deconstruct their floating base in minutes, allow the currents to scatter them, with the occasional help of friendly orcas.

'Humans First' movements hated her the most, and she found great satisfaction in that.

More than once, vigilantes from anti-whale groups attacked them, with weaponized drones and small helicopters. Such attacks were never surprises, always given away by internet traffic, monitored with little effort by friends of Niemi's following. By the time the drones arrived, the flotilla would have vanished, dispersed as if it had never been.

Save one vessel, a small submersible, floating among the black and white bodies and vaporous spray of orcas. If the attackers had looked closely, they would have seen that the largest orca female had a gray marking on one fin, in the shape of a human hand. When the drones fell upon them, they dove straight down, gone in seconds, beyond the reach of weapons and soon beyond the reach of air-based radar and sonar.

The attackers waited. They must rise for breath. They pursued did rise, single whales rising to breathe and dive again in dozens of locations miles apart, and Niemi's submarine was not among them.

But the orca attacks on fishing ships became more sporadic, the losses less important.

The scarcity economics that spread in every continent brought more famine, more disease, and more anger. The world was coming to war, and Niemi's pesky social experiment was forgotten for a time. It became a dim, distasteful memory to most. But to some, a legend.

Her following, hidden in ocean shadows, continued to grow. And with less food competition from other whales and sea predators, the numbers of orcas and the few dolphin species grew with her following.

●

On a day of gray skies, Mileva lingered by Grayfin, not venturing out, not blowing vapor well up to splash on Niemi where she ate her sea greens, not following the others as she had come to do, watching the younger ones hunt the seas and return to the old grandmother with a hunk of flesh. The time had come for her to pass on, and knowing it was coming still hadn't prepared Niemi.

Twenty-five years had passed for them together. She had loved this whale woman more than her own mother. The connection between them — this was the fabric of heaven, the hope of eternity, the bond of hand to flipper, bodies, worlds, universes.

Mileva — a Slavic name meaning 'gracious'.

Mileva's steamy breaths came slower and shallower, until they just ceased. Her body rocked against Grayfin's hull, as against a lover.

Soon, several big females came to grasp the elder mother by her fins and pull her away, to where Niemi never knew.

Niemi had not wept in many years. But with this loss, she remembered how.

●

The years passed, like cool ocean waters passing over the skin, leaving the sands and stings and memories of great swims.

They are thousands now, living on a floating island caravan just within sight of the coast, where lay the war-damaged cities and their damaged people. Ropes of kelp and knots of barnacles and coral cling to the old fishing nets and foam plastic balloons lashed beneath, providing ballast, stability when storms rage against it. Gardens spring from the sand and dirt they've collected, seeds and feces dropped by birds, thousands of them. Shimmering fish pinwheel in swarms around and beneath the island. The caravan moves on the wind, nudged at times by those who built cloth sails and turbine masts, holding it in favorable waters.

Guarded by orcas; guided by the moon, the stars, the sun.

It is a warm night.

Niemi climbs from the tarnished and dented and welded hull of Grayfin to gaze upon the caravan a quarter-mile away. A floating city-state it has become, nothing she ever imagined or wanted, a thing sprung from the harmony of being, the harmony of beings. She may have inspired it, but she isn't part of it, is she? Haven't they come for themselves, thinking of her as an idea only? She walks among them sometimes, the hushed tones as she passes, the orcas ever-present. The symbol of the mother orca Mileva is sown into many of their sails, with the gray, human hand pattern on her fin.

The night sky is brilliant, bisected by the pale ribbon of the Milky Way. Her sense of smell is going the way of her body, her sight, her strength, yet the sea air is alive with salt and life, and the hint of death, the ultimate certainty. There is harmony even in the smell of the sea.

How many worlds out there have lost their harmony? How many have lost their whales?

This is the ocean; a pool of interaction, living and passing on, woven lives and minerals and elements. Harmony, in a word. One cannot escape it, not without leaving most of oneself behind, in the infinite song that bounces from shore to shore, island to continent, depth to sky.

Come back, lights, bring our people back home.

The sky remains quiet, the lights do not come. They stopped coming decades ago.

Away over in the colony, flutes and horns, stringed boxes and deep drums begin to play a lilting song — not a song, really, more a feeling, a yearning, a reaching out for ears and jaw teeth to hear. Wailing, whistles, clicks of wood and stone and metal rod. Language in every form, every pitch, vibration in every frequency.

Beneath her, the orcas speak, respond to the music, join the conversation. Niemi has listened to their voices for so many years now, decades, that their language has become her own, like it was her first. She hears every sound, every idea, every dream.

They are thousands now, on hundreds of floating pods in every sea and ocean, around and near every port, the human-orca communities, in salty seas all over the planet, patrolling the shoals, monitoring the sea farming, keeping it within sustainable boundaries. There is spill-over, communities on land springing up, the harmonizing of humans with other primates, elephants, even forests, nearly doomed at one time, but sprouting back to life. The movement was now a tidal wave.

It all started with a few real believers dipping into the water, a ritual they all performed now, to leave the security and technology behind for a short time, to become one with the sea, one with the orcas, to be completely vulnerable. To have a faith like no other, the faith in the impossible community of living spirits. They didn't call it a baptism. The didn't call it anything.

The pain hits Niemi again, this time too hard to ignore, the malignancy that spread from her lungs — micro-dust sarcoma, doctors explained, a condition even bathing in the nurturing salt waters can't cure, so many afflicted with it now. If only she'd had more time to build the sky pods — communities of humans and birds, to patrol and scour. She tries to breath, but great invisible hands crush her from both sides.

"Niemi?" Tanya hears her fall, rushes from Grayfin's cabin, is there, grasping her shoulder.

"It's...huh...time, sister."

"No —"

"Yes. I need...to be...in the water."

Dark fins cut through the ocean soup in the twilight — they always know somehow, the tall black fins of the males, the shorter, sometimes curved dorsals of the females. And there among them, Seaflower, tulip-shaped patches of white on her flippers. They always know, these great beings, these wise ones of the sea. They know when one of their own is about to pass.

"Help me...get these off." Niemi struggles to unbutton the shirt and trousers, but Tanya is there to help.

Many more orca come, as Tanya helps her ease into the cool water, so nice, so delicate a caress on her skin.

"Where...are the lights?" Niemi studies the sky, knowing they are coming, coming to bring their friends, their other peoples back home. The world is better, ready for them. There is harmony now. Isn't this enough?

"What, Niemi? I can barely hear you."

No matter. She can't draw the breath to talk. The whales are around her in the water now, buoying her up, nuzzling her, holding her up to the crisp air as they would a newborn calf. Funny that the air bites her lungs so. Funny how the sky darkens. Is a storm coming?

There. Lights in the sky, moving across the stars, no satellite or abandoned space station. No, these lights are falling, growing brighter as they sink through the miles of atmosphere. Great tankers of water, carrying the children of those huge beings who left before. They are coming. She has done enough.

Her peoples are coming home.

C.J. Erick's story "Saving the Whales" was originally published in Metaphorosis on Friday, 24 November 2023. See magazine.metaphorosis.com

About the author

Chemical engineer C.J. Erick writes in multiple genres, publishes novels in a space fantasy series, and dabbles in poetry. He lives in Dallas area with his wife and their rescue superhero dog Saber-Girl, calls his sourdough bread starter "Ursula" (K. Le Guin), and cooks crazy-good Cajun food for a Midwest Yankee.

www.cjerickfiction.com, facebook.com/cj.erick.9, Instagram: cee_jay_erick

Copyright

Title information

Scientists of Metaphorosis

ISBN: 978-1-64076-307-4 (e-book)
ISBN: 978-1-64076-308-1 (paperback)
ISBN: 978-1-64076-309-8 (hardcover)

Copyright

Works of fiction

Publisher

Metaphorosis
a magazine of speculative fiction

Metaphorosis Magazine is an imprint of
Metaphorosis Publishing
Neskowin, OR, USA

www.metaphorosis.com

"Metaphorosis" is a registered trademark.

Discounts available

Substantial discounts are available for educational institutions, including writing workshops. Discounts are also available for quantity purchases. For details, contact Metaphorosis at metaphorosis.com/about

Metaphorosis Publishing

Metaphorosis offers beautifully written science fiction and fantasy. Our imprints include:

Metaphorosis Magazine

Plant Based Press

Verdage

Vestige

Joyful Heave

You can also find us:
@metaphorosis.bsky.social (Bluesky)
@Metaphorosis@writing.exchange (Mastodon)
www.facebook.com/metaphorosis

Help keep Metaphorosis running at
Patreon.com/metaphorosis

See more about some of our books on the following pages.

Metaphorosis is an online speculative fiction magazine dedicated to quality writing. We publish an original story every week (2016-2023) or month (2024), along with author bios, interviews, and notes on story origins.

We also publish monthly print and e-book issues, as well as yearly *Best of* and *Complete* anthologies.

Come and see us online at magazine.Metaphorosis.com.

The Metaphorosis Library Collection

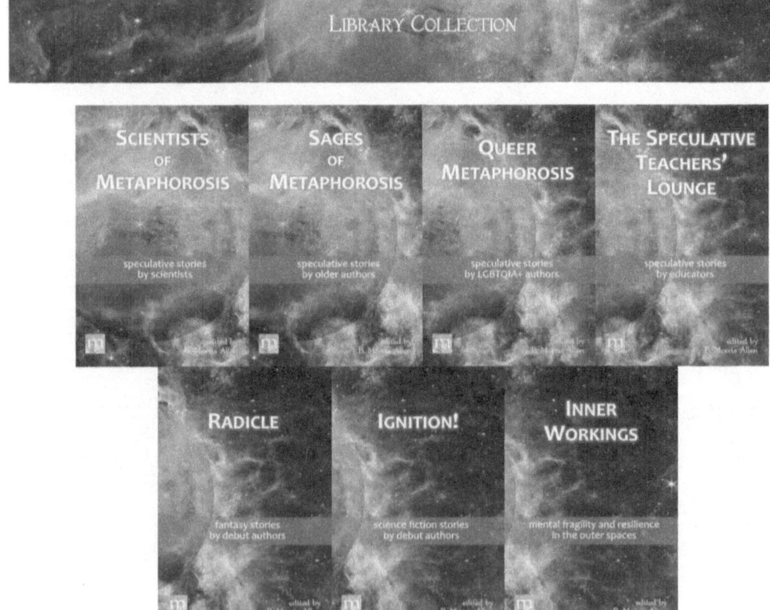

Plant Based Press

Vegan-friendly science fiction and fantasy, including anthologies of the year's best SFF stories, from 2016-2020.

Chambers of the Heart
speculative stories
by
B. Morris Allen

A heart that's a building, a dog that's a program, a woman sinking irretrievably — stories about love, loss, and movement.

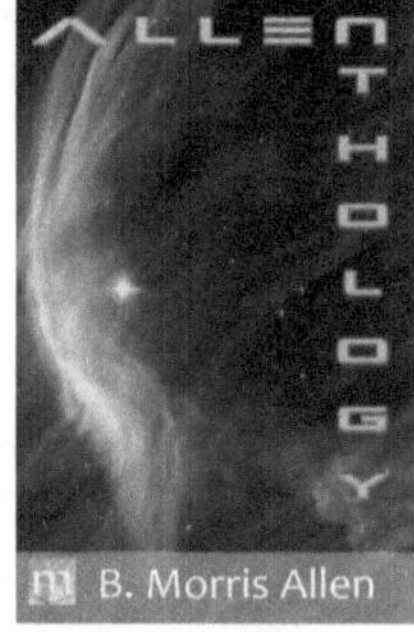

Susurrus

A darkly romantic story of magic, love, and suffering.

Allenthology: Volume I

Including three full collections of SFF stories.

Verdage

Science fiction and fantasy books for writers — full of great stories, often with an additional focus on the craft of speculative fiction writing.

Reading 5X5 x3

Changes

How do stories move from 'maybe' to published?

Here are 15 case studies of stories published in *Metaphorosis* magazine.

Reading 5X5 x2

Duets

How do authors' voices change when they collaborate?

A round-robin of five talented science fiction and fantasy authors collaborating with each other and writing solo.

Including stories by Evan Marcroft, David Gallay, J. Tynan Burke, L'Erin Ogle, and Douglas Anstruther.

Score

an SFF symphony

An anthology with an emotional score from the heights of joy to the depths of despair — but always with a little hope shining through.

Reading 5X5

Five stories, five times

See how different writers take on the same material.

Reading 5X5

Writers' Edition

Two extra stories, the story seed, and authors' notes on writing.

Vestige

Novelettes, novellas, and novels by Metaphorosis authors.

The Nocturnals
Mariah Montoya

Night is Dangerous. Day is deadly.
Where day and night last thirty years, humans move constantly stay ahead of the night and cruel Nocturnals that call it home. But a boy is lost out there.

Science fiction and fantasy anthologies with innovative and unusual themes.

Museum Piece
an unusual collection

A gallery of the strange and outrageous

Step right up and enter a world of wonder and oddities! These museums are not your typical tourist traps. From the Museum of Lost Dreams to the Museum of Fine Regrets, each exhibit will take you on a journey you won't soon forget.